AMERICAN BEAUTY

EDNA FERBER

American Beauty

PUBLISHED BY

P. F. Collier & Son Corporation

BY SPECIAL ARRANGEMENT WITH

Doubleday, Doran & Company, Inc.

NEW YORK

Manufactured in the U. S. A.

TO

MORRIS ERNST

without whom this book might have been
finished six months sooner, and to

WALTER LIPPMANN

who pointed out that first young Pole
walking toward us in the sunset
at Wading River.

New York
June, 1931

CONTENTS

1930

CONTENTS

1930

AMERICAN BEAUTY

I

1930

OLD TRUE BALDWIN and his daughter Candace were whirling up the brisk little hills and swooping down into the rich green valleys of that spectacular part of Connecticut through which the Still River flows, and the storied Housatonic. They had started from New York at eight, for old True had never lost his farm-boy habit of early rising. Up through the pleasant Parkway at a smart clip, flashing into Westchester and out like a streak of green light, past New England villages whose prim clapboard houses, grayed by the two centuries that had passed over them, shrank in withered dismay from the vulgar red stare of gas filling stations, now become their neighbors.

Candy Baldwin drove with that relaxed insolence which marks the expert. Her father, after preliminary panic, had learned years ago that he could sit at ease beside her, serene in the knowledge that, though the car just ahead threatened hideous oblivion, it would always next instant fade meekly into the background.

The monster in which they now pounced upon Connecticut was inadequately advertised as a super roadster phaëton. That negligible portion of it occupied by Candy's slim body and True's old hulk seemed but an afterthought on the part of its designer. Its voracious maw swallowed a hill at a gulp. One hawk-like swoop, and a meadow lay inert behind it. The rubbled country by-roads, built more than two hundred years ago for rude ox carts and the iron-shod hoofs of horses, bit at its plump tires in vain.

All about them, brilliant emerald in the summer sunshine, lay the tobacco fields of the Housatonic, a rich and heartening sight. True Baldwin, who had been sitting slumped and inert, the wrinkled crêpe of his eyelids half closed over his lack-luster eyes, now slowly began to stir and look about him, this way and that, like a weary and ageless reptile who, feeling the good warm sun on his clammy skin, slowly uncoils, muscle by muscle, and regards with unblinking and disillusioned gaze a world which he well knows and has, in his wisdom, rejected.

From time to time, as they sped along, Candace had

flashed at her father, out of the corner of her eye, a look meant to be searching, though secret. This, finally, irked him.

"God's sake, Candy, stop hovering! D'you expect I'm going to have a stroke?"

"Why, you ungrateful old party, you! I was just being companionable. Looking to see if you were liking it. I never knew this part of Connecticut was so lovely."

"Certainly wasn't, as I remember it, nearly fifty years back. Can't understand it. Look at those fields! Tropical, darned if they're not."

"Oh, call them lush, Mr. B. There's a word I've always wanted to use. The Connecticut landscape is lush—would you believe it?—and that's werry odd, because I'd always been told it was grim and barren as a New England spinster."

"New England spinster yourself," her father retorted, gallantly, "once removed. But you're certainly right about its being surprising. Time I was sixteen I pulled rocks out of those fields till my back——" Then, suddenly, sitting up very straight, "Holy mackerel!" He leaned forward. His eyes took on the alertness of the days before his illness. They swept the fields hedged in by the old stone fences so painfully built out of the back-breaking rocks of the fields themselves. He waved his arms. "Look at that, will you!"

"Look at what?"

"Women. They've got women working in the fields."

Over the vivid green of the young tobacco plants in the fields there bent, not only the sturdy figures of men, but the broad, petticoated backs of women, the less bulky forms of young girls, and even the spindling shanks of children scarcely taller than the plants they tended.

Candace beheld this undismayed. "Well, why not? It can't be harder than washing clothes or scrubbing floors, and those have always been considered nice womanly occupations."

"Women working in the fields, like men! It's Russia, I tell you. Black Russia."

"Red's the color you use with Russia now, darling. And anyway, not Russia. Poland, remember." For she had tried to call his indifferent attention to the strange names painted crookedly on rural mail delivery boxes as they flashed past the roadside posts outside each old farmhouse. Markiewicz, in crazy lettering. Krupa. Halicki. Borek. Wroblewski. "The Poles seem to have bought up a lot of the old places, don't they? I must say they've done well by the farms. Now, do sit back and relax, Dad. You know what the doctor said."

"Doctor be damned! Women working the fields of New England like cattle. It's these Polacks. What right have they got in New England, anyway? Shades of John Winthrop and Roger Conant and Orrange Oakes!"

"But, dear, the Poles must have paid their hard-earned dollars for them. And anyway, when you come right down to it, how did you precious Puritans get your land? Grabbed it from the Indians, that's how."

"Talk like a fool, Candy. Any child with a primer knows they went through the hardships of hell for this land. Cleared it and planted it and reaped it——"

"And beat it. Beat it, as fast as they could, for Ohio or Texas."

"Well, suppose they did. It shows the spirit of adventure in 'em. Pioneers."

"Tell you what I think, Dad: I think those early New Englanders hated New England. They weren't farmers by nature, poor darlings, but from necessity. They didn't really love what the dreary writers call the Soil."

"Didn't, huh! And where did you get all that?"

"Book larnin'."

And to herself Candace thought, Well, I've managed to get him interested, at any rate, a little. That's something. Oh God, I hope it works!

Certainly, for the first time in a year, something of the old force seemed to animate True Baldwin. "You and your flip generation! You wouldn't have lasted a week, living the lives those women had. Cooking and spinning and soap-making and Indian-fighting and child-bearing."

"Isn't it so!" Candy exclaimed, with mischievous meekness. "And withal, how genteel and re-fined. Look at the pictures. Always going to church in the snow—capes, flat collars, and a prayer book. Or sitting dreamily in a

[5]

draught with a spinning wheel. Me, I don't believe it."

"The flower of America," trumpeted old True, now thoroughly aroused, "sprang from New England."

"Gone to seed now, darling, you must admit. They certainly let the farms go back to the primal ooze or thereabouts."

True Baldwin, with a wave of his arms, included the entire landscape. "Primal ooze, huh! Look at that garden spot."

"But that isn't Yankee. That's Polack. Whole families digging their toes into the dirt. Why, look at you! You're a runaway farm boy yourself, True."

True Baldwin pushed the hat back from his forehead. "I'll show you who New England belongs to, by God, if I have to buy up the whole state of Connecticut."

"Three cheers!" cried Candace. " 'At a boy! Now you're talking!"

True Baldwin, a year before, had been one of those lean, wiry, and seemingly indestructible old Chicago millionaires who make a point of walking a brisk mile or so on their way downtown to business, mornings, the Rolls drawn up at the curb to meet them at the corner of, say, Michigan and Scott. The physical collapse of this fine old structure had been as swift and inevitable as the Wall Street debacle by which it was timed. He became, suddenly, a shrunken and wattled old man who seemed mistakenly to have donned the garments of someone twenty pounds heavier than he.

Science took him in hand. By the time the specialists had finished with him he had aged ten years, which made him appear a good seventy-six. They stood him in front of a glass-faced thing mellifluously called a fluoroscope and resembling an oversized public telephone booth. This revealed to the world such portions of his inside as had not already come under the X-ray's godlike eye. He was stood up and slapped; sat down and pounded; laid down and poked. They analyzed his most intimate mental, psychic, and physical functions. They delved into his private and anatomical past. They counted his blood cells, red and white (he said he boasted no blue) ; gauged his metabolism, ascertained his blood pressure, weighed him, measured him, fed him test meals of which later they indelicately deprived him.

"Death," he demanded, not very humorously, when they had quite finished, "where is thy sting!"

"Death—nothing!" retorted the paternal young super-specialist who had ordered a flock of sub-specialists (all his seniors) throughout the performance. "You're at least twenty years ahead of it, with that cast-iron con-stitution of yours. Only——"

"Only," echoed old Baldwin, grimly. "I knew there was a catch in it."

"No, my dear Mr. Baldwin, there's no catch in it. You've got to live more quietly, that's all. No more Wall Street. That's out. And this commuting between Chicago and New York, and juggling millions in a compartment

[7]

on the Century, that's out, too. I want you to promise me you'll get away."

"A trip, you mean?"

"No. I mean get away and stay away. Live where it's quiet and peaceful."

"Rot on the Riviera, I suppose. Go and bleach my bones in that damned sunshine with the other old cadavers."

"The south of France isn't the only place that has sunshine."

"I hate southern California!" snorted True Baldwin, with more venom than the statement seemed to demand.

The young specialist had a singularly soothing way with him. It was this, perhaps, that accounted largely for the fact that he had, at thirty-five, the medical practice of a man of fifty. He did not chide, he did not bully, he did not threaten. He used no Latin phrases. When in deep thought he sometimes moved the blotter, penholder, prescription pad, and cigarette box from the right-hand side of his desk to the left. The disturbing problem solved, he moved them back again. The first he now did, quietly and thoughtfully.

"You told me you used to be a farm boy, born on a farm. Have you never thought of going back to it?"

"You're crazy."

The young man laughed as though True Baldwin had said something pleasantly witty. "No, I'm not. If I were you I'd buy a farm in the region I grew up in. Not a toy farm—a big one. I'd make a business of farming. George Washington did it, after the most important career this country has ever known. He rode over his farm every day, overseeing everything."

"Yes, and what happened to him! Got his feet wet, took pneumonia, and died."

"Dear Mr. Baldwin, I'm serious about this. You're a builder and a worker. You could travel, but idling is no good for an active man like you. If you want to travel and play around part of the time, all right. But living in the city—Chicago or New York—that's no good for you. For that matter, no one lives in big cities any more unless they have to. If you start putting things into the ground and watching them come up, you'll find there's as much thrill in that as in watching the tape come out of the ticker."

"That's right. Bring *that* up."

"Oh, now. Forget you've only got a miserable two millions—or is it three?—left from the smash. I promise you that if you go back to the Illinois farm where you were born you'll get a thrill——"

"Illinois! Me! Why, you young fool, I'm no Sucker! I'm a Yank—a Nutmeg. I was born in Connecticut, up in the hills way back of Stonefield."

"Really! Well, that's interesting. Hardly a two-hours' run from New York. You've probably been back often on your trips East."

True Baldwin slumped a little in his chair. Into his

eyes there came an odd look. One might almost have said it was a look of defeat. He spoke in a tired voice and spiritless.

"I've never been back. Funny. I'm not even sure I could find the house I was born in, if it's still standing. My daughter Candace gets up around New England a good deal, because of her work. Interested in those old houses, of course, being an architect. She says the Polacks, Hungarians, and so on have swarmed in there and bought up the whole north end of the state. Massachusetts, too. She says they're raising tobacco and getting rich. Candy says some of the old New Englanders are even working for them as hired men now, and glad to get this job. I can't believe it. That couldn't happen in New England."

"Take a run up and see for yourself."

"What for?"

"Reclaim it. Lots of people are buying Connecticut farms. They're glad to get away from the city. I have some friends whose ancestors came from there; and now they're going back."

"After almost fifty years, back where I started from! There's defeat for you."

"Not at all. You'll have made the complete circle." Then, as True Baldwin made an impatient sound preliminary to departure, "Just why did you leave the farm when you were a boy? How did it happen?"

Baldwin rose. "I'm not going all over that again. You've got it down on those papers you fellows were always scribbling at when you put me through that third degree—why was I born; did I hate my father; did I love my wife. You said you had to know in order to cure me. Well, now you know, and I feel worse than ever."

The young specialist gravely transferred his desk gadgets from the left-hand side back to the right. "Tell me again, won't you?" he asked, coaxingly. "Let me see— you ran away, wasn't that it? Why?"

True Baldwin seated himself again, reluctantly, yet with that air of complaisance usually worn by one who is asked to tell the story of his life.

"Why does any boy leave the farm? To make his fortune, of course. Though I guess maybe that wasn't all. I ran away when I was eighteen because I was as poor as the dirt of our farm and crazy in love with the Oakes girl—Jude Oakes. The Oakes were aristocracy. They lived in a big brick house—falling to pieces—up toward the end of Oakesfield. The district was named after them. It was the only brick house for miles around, and it looked like a palace to me. They say that back in 1700 old Orrange Oakes built that house out of bricks made from the clay of the farm itself. He must have been quite a fellow. Judy's family were high and mighty and gave themselves airs—though by that time they were as dirt poor as the rest of us. They had that house, and the land —originally I guess it was a thousand acres, or nearly, but it had dwindled to three or four hundred. No one to work it properly, and gone to seed. The Oakes crowd traced their family back to some English lord or other, and beyond. Anyway, he was the original Orrange Oakes, and they were always bragging that he was beheaded by Cromwell. They had a picture of him in the hall. Funny thing to brag about. Nowadays you don't hear people bragging because somebody in the family was hanged."

"Was she pretty?"

"Pretty? Oh, Judy. Well, no, I don't suppose you'd have called her pretty. No, pretty isn't a word you'd ever have used for Jude. She must have been two, three years older than I. I don't know what it was. Something kind of, uh, stormy about her, and what you'd call magnetic, I suppose. Black hair, thick and vigorous, and strong black brows, and gray eyes that didn't go with black hair and yet did. And a kind of wide mouth. I kept thinking about it. I was only eighteen. Funny how I remember it, or how I ever got a good look at her in the first place. I hardly ever saw her, except in church. The old church had a colored glass window in it, with saints and so forth. They say old Orrange Oakes had it sent from England, piece by piece, as if it was jewelry. I suppose it was, in a way. Red and yellow and blue and purple. The colors used to make a kind of halo around Jude's head as she sat in the Oakes pew. They sat way forward, and my folks sat way back. There's the caste system for you, in America. I'd look at her and worship her instead of God. I remember she used to wear a velvet hat kind of thing with a bunch of currants on the side, to church. She looked like the Queen of Sheba to me. Once she must have felt me staring—they say you do—and turned her head, all of a sudden, and caught me. It was as if I'd got an electric shock of a million volts. I guess I got red, but by gosh, she did, too, way down to where her collar covered her neck. That made me feel good, I don't know why."

He paused. The young specialist sat very still. "And then, what?" he finally said, gently.

True Baldwin gave a little start. "Then? Then nothing. Jude's younger sister skipped out one day with a peddler named Ping or Pring or something like that, who used to come by once a month with notions and gimcracks for the housewives to buy. No wonder she went. There wasn't a man for miles around except young farm louts like myself, and this girl—Rilly, they called her, I remember—short for Amaryllis—was a pretty little foolish thing with a pointed face and lots of kind of light-colored hair blowing around, and little freckles like gold. Not a bit like her sister, Jude. Well, sir, the mother carried on like crazy. They seemed to breed mostly daughters, the Oakes family. After that happened Judy might just as well have been a Turkish girl in a harem. Her mother wouldn't let her out of the house, scarcely. I used to walk miles out of my way just to go past the Oakes place, but I hardly ever saw her. I got desperate.

I planned to run away from the farm—and did—and make my fortune—did that, too—and come back for Jude Oakes in a carriage with two black horses, and a gold watch and chain across my middle, and shiny boots."

"Dear Mr. Baldwin, why don't you do it now?"

Old True flushed like a boy. He rose, heavily, picked up his gloves from where they lay on the doctor's desk. "I wear a wrist watch. The only carriage I know of is the one in the exhibition gallery at the Grand Central station. And I haven't seen a carriage horse in years, black or white." He stood a moment, looking down at the gloves in his hand. "Funny, isn't it, how your whole life goes by while you think you're only planning the way you're going to live it? She'll be an old dried-up New England spinster of nearly seventy now—or, more likely, a mound in the Oakes lot." He held out his hand in farewell. "So, Doctor, if all that's any use to you, put it down in one of your charts, and I hope it'll do you more good than it has me."

The young specialist laid a fatherly hand on old True's shoulder. "It's going to do you a lot of good. You wait. You'll see. And promise me you'll take a run up there into Connecticut with Candace some time this summer, won't you? And look around?"

"No," snapped True Baldwin. "If I'm going to die, I'll die right here in Chicago with my spats on."

But no sooner had he gone than the young doctor said, in the telephone, to his secretary in the anteroom, "Get

me Miss Candace Baldwin, of Barnes & Halperin, archi-
tects." And, a moment later, "Candy, this is David. He
has just left. . . . Well, no, he didn't exactly promise.
But I'm inclined to think that if you'll talk to him from
time to time, and make a trip to New York with him
when he goes East . . . He talked a great deal about
that Oakes girl and the brick house. . . . If it's still
standing, and you can find it and get him to look at it and
perhaps even buy it, and the land, he'll probably live a
long . . ."

He and Candace Baldwin had had confidential talks
before ever True Baldwin was put through the medical
mill. To Candace, in fact, belonged credit for the Connecticut farm idea. She was almost as glib with her
psychiatric terms as the young specialist himself.

"That old brick house has been in his mind all his life,
hasn't it? It represents frustration—that and his love for
Jude Oakes. Poor darling. He probably piled up all those
millions simply as compensation and doesn't know it."

The young doctor had listened politely. He and Candace liked each other in a cool friendly way. Candace
Baldwin, at twenty-six, was unmarried. She was the type
of American girl that came into fashion after the War—
chic, but not pretty. Paradoxically, she was said to have
the most beautiful head in Chicago, which was, perhaps,
faint praise. You saw it pictured even in New York
magazines that told you where people were during
February. Certainly that fine head gave this girl an air

of distinction that frequently made a roomful of authentic beauties look commonplace. She was, by profession, an architect, which people thought odd.

"Women," she said, somewhat bitterly, "don't want women to plan or build their houses. Isn't that cockeyed! They use a house more than men do. They entertain in it, they bring up their children in it, and run it. Closets and bathrooms and kitchens and bedrooms are all planned for women. But they want men to build their houses."

Still, she had persisted. At school she had worked with a kind of ferocity; later, had served as apprentice draughtsman in the hive-like offices of Barnes & Halperin; had predicted that Chicago's near North Side would be reclaimed; and got into all the New York papers by stating that within ten years Negro Harlem would be transformed into the smart residence district of New York. Candy's clothes were audacious and simple; she had beautiful teeth, fine eyes, a sallow skin; was angular, graceful, warm-hearted, and extremely adult. She practised few conscious wiles. Men rarely fell in love with her. Those who did carried scars.

In her talks with the young specialist on the subject of her father she had been rather revealing about herself. She was not, however, plaintive.

"Woe," she said, "is me. I am the child of a loveless marriage. Mother was plain and powerful and had a lot of old Chicago family behind her. I inherit my plainness

from her and my charm from Father. Once she made up
her mind to have him he never had a chance. Not a living
chance. You ought to have seen that family all together.
Prominent teeth and sort of protuberant eyes. In a roomful of them you had no more of a break than a mouse in
a den of lions. Dad made his pile pretty early—for so
much, I mean. They were always very polite and respectful to each other, but I don't remember ever having seen
them kiss. They wanted me to be a boy. There were no
other children. Mother died nine years ago. I used to
think Father might marry again, and worried about it a
little, though I never would have interfered. I'm glad
he didn't. I know that's selfish. I feel so sorry for Dad.
He hasn't had much fun. I think he has always meant
to—and now, suddenly, he's sixty-six. I suppose Father
and I are really in love with each other, in a perfectly
nice way."

He considered this gravely. "Do you think that's why
you've never married?"

"Probably. That, and the fact that I'm the kind of
girl who wants to be hit over the head. Unfortunately,
I don't look the type. Still, who is there to marry?—
saving your presence. Brokers, and run-down third generation packers' sons, and interior decorators. I like
traffic cops, taxi drivers, truckmen, and steel riveters.
And I meet so few of them, socially."

So it came about that now, a month later, old True
Baldwin and his daughter Candace were driving through

Connecticut in search of two houses which one of them
had not seen in almost fifty years, and the other had
never seen at all. They sought the old gray clapboard
farmhouse where True Baldwin was born, and the red
brick mansion in which Jude Oakes had lived. They
scorned the help of local realtors, preferring to do their
own discovering. This had got them into difficulties.
Twice they had been hopelessly lost. They had even
stooped to asking direction from two wayside travelers,
for very few passed those byways, and they had tried to
keep off the main highways. Their queries had met with
discouragement. Sunburned, broad-fisted, the men ac-
costed had replied, stupidly, "You want farm? I ain't
know."

"Poles," Candace said, shifting gears. "Never mind.
We'll find it. He was good-looking, wasn't he?"

By now old Baldwin had slumped, disconsolate. The
sun was hot. He had breakfasted early. He was hungry.
He needed a drink. The sight of the Polish women in
the fields had served to arouse his interest. Then, suddenly, the landscape, the old houses, had begun to take
on a sort of familiarity.

"Look! That's the old Jonathan Mapes place. . . .
Medad Pynchon lived over there, in the valley. Is that
--yessir, I'll bet that's the old Elijah Tuthill farm. He
was a skinflint. We boys used to steal his apples just to
make him mad, though we had them rotting on the
ground on our own places. . . . Amos Peck . . .

Timothy Bennett . . . Thornhill . . . Dibble . . ."

But the name on the metal mail box outside each farmhouse had a foreign flavor far remote from these homely New England names that came faster and faster from old True's tongue. Jackowski where Mapes had been; Franek instead of Pynchon; Stanislaw Sekowski; Osniak.

He became more and more disconsolate. She began to think that she had made a mistake in bringing him here at all. She even hoped that the old Baldwin farmhouse had vanished—that they would never come upon it. Craftily, she tried to prepare him for the shock of disappointment.

"I think I really hate these New England houses. Little postage-stamp windows, little tight mean stairways, little low ceilings. I know they're supposed to be very pure and native; but when you come to look at them, how scringing they are, and prim and sour, staring out at the roadside."

"You're a hell of an architect, you are, if you don't know that they built close to the roadside for company and convenience, and low ceilings because they couldn't warm the rooms otherwise, with nothing but draughty fireplaces in bitter winter weather; and narrow stairways——"

"I know, darling, I know. And very bright of them, too. Only, why anyone wants to live in them now I can't imagine. And as for that early American furniture! It's the ugliest native handicraft ever devised by man. I know they had to make it in a hurry, out of the pine of the forest, but it certainly is as stern as Judgment Day, and about as comfortable."

Suddenly, "There!" he shouted, interrupting her. And then, in a sort of croak, "Oh, my God!" She stopped the car; he was pointing to an ugly little house by the road-side. It had not, originally, been a bad example of the old New England farmhouse. But now it was defaced with a cheap porch tacked on the front. There was a tin garage at the side. Three dirty children, all apparently of one age, were rolling about the yard.

"Oh, willa-walla," thought Candace, dashed. "So that's the old Baldwin homestead! And for years I've been snooty about it to the stockyards Chicago society gals." Aloud she said, "Why, True, you're wonderful to have found it. Come on, let's get out. Let's see if they've got a bronze tablet on the wall of the room where you were born."

Heavily he climbed out of the car, dejectedly he fol-lowed her around the dirt path to the back door. A vast Polish woman seemed to fill the kitchen. She came to the door, amiably enough, and answered their questions, though she was formidable of aspect. "Is Rzepkowski farm. August Rzepkowski. Ain't here. Is working in tobacco." She had abundant hair, great breasts, bad teeth, was probably not yet thirty, looked fifty; incurious, unimpressed by the glittering motor drawn up at the roadside. Were there not two good cars in the tin garage? "You look for farm to buy? Is farms for buy but not here. People is coming from city now for buy farms."

"No, we don't want—that is, could we just come in and look at the house? My father was——"

"No!" shouted True Baldwin. Wheeled suddenly and left Candace standing there by the kitchen door. She murmured an excuse and flew after him. He was climbing into the car, heavily.

"I'm so sorry, Dad."

"That's what comes of opening graves and looking at something that's been dead for years. That damned doctor!"

"Don't feel that way about it. Poles don't care about houses. It's the land they want. I'll bet the Oakes house——"

He closed his tired eyes. He dismissed the Oakes house—the whole countryside—with a wave of the hand. "I don't want to see the Oakes house. It probably has been turned into a cow shed. I don't know where it is, anyway. I forget. The hell with the Oakes house. I'm sick of Connecticut. I want to go home."

She drove in silence for a moment, thinking. Her glance swept the landscape, right and left. It can't be far, she thought. But it's probably terrible, too. "We both need a good big lunch, that's what. I wonder if there's anything besides those chicken-dinner horrors we've passed. Honestly, True, I think Connecticut's lovelier than Kent.

They came from Kent, didn't they—a lot of those old Puritan boys and girls. In another ten years I'm afraid it's going to be fashionable. I'll bet I could make the most divine place out of one of these farms. No early American nightmares, but beautiful Colonial and English furniture, and imported chintzes and pine paneling and rows and rows of books, and millions of fireplaces and bathrooms—— Ooh!"

She shoved on the brakes so abruptly that True, his eyes still wearily shut, was all but catapulted through the windshield.

"Hell's bells!" he shouted.

"Look!" Now it was Candy who pointed toward a house. It was a large brick mansion in shocking disrepair set well back from the by-road on which they were traveling. "Look at that! That's the most beautiful house I ever saw. It's the most beautiful house in America. It's got dignity and strength and grace. I want it. I don't care how many Polacks own it, True, you've got to buy me that house and let me restore it, because it's the most beautiful house I ever saw. God, it's beautiful!"

She was out of the car and up the path between two giant elms. He clambered after her, suddenly agile. "Heh, Candy, wait! I told you, didn't I? Didn't I?"

"What?" absently. Her architect's gaze was on the fanlight over the front door.

He caught up with her, panting. "Oakes. Oakes. It's the old Oakes place."

"No!" Awe was in her voice. "Father, I apologize. It's perfect. Look, will you please, at that fanlight! It's made of lace, I tell you. It's as pure and exquisite as a frosty morning. It's the most beautiful fanlight I've ever seen. It's the most beautiful fanlight in America. Wait. Where's the doorbell? Oh, no bell, of course. How silly of me. Knocker. Oh, my gracious, look at that knocker. It's an Adam, gilded with water gilt. It's the first I've ever seen on a door. They have them in museums. Water gilding is a lost art. It's the most beautiful knocker in America."

She now clapped the knocker smartly, though reverently. They waited. No sound came from within. Suddenly, as they stood there, their hearts beating fast, old True put his hand over his eyes. She rushed to him, put her strong young arms about his sagging shoulders. "Dad. Darling. Are you ill? Here—sit down."

"Don't want to sit down," True said, gruffly, but sat a moment beside her on the doorstep, nevertheless.

"Better?"

"I'm all right. I'm fine. I don't know—I had a funny feeling, as if something had loosened up inside—that had been too tight. Maybe I'm excited and don't realize it —about coming back here, I mean. Huh?"

"Maybe," Candace agreed, gravely. They sat there a moment, the two, her strong brown hand covering his as it lay on his knee. Presently Candace rose. "I'll try again." She clattered the knocker, smartly. Echo only. Then the bark of a dog from somewhere at the rear.

Old True got to his feet. "We'd better go round to the back. Careful of these farm dogs, though. They bite. Here, let's get into the car and take the driveway round."

Thus they grandly and prudently approached the kitchen door of the old Oakes house to find it shut and guarded by an English setter of excellent points, enchanting aspect, and delighted to see them. Between him and Candace it was love at sight. The demonstration went on until True said, not too mildly, "Did we come here to see a dog or a house?"

They knocked at the back door. They lifted the old latch. The door was unlocked. Love or no love, the English setter gave a growl of protest. They shut the door, hurriedly. They peered in at the window. A vast kitchen, pine-paneled, with great cupboards. That which had been an enormous fireplace at one end was boarded up, and in its place stood an old-fashioned kitchen stove. On the kitchen table were plate, cup, and saucer, neatly ranged, and beside them an open book, face down, as though a breakfaster had read as he ate, and meant to read again, at noon.

Candace knocked again, though hopelessly. Old True faced the door with something like apprehension in his gaze. Perhaps he dreaded to see the figure that would emerge to replace his memory of the stormy black-haired girl with the strong brows and the gray eyes. He put one hand on the brick of the old house, hot in the noonday sun. The original paint still showed in patches, mellowed to a faded Italian pink.

"Maybe they're in the fields," Candace suggested. "There's a wagon road leading round past that barn. Let's follow it."

They entered the car again, followed the wagon road past a shed in which stood a Ford; jolted over the furrows.

"They'll be out in the tobacco," Baldwin suggested. "If the Polacks own this place, the whole family'll be out there, I suppose."

"It didn't look it. That kitchen was spick and span. And that dog—he's no Polish farmer's dog. He's thoroughbred."

Now they saw, in a distant tobacco field, a solitary figure bent over the plants. They bumped along toward it in the fierce noonday sun. The figure unbent, straightened. The man turned toward them, shading his eyes with his broad straw hat.

"Good God!" exclaimed True Baldwin. "The man's naked!"

"Not at all. He's got on bathing trunks." She brought the car to a stop within twenty yards of the figure. She had been right. He was working in the Connecticut tobacco fields on this hot July day in swimming trunks. His upper body was bare, brown, and shining with sweat. He came toward them, quite self-contained.

"Cover yourself, young man!" roared True Baldwin from his seat in the roadster.

The man came on. "I haven't got anything to cover myself with."

Candace Baldwin looked at him with the appraising and unstartled eyes of a young woman who has seen thousands of young men on the sands of countless bathing beaches from Florida to Antibes. He was slightly above medium height, with unexpected blue-gray eyes in a warm brown skin; a long English head, a slightly aquiline nose. He took off his hat. His hair, chestnut and very thick, was bleached now by the sun almost to golden. In his hand he had a grimy towel with which he now mopped himself without embarrassment. This done, he draped it over his shoulders, negligently.

"Topping tobacco," he explained. "It's hot work. I usually take a swim in the river yonder, before dinner, when it's like this." He looked at Candace, cool and pink-garbed and scented. She looked at him, warm, wet, a soiled towel over his bare shoulders, a ridiculous tattered straw hat on his head.

True Baldwin spoke in the tone of the man of millions, and accustomed to them.

"What's the name of the people who own this place?"

"Olszak."

"Ol——" He was stricken with disappointment. His tongue refused to form the foreign word. His face grew red. Candace laid one hand, in its white pigskin glove, on his arm. He swallowed hard, once. "I knew it when it was the Oakes place."

"Oh, yes."

"There was a—do you know if—do you know of a Miss Oakes—Miss Judy Oakes? Judith, it is, I guess."

The young man stared. "Miss Judith Oakes? Why, she's dead. She's been dead years and years."

At the look on her father's face Candace now spoke up.

"My father is interested in land around here. Is this place for sale?"

The man flushed beneath his tan. "Yes." Hesitatingly. Then, more firmly, "Yes."

"Well!" True Baldwin's face took on a new animation "My name's Baldwin—True Baldwin, of Chicago. I lived around here when I was a boy. Old Captain Orrange Oakes got this farm a grant from the Indians more than two hundred years ago. Four, five hundred acres, isn't it?"

"Only three hundred and sixty now."

"Work here?"

"Yes."

"Well, I'd like to talk to this Polack. Does he speak English—this—this—uh—Ol—uh———"

"Olszak."

"Olszak. Do you know where I can find him? No one up at the house. At any rate, nobody answered."

"I am Orrange Olszak," said the man.

II
1700

IN A day when the test of the well formed man was
his ability to keep his breeches above his hips and his
ungartered stockings above his calves, Captain Orrange
Oakes walked triumphant. On horseback he alone was
as good as a parade—though who ever saw him ride
unattended? He was, certainly, the most splendid figure
in that small but rich company which gave to eighteenth-
century Connecticut, in those years between its first
Puritan meagerness and its later decay, a brief period of
lavish magnificence.

Captain Orrange Oakes easily kinged it. Picturesque
and powerful as he was, he must have been something of

a terror, too. It was said of him that he was regarded with such awe by his grown sons and daughters that when on horseback they never presumed to ride on a line with him. Only his wife, Judith, and his little daughter Tamar, aged fourteen, had the temerity to keep their horses abreast of his.

Bound for church on the Sabbath, the Oakes household made an imposing cavalcade. As they swept, clattering, down the crude country road in their scarlet and blue and brocade and silver, they were an animated frieze flung across the somber background of Pequot Ridge, its slopes black with hemlock. Puritan Massachusetts would have held up its hands in holy horror—but then, that was why Orrange Oakes and the whole vivacious company had left Massachusetts behind them.

Captain Oakes always rode well in front, his wife Judith on one side, his adored Temmie on the other. What a woman, this Judith Oakes, with her high brow, her wide mobile mouth, her black hair, her strange gray eyes, and her stranger knowledge of Latin and French and astronomy, in a day when the woman who could read and write at all was considered a bluestocking. After producing a whole houseful of grown sons and daughters she had calmly brought forth Tamar, beloved offspring of her husband's middle age.

Behind Orrange and Judith rode their five sons, with their families; their four daughters, with their families; the servants of the household, white; the field hands; the servants of the household, black. They were summoned to the meeting house by the beat of the drum throbbing over the hills, across Pequot Ridge and into the valleys. And the valleys sent the sound up again, tossing it back, like a bouncing ball, into the hills. An unsecular sound and exciting to the senses, so that this aristocratic congregation, arriving at its place of worship, was frequently surprised and more than a little alarmed to find itself filled with such élan and vivacity as to make the proper Sabbath-day decorum difficult. The drum call was a trick learned, innocently enough, from the friendly Weantinocks. Their bland old chief, Waramaug, it was who had sold to Orrange Oakes the very land on which he had built his incredibly handsome house.

"I do declare, Captain Oakes!" Judith would exclaim, in that thrilling contralto voice of hers, as she slipped decorously off her horse with a little rustle of silk and a brief flash of bright morocco shoe, "a morning's ride in this Connecticut mountain air is as good as a glass of sherry—or as bad, I should say, as it's Sabbath morning. I'm all of a glow."

As for fourteen-year-old Temmie, the captain's spoiled darling, a high-spirited young lady at best, she was so affected by drumbeat and sparkling air that it always took her father's most martial manner and her mother's sternest brow to restrain her from breaking into an unsabbatical gallop, giving an Indian war whoop, and behaving altogether in a manner unbefitting the Day and an Oakes.

There was something touching, something magnificent, in the sight of this elegant company, in the midst of forest and hill, of Indian and bear, of bitter winter and blazing summer, still clinging to the refinements and elegancies of a European civilization; still redolent of the English court to escape whose less pleasing odors they had fled to America. You saw the women a-horseback through the wild grandeur of the Connecticut landscape in fine shoes of flowered russet or red morocco; silks and velvets and brocades fashioning the gowns under their favorite cloaks of scarlet. The men, too, in cloaks of fine red cloth, with long vests of plush in gay colors, and plush breeches. Captain Orrange Oakes dressed more quietly than most, with a kind of somber richness. Though his buff coat was of dressed leather, the hand-fashioned hooks and eyes down its front were of real silver. His falling collar was of linen, but it was tied with little tassels. The feather in his hat was dark in color—brown or black—but thick as moss, and his long doeskin gloves were embroidered in gold threads and colored silks. He actually paid fourteen pounds for every pair of his handsome doublechanneled boots. There was leather enough in them for six ordinary pairs of shoes. The great hand-made square-toed casings would last years—in fact, did become heirlooms. Oliver Prudden, of Wethersfield, made them for him. Altogether a fine figure of a man, this Captain

Orrange Oakes, looking more than his height perhaps because of his long English head and the proud arch of his aquiline nose.

"His boots," Captain Oakes was wont to declare, "proclaim the man. Show me scuffed leather and a pair of run-down heels below no matter what yardage of velvet and satin and camlet, and I'll show you a second-rate fellow."

But then, he did everything on a grand scale, from the boots he wore to the house he built. Centuries later, in the rat-ridden attic of the old house, Candace Baldwin actually came across a pair of those very boots, and even in their dirt and debasement they still bore the aristocratic impression of his high-arched instep. As for the house itself, now, after almost two hundred and fifty years, it seemed as amazing, as inexplicable as the Pyramids.

That portion of the Oakes family which had fled to America had, since 1634, or thereabouts, been living (rather restively) in Puritan Massachusetts. Accounts of this new Quaneh-ta-cut began to seep into Plymouth, but little heed was paid to them. But by the time this second American Orrange Oakes was well past middle age these accounts had grown so frequent as to be no longer a novelty, and so glowing as to prove, to him, irresistible. Orrange Oakes, by now, was thoroughly sick of Massachusetts in general and Boston in particular. Primness, blue laws, witchcraft, repression—it was worse than the

England from which the first Oakes had fled. Now, in this Quaneh-ta-cut—the Long Tidal River—there were vast tracts of land to be had almost for the asking; rivers swarming with shad, salmon, mackerel; mountain air and valley shelter; primeval forests awaiting the ax; great areas of meadow and stream that were like English parks made to hand, all greensward and mammoth oaks and elms and trout brooks. It was Kent, they heard, transported to the wilderness, and a thousand times more desirable. Orrange Oakes had come from Greenwich, in Kent.

Anne was throning it in England, the last of the Stuarts. And England herself had proved faithless as dear, for even now these settlers began to realize that their bitterest foes were to be not the Indians whose lands they now possessed, nor the French who coveted them, but the English government itself, across the Atlantic Ocean.

As they had fled from the oppression of England, now this little company, headed by Captain Orrange Oakes, fled from the grim repression of Massachusetts. Oakes, and his giant cousin Noel Champion, together with a company of twenty, made the preliminary trip to the proposed settlement and negotiated the opening terms with the friendly chief Waramaug, of the Weantinocks. So enthusiastic were they, so overwhelmed at the beauties of this Connecticut, as they came to call it, that they returned at once for their families and their household goods, their servants and treasure, though the last agreement was still to be made, the final papers to be signed, the money and trinkets to be paid over.

Back again in Connecticut the men of the company installed their families and chattels in crude though fairly comfortable temporary quarters in the settlement of Fenwick, and prepared to ride off on the short journey into the country of the Weantinocks. Part of the payment money they took with them, but not all. Captain Oakes was for taking the entire stipulated amount and done with it, for a liking and a mutual trust had sprung up between this English élégant and the foul-smelling, friendly, and shrewd old Chief Waramaug. But the others objected so hotly that he gave in, graciously enough. After all, perhaps all papers should be in order before so important a thing as money could change hands. Coinage was scarce and precious in this new land.

As this point Captain Oakes showed that besides being a magnifico he must have been more than a little mad, as are most great men. For just as they were about to ride off, with a last wave of farewell, out rushed little Tamar, whom he worshipped. It was scarcely daybreak. She was supposed to be in her bed and asleep. But she was dressed in gown and hat and feather. She rushed to his horse's head, held up her arms to her father, wept real tears, went into a fine frenzy, and begged to be taken along.

Judith Oakes, stern of brow but smiling of lip, marched on her overwrought youngest.

"Take me too, Father! Take me too! I want to go with you to the camp of the Indians."

"Stop this nonsense, Temmie," commanded Judith, more amused than angry. "Get along with Debby in the doorstep and hush your crying. Hush it, I say, or there'll be no Indian pudding for you at dinner, and real cream with it. Come along now, do. I'm ashamed of you."

Temmie Oakes was both strong-minded and high-strung—a terrible combination. She now set up a piteous wailing and a stamping of the feet. She threw her arms about the neck of her father's horse, causing that astonished animal to shy and curvet. She clung there, seeming in momentary danger of being trampled to death. Her gray eyes, flecked with brown, were turned on her father in agonized appeal. Temmie could always be counted upon for a superb performance.

Captain Oakes said a surprising thing. "Oh, let her go, Judy. 'Tis but a few hours' ride. We'll be back by nightfall."

Between the two of them they overrode Judith's misgivings, though they did not overcome them. Having won her point thus far, Temmie refused to sit a pillion behind her father but must have her own horse and ride at her father's side. Off they swept, with a clatter of hoofs and a waving of farewells, to where old Waramaug sat awaiting them with his sachem, his sub-chiefs, his wisest and bravest men. A final flirt of the hand. The forest swallowed them.

To Judith Oakes and Mistress Noel Champion, and the other ladies of the company it was a long day until sundown. But at sundown, right enough, they heard the welcome clatter of hoofs. Judith Oakes, in her gown of blue and her camelot cloak billowing blue and scarlet behind her, ran toward the returning cavalcade. Her eye leaped to where the slim little figure in riding skirt and feathered hat would sit the horse beside her father's.

She was not there. Judith looked behind—before—all about the party of horsemen. Then her frantic eye leaped into the dimness of the woods beyond. No tardy little insolent figure, drooping perhaps a bit with weariness, emerged from their dark fastness.

Judith Oakes ran forward, stumbling. "Captain Oakes. Captain Oakes! Where is Temmie?"

Orrange Oakes was off his horse and strode toward her, his arms out. "She's all right, Judy. Temmie's safe enough."

But she saw that it was as though a coating of gray paint overlay the ruddy English coloring of his countenance. For the first time in her life Judith Oakes swooned away.

The story, frantically demanded now, came quickly enough. The company had been received with every courtesy. Final terms were discussed, agreed upon. Old Chief Waramaug, very smelly and dignified, had gravely handed to Captain Oakes the bit of turf with the twig stuck in it—ancient Indian ceremony of turf-and-twig, indicating that the soil, and all it sustained, was now handed over to this English company forever. Now the money and the trinkets. But, the English explained, they had brought only part of the money. The remainder would be paid later. The Indian faces grew statuesque, were frozen with anger and outraged dignity. They had performed the ceremony of turf-and-twig. They had made the last gesture of trust. Now they had been tricked by the English as they had often before been tricked by the French. Protests were unavailing. They withdrew, conferred, returned with their decision. The money must be paid next day. As proof of good faith one member of the party must be left behind with the Indians in their camp. The others must ride away to Fenwick and return. They had chosen as hostage little Tamar Oakes.

Horror in the English ranks. Protest, pleading. Captain Orrange Oakes immediately pleaded that he might stay. They did not even smile their contempt. Noel Champion, the huge, would stay as hostage. No. The whole company would remain, excepting only two who would ride as swiftly as might be back to Fenwick and return at once with the money. No. The Indian dignity, the Indian tribal custom, had been outraged. Tamar, and Tamar only, most precious treasure of Captain Oakes, or the land agreement was void. She would be given every comfort that the camp afforded. No harm would come to her. They were quiet, polite, immovable.

So the company had galloped off, broken. They rode at a terrible pace. As they approached Fenwick their faces were like masks of putty. At sight of Judith Oakes, and their wives and their children, their hearts turned to lead in their bosoms.

Now, dead tired as they were, they called a meeting, secured the remaining sum of money, wheeled and were off again into the forest. They lost their way once, in the blackness, and their utter fatigue. But at sun-up they arrived at the camp of the Weantinocks. There they beheld Temmie, unwashed and completely happy, playing at a game resembling bean bag with the small fry of the tribe. She was having a marvelous time of it; announced that she intended to stay, having made (in the sign language) various enchanting plans for the day—the week, in fact—with the other children. At the announcement that she was to return home at once she now kicked, screamed, and behaved altogether abominably, to the intense surprise of her new-found friends.

So the land deal was consummated. The Weantinocks gracefully withdrew from this magnificent section of their hunting ground. The little colony of aristocrats found themselves possessed of many miles of rich intervale land lying between Pequot Ridge and Wepawaug Ridge, with the wide swift Housatonic and the dimpled little Still River flowing therein. The ridges were sheltering arms within which the fertile meadows lay, serene.

Captain Orrange Oakes, the leader, and his vast cousin

Noel Champion had got their land deeds separately from old Waramaug himself. The Oakes land was the richer and more splendid, embracing in all about one thousand acres.

The colonists had planned, for the most part, and cannily, to build tight clapboard houses out of the oak of the forest and the white pine. Their ceilings were low to hold the precious heat in winter; their stairways were pinched and boxed to keep out the draughts that swept through during the bitter New England winters. They placed them timorously by the roadside for companionship and convenience, and gave them huge central fireplaces, four-square, to save labor and heat. The houses had a purity of line, for all their primness, and a grace, too, and proper proportions, for these were English of taste and background. There was, indeed, something dark and French about these adventurers into the New World, for theirs was the Norman, not the Saxon blood. But of outer elegance their houses had little, though big Noel Champion's house promised, at first, to be the finest for miles around. Built of wood like the others, it was broad-fronted, deep, and spacious—a manor done in the Colonial style. The other frame houses showed plainly that they had been built by a brave—though somewhat frightened —people, in a new and hard country, huddled as protection for each other against cruel winter weather and Red Indians and bitter loneliness. But then, Cousin Noel Champion's physical oddity alone would have decided his type of dwelling for him. Almost seven feet in height, with shoulders like a bull, he would have cracked a low ceiling with his head. The colony well understood his rather grand house plans, and accepted them as a matter of course. They marveled, indeed, how any house could be built big enough to hold Noel Champion in comfort. Beside him even Orrange Oakes, a fine enough figure of a man, dwindled almost to dwarfishness. This Behemothian quality in Cousin Noel Champion was, no doubt, a glandular thing, for every other generation or so there cropped out in the family one member who seemed to have sprung from some prehistoric race, so vast, so out of all proportion to his fellow men. In strange contrast to his elephantine build and enormous strength this family giant (or giantess, for the mark sometimes descended on a woman) always had, oddly enough, a skin like a girl's, pink and white and delicate as a wild rose. Big Noel had it. Big This or Big That had always been prefixed to that member of the family upon whom this heritage of vastness had descended. During the reign of Henry the Eighth one of the Oakes women (Lady Arabella Marvell) had been a famous figure at court. It was said that the other ladies could get their two feet into any one of her shoes, and that her sleeves could be pulled on over the whole of their slim bodies. She was one of the sights of the court, and no joust or feast or revel was complete without her. Poor lady, she was shy of temperament, and sensitive, and very kind. It must have irked her to be known as Big Bella, and to be gaped at wherever she went. Oddly enough, whenever one of these giants turned out to be a girl-child she was automatically named Arabella; every century or so there was a Big Bella striding the Kentish countryside or riding to hounds on a horse of Trojan proportions, so that in breadth and wind and legs he could be equal to the burden he must carry.

So now the colony well understood Big Noel's house plans and approved them as a matter of course. They accepted the fact that, hot or cold, an Oakes refused to huddle. But this mansion of Captain Orrange Oakes! As he set about building this structure, the countryside stared, aghast.

"I'll live in no sniveling cottage," declared Orrange Oakes, "but a proper house, such as the Oakes have always had. A house for a gentleman and a gentleman's family. Not so large, perhaps, as Oakes Lawne, in Kent, but large enough, b'gad! I'll live in no keeper's cottage sort of dwelling so that in every room in the house your nostrils tell you what's for dinner."

He had a kiln set up on the place, and the Negroes dug, moulded, and baked the red clay on the very grounds, so that actually the Oakes house was made of bricks shaped from the very earth on which it stood, the wood in it was hewn from the forest's timbers, the gigantic foundation stones were wrenched out of the soil or torn from its ledges.

Two hundred years later the cellars and foundations

of the house were a mystery to students of old dwellings. They were evidently made of field stones and ledge rocks left by prehistoric glaciers to break the backs of thousands of toiling, stiff-necked New Englanders. But one of these foundation stones, by actual measurement, was found to be twenty-two feet long, two feet wide, and fourteen inches thick. There were many others between ten and twenty feet long. It was a legend in the neighborhood that these monoliths had been broken into proper size by a phenomenally powerful Negro slave named Esau who had shaped them by dropping a huge boulder upon them, which stone he first balanced on his head. In lieu of a suitable tool of harder metal, great Esau's skull and the black marble pillar of his neck seemed to have served very well. The ledge from which these great shafts of stone were torn was traced to a spot fully ninety yards distant from the house site. They must have been transported by stone boats on rollers, in itself a herculean feat.

Candace Baldwin, many, many years later, measuring and marveling as she measured, exclaimed, "There were giants in those days." Then, when she began, with reverent but necessarily ruthless hand, to tear down partitions in remodeling, "I'll bet a million dollars that Wren himself had a hand in this house. It's as unmistakable as a Rembrandt."

She was right. For as Orrange Oakes had gone about directing the building of his dwelling he had carried certain detailed plans in his hand, which he consulted and studied throughout each day. He had, indeed, sent to England to ask of his old friend Kit Wren his opinion as to what an American country gentleman's house should be. With this request he had forwarded some description of the hills and forests and streams and meadows of the lovely Connecticut countryside.

"It has, my dear Kit," he had written, "a resemblance to our own Kent, but it is different. It is grander, bolder, vaster, more sweeping. The sky looms larger, the trees grow higher, the rocks seem more grim. It has, I may say, quite another kind of beauty. A kind of American beauty."

Promptly as could be, certain plans were forwarded him from England. In one corner they were neatly signed, "Sir Christopher Wren."

So it was not entirely an English house, for it took some account of American climate, American soil, American needs. It stood so that two giant oaks guarded its doorway like sentinels. Under its eaves, when it was finished, ran a hand-carved cornice in an exquisite pattern of oak leaves. The great beams of the house were solid oak, put together with hand-made oak pegs. The wood was so hard that, centuries later, modern carpenters and contractors cursed deeply as the resisting oak actually bent their shoddy metal tools.

There were twenty rooms and twenty fireplaces in this grand house in the Connecticut wilds. During the winter it took quite a tidy little army of Negro slaves just to keep these fires burning. Day and night they went softly to and fro carrying neat stacks of logs in rough canvas holders; replenishing the flames, tidying the hearths, gently shoveling the ashes. The ceilings of those rooms were fully fourteen feet high, and through the house, downstairs and up, ran a broad central hallway into which you might have stuffed the whole of any one of the salt-box dwellings thereabouts. The place was chill as a tomb, and Judith Oakes, poor lady, must have felt many a shiver agitate her sloping shoulders during those long bitter winters.

To have built this brick house at all was a thing remarkable enough, and not so faintly akin to feats in mythology and the Bible. But not content with this, Orrange Oakes must needs enhance it with all sorts of oddments and elegancies. The stairway leading up from the main hall had a twisted newel post of mahogany with undercut carving, and the banisters too were of mahogany, and turned, at that. On the second floor the large square hall off which the chambers led was called the "saloon." It was almost an upstairs drawing room, with its books and plants and sewing table and mahogany and cherrywood chairs. In the sleeping chamber of Orrange and Judith Oakes the posts of the great oak bed were mortised into the floor and extended to the ceiling, supporting a framework from which hung the lustrous damask curtains. Wall papers, rich and heavy, were imported from England.

It was a little later that Captain Oakes had built for his gifted wife a glass cage attached to the house and so situated that it caught the sun from dawn to dusk. There, like an orchid, that remarkable woman sat, reading and studying. She had learned French and Latin as a child in England, and now she took up the study of Italian. She wrote poems, too, was an astronomer of parts, and played the piano—the first and only piano in Connecticut.

There was no end to the wonders of that house. Take the saddle room, off the main hall. It was called a closet, but was certainly large as many a room; and here, on long wooden hand-made oak pegs, hung the fine silver-mounted saddles of the family, too precious for mere stable shelter. Take the four huge baking ovens down in the vast kitchen, testifying to the abundant hospitality of the house. Any one of these things, in 1707 Connecticut, was a seventh wonder. But it was, perhaps, the fanlight over the front door that gave the structure its final touch of utter completeness.

In design the fanlight was a crown, forming the base, from which, in delicate pattern, there sprayed the symbolic shamrock, the thistle and the rose. The effect was breath-taking in its airy grace, as when a fan of real ivory and lace is held up before the features of a ravishing beauty, its transparencies enhancing, but not concealing, those features.

In the cool half light that this jewel cast upon the main hall there hung the treasured portrait of the

romantic and ill-fated Sir Orrange Oakes. The ship
Abigail had brought him to Boston in 1635, and there
he should have stayed for his own good, poor gentleman.
But back he needs must go to England. You now saw
portrayed long dark curling locks on suave black satin
shoulders; great gray eyes with brown flecks in them;
the whole relieved by the high light of a lace ruffled shirt.
More visionary than fighter or statesman—it was this
that had brought about his doom. For beneath the portrait was a neat gilt-lettered placard:

SIR ORRANGE OAKES THE YOUNGER
1612–1657

REPUBLICAN AND PURITAN

He was of a turbulant and visionary temperament and came into
collision with Cromwell.

Beheaded on Tower Hill 1657.

A grim and glorious epitaph. He who had come into
collision with Cromwell now looked down upon his
descendants' peaceful hall and dominated it with his elegance, his courage, his gray poet's eyes.

III

I T WAS late autumn a full year after their coming to
Connecticut that the house was completed, and ready
for occupancy. And the week of the great house-warming
it was that Tamar Oakes died. It is almost impossible to
tell the story of the sandstone slab that forms the hearthstone before the fireplace in the dining room. For that
hearthstone gives to the old Oakes house such a touch of
the macabre that one who has not seen it cannot quite
believe it.

Temmie Oakes, child of their late love, had always
been an elfin sort of creature, with her little pointed face,
her small-boned body, her great gray eyes with the golden
flecks in them that seemed akin to the little golden
freckles that dusted her nose. Any woman less balanced,
less altogether admirable than Judith Oakes, might have
known resentment and even jealousy at her husband's
adoration of the girl. Both worshiped her, but Judith's
love was tempered with sound maternal judgment.
Neither quite understood this odd sprite which they had
brought forth after love's ardors were long supposed to
have cooled.

Sometimes Temmie appeared to revel in such luxuries
as her father's abundant means allowed; at other times

she seemed to rebel against the prunes and prisms of a young miss's well ordered life. One day she exclaimed with delight at the gay chintzes of the bedroom which was to be hers. The next she pouted and protested that she wanted no such suffocating stuffs about her; she was all for living in a tent, like the Indians, and sleeping on a bed of skins. She spoke often of that night of her enforced stay with the Weantinocks; regarded it as the high event in her quite eventful enough young life. In common with her father she had a genuine regard and liking for the friendly Indians of the region. On the rare occasions when old Waramaug, blanketed and saturnine, visited her father briefly, speaking through an interpreter, she was always to be found, somehow, in the group, or near it, drifting in and out of the conversation, pulling at Waramaug's blanket, admiring his elaborate moccasins, smiling her brilliant smile straight into his stolid face. She had implored her father a hundred times to be taken back to visit her Indian playmates.

The four great ovens were going full blast, the house was all astir with preparation, the whole district of Oakesfield was agog with anticipation, when it was noticed that Tamar was missing. She had expressed in no uncertain terms (being her father's own daughter, and her strong-minded mother's) her dislike of all this bustle and fuss, and had flounced out of the grand new house in a huff, declaring that she wanted to be alone for a while. She had gone down to the river bank, they thought, or was idling on the outskirts of the near-by wood, though that was forbidden.

When she failed to appear at midday dinner there was anger in the household but little alarm. By four the household was definitely uneasy, by six terribly alarmed, by nine frantic. The bell in the loom house was tolled. The men of the household, the servants, slaves, the men of all Oakesfield joined in the search for her. The river was searched, the forests, the near-by hills. They went to the camp of the Weantinocks, many miles away, their faces stern, but there they found nothing. Waramaug and his braves themselves joined in the hunt that lasted all night and all next day. Preparations for the great house-warming were, of course, abandoned. It was Waramaug himself who with Orrange Oakes close beside him had come upon her at nightfall, lying dead. She had run off to join the camp of the Weantinocks, no doubt, in a childish prank, and had died of exhaustion, or fright, being an overwrought and delicate child; or perhaps of exposure. It was old Waramaug and Orrange Oakes who brought her home to the grand new house.

All that night, over the hills, across Pequot and Wepawaug Ridge there came, faint and faraway, the slow muffled beat of the Indian drums—slow . . . beat . . . beat . . . throb . . . throb . . . a sound as inexorable, as unescapable, as the footsteps of fate.

Orrange Oakes shut himself away from everyone; from his wife, even. He sat alone with the dead child,

a broken old man. Judith Oakes did not reproach him.
Toward nightfall he called her.

"Forgive me, Jude."

She took him in her arms as though he were a child
given her to take the place of the dead child upstairs in
the cold still chamber with its gay English chintzes.

They sat closeted together for a long time, talking,
talking, in low tones. Those outside could hear the sound
of his voice, hoarse with grief and weariness, and hers,
patient, tender. Then, suddenly, a sharp cry of horror
from her—a scream, almost. Then sobs. Then these, too,
checked by this amazing woman. No one knew what they
spoke about, but within twenty-four hours it was easy to
guess, for by that time Oakesfield was agog with it, and
the news spread throughout all Connecticut and even
sped to England by the next boat.

The two now emerged from the closed room. She was
so white in her swathings of black that it was as though
she, too, had died. He stumbled, gropingly, like a blind
man.

Judith Oakes gave her orders in an even voice. "Captain Oakes is badly in need of sleep. Turn down the bed.
Get the warming pans. Mend the fire. Debby, tell Zeb
a hot toddy, with plenty of rum."

Judith Oakes sat sentinel, taking no part in the bustle
and stir below stairs. The house hummed with hushed
footsteps, with sibilant hisses of sympathy, with the muted
whir and clatter of preparation for the funeral baked

meats that were to have been spread for a quite different occasion.

Captain Oakes slept heavily, a tortured, murmuring sleep. At dusk there appeared, silently and suddenly, a tall blanketed figure that stationed itself beside one of the giant oaks that guarded the entrance doorway. Judith Oakes went to her husband's bedside. She placed a hand on his shoulder, gently.

"He is come," she said, between white lips.

The rest is legend. Tamar Oakes was cremated in the kiln which had been built for the firing of the bricks of which the house was made. All night long the fires burned. Captain Oakes kept watch out there, and old Waramaug, the Weantinock, and Big Noel Champion, and black Esau, the Negro slave. Judith Oakes sat in her chamber, a statue. The child's ashes were placed in a white jade box that had come all the way by sailing vessel from China. Orrange Oakes could not bear to have his darling taken from his house. She must stay near him, even in death. So they removed from its place the great red sandstone slab, quarried from native rock, that had been the hearthstone in front of the vast fireplace in the dining room. The slab was duly inscribed and put back, for under it they had placed the jade box with its ashes that had been the body of Tamar Oakes.

The casual caller, years later, standing at ease on the hearthstone, warming his coat tails before the dining-room fire, glanced casually down to find his eye caught

by an inscription carved into the slab on which he stood
balancing comfortably, heel and toe. Reading it, idly, he
was likely to leap from the spot with the haste of a
tripper at Westminster Abbey who finds himself standing
on a Name.

TAMAR OAKES
1693–1708
Aged 15 yrs. 7 mo. 21 d's.
We shall not weep for thee since thou hast gone unsullied back
to Heaven.

Feeling this dining-room slab something in the nature
of a skull at the feast, visitors were wont to experience
that prickling of the scalp, that pimpling of the skin, that
comes with sudden panic; but the Oakes family, in time,
came to take it quite as a matter of course, like any other
bizarre feature of this amazing house.

They were a large family, the Oakes household; yet
now suddenly the rooms seemed empty. The spoiled elfin
child had been the center about which the whole spirit
of the place had functioned. In the day's routine she had
provided the elements of suspense, excitement, irritation.

Captain Oakes issued an order that might well have
caused more than a flutter of remonstrance from any lady
less spirited than the redoubtable Judith Oakes.

"I wish this to be understood," he had said, the members and servants of his household gathered about him—
and quite a sizable little army they made, too, massed
together in the main lower hallway. "There is to be al-

ways a fire kept burning in the oak room of the east wing, and the door left unlatched summer and winter. The fire, in winter, is to be piled high with wood, and an extra stack beside it in case that a wayfaring Indian, original owner of this soil, should chance to pass by."

There was a stir of wonderment and something resembling protest at this, but an order from Captain Oakes was a command. In time it came to be in no way unusual to learn that several Indians had spread their blankets before that hospitable fire on stormy or bitter winter nights, and had departed silently as the dawn came.

"But I wonder at you, Mrs. Oakes, I do indeed!" the lesser ladies of the community would declare. "However do you manage to sleep, or even close an eye, for that matter, knowing that those savages are there in your very house, plotting who knows what manner of murder without mercy and you helpless in your bed?"

Mrs. Oakes was considered queer, at best, though regarded with as great a degree of respectful awe by the ladies as was her husband by the men. "We've still our scalps, you see," she replied, giving her head a little toss, for she was justly proud of her mass of intricately coiled black hair. "One night last week Captain Oakes informed me that old Waramaug himself was there, squatting by the fire with his pipe. I could not close my eyes that night —venison steaks for supper, and I am but a poor hand at digesting these queer wild meats, and always shall be —or perhaps it was that thoughts of Waramaug always bring to mind more clearly than usual our little Temmie. Or it may have been the stars kept me awake."

"The stars!" murmured the ladies, in polite wonderment, and darting glances at one another.

"So I dressed and came down with my candle, and there he was by the fire, rolling a great leaf of this tobacco they raise. When he saw me he rose and motioned me out of doors. I followed him. And what do you think!"

"What?" said the ladies, breathlessly, putting down their teacups and leaning forward, aquiver.

"Orion was in the ascendant."

"O'Ryan!" echoed the ladies, utterly mystified at the sudden introduction of this Irish unknown into their midst.

"Orion—the constellation. I've never seen it so brilliant in all my days—nights, I should say. There he was the great Greek beauty, hunting across the sky, and his girdle so bright that it fairly dazzled one's eyes to look at it."

Small wonder they thought her queer, with her Orions, her glass cages, her poetry, her Italian studies. Astronomy —they said, repeating the tale the length and breadth of the settlement—studying the stars, mind you, with a dirty savage, in the middle of the night. Well!

But though they gossiped not a little about this strange Oakes household, and wondered about it, they looked up to it, too, and copied it as best they might. Undoubtedly they all knew many aspects of hardship, but there was about their manner of living in this brief period of Connecticut's history a kind of splendor and lavishness that were not to be met again. They were, for the most part, a well-to-do group in the beginning. In every household there were bins of cornmeal, rye, buckwheat, and wheat flour. Festoons of dried apples hung in the attics and kitchens; and herbs for flavoring and for medicine. There were partridges in the woods, pheasants in the brush. In the poultry yards were chickens, turkeys, geese, and ducks. The turbulent Housatonic River was so crowded with shad that one could all but scoop them up by the handfuls. It was the most prosperous and comfortable period of Colonial life in America. Merchant ships from China and the Indies brought rich silks, tissues, embroidered gauzes, porcelain and tapestries. From England came fine clothes made by fashionable London tailors, wigs from popular wig makers. Fashions in Oakesfield, wild and remote as it was, were never more than a year behind those of London. Orrange Oakes had sent to New York for the Dutch painter, Van Oogstraat, in order to have a portrait of Temmie (this was just before her death) in the highly unpuritan costume of a court lady—stiff stomacher, ruffles of point lace, necklace of pearls, a fan in one hand, in the other a rose. She had rebelled at the costume, and her piquant, humorous, pointed little face mirrors that laughing rebellion. He had hung it in the big chamber upstairs, over the fireplace, so that his eye fell on it first when he woke in the morning, and last when he slept at night.

These wealthy emigrés ate and drank much as England ate and drank, but they knew, too, the tang of New World food over which the gourmets of the Old World had never smacked their lips.

At the Noel Champions they ate very well, for Big Noel was a huge feeder, but hospitality reached its peak in the Oakes household. Of its four great ovens, one was seldom idle. From the Sound at Lyme or New London came kits of salted shad, mackerel, and salmon. In the cellars were barrels of corned beef and salted pork; lard, sausage, and head cheese. In the dark, earthy-smelling root cellars were bins and barrels of apples and winter pears and vegetables. The choicest apples and pears were wrapped in tissue paper for use at Thanksgiving time and New Year's. In the smoke house were hams, bacon, and dried beef. Butter and cream were used as freely as though they were condiments. Other cooks might make shift with what came to hand, but no mere cider ever went into the making of the Oakes' mince pies, to spoil the flavor of brandy and sherry.

Witness to the romantic connection between these bleak New England settlements and far-off China and the West Indies were exotic jars of ginger and tamarind brought in by Yankee captains of full-breasted sailing vessels bearing prim Puritan names—the *Abigail*—the *Sarah Mariah*—the *Mehetable Barnes*.

For that matter, Judith Oakes actually boasted a great cloak of darkest sable skins, most precious of furs, that had come all the way from Russia. Orrange Oakes had ordered it through Captain Zophar Bunce whose sailing vessel had brought it from northern China. A magnificent garment in any place or climate, it was a last lavish touch in these Connecticut wilds. It came to know strange and degraded usages as the decades rolled into centuries.

Not the Indies and China alone, but Africa, too, laid a hot dark hand on this virgin land. There were a full hundred slaves on the Oakes place. The Connecticut settler, abhorring political or religious slavery, saw no objection to human family slavery so long as it paid. Outside Captain Oakes' study door in the daytime and his chamber door at night was always stationed on duty one of two little black page boys. It was the duty of these buttons to run errands, carry messages to stable or field, or to other members of the Oakes household above stairs or below.

"Tell Hannah a glass of sherry for Captain Oakes."

"Black Prince to be saddled and brought round at eleven."

"Zeke is to present Captain Oakes' compliments to Mr. Noel Champion, and will he and Mistress Champion take dinner on Wednesday next at three."

A slave sold for from sixty shillings to twenty-five pounds. Later, of course, the price rose to one hundred pounds for really choice goods. Captain Medad Pring always took his vessel to Africa after he had made his trip to the West Indies, and gathering up a load of Negroes there he did a brisk trade in New England. Even Deacon Jared Dibble kept two slaves in a little cabin on his small place. For that matter, the following blithe advertisement appearing in the *Connecticut Gazette* went as unremarked as many another like it:

To be sold, a strong and healthy Negro man, 29 years of age, and brought up in the country to the farming business. Also an able body'd wench, 16 years old (with sucking child) can do all sorts of housework . . . . for no other fault than her breeding. Enquire of printer.

Land and slaves; peace and plenty. More and more tight little white clapboard houses sprang up in the vicinity of Oakesfield, and the admonishing fingers of church spires shone more thickly among the black tips of the hemlock forests. Wool and fustian began to come in; the great places, like Oakes Farm, were self sustaining, but for the small man there was now the need of the crossroads blacksmith, the carpenter, the peddler. New settlements had sprung up not far distant, and they bore names as English as Oakesfield: Windsor, Windham, Litchfield, Groton. They planted the fields in corn and fertilized them after the Indian fashion with fish—thousands of shad to the acre, hauled in nets out of the Housatonic and the Sound, and the fields stank to heaven. Apprentice workmen and hired hands refused to sign a contract which stipulated that they were to be given shad or mackerel as provender more than twice a week. And soon the rivers were to be free of fish, and the rocky fields barren.

Captain Orrange Oakes and Judith had grandchildren now older than their own Temmie had been. The Oakes house, big as it was, began to be too small for the sons and daughters of their sons and daughters. Or perhaps it only seemed too small to contain the growing mood of restlessness that had come upon this third generation. The two old people tried to curb it. Captain Oakes, with the years, had lost much of that iron indomitability which had made him so awesome a figure of leadership in the old days. But life seemed to hold no fires fierce enough to melt the metal of Judith Oakes' resistance.

It was she who insisted on packing her granddaughters off to boarding school in spite of the fact that women's education was supposed to be quite complete as found within the four walls of their home.

"Boarding school," insisted this terrific old matriarch, herself mistress of three languages, and steeped in the stars.

"Boarding school!" echoed the ladies of Oakesfield, who never ceased to be astonished at each modern pronouncement of this, their social leader. "Boarding school —for young ladies!"

"Certainly," snapped Judith. "There'll be a time when schools for women will be as common as schools for men —colleges, too, and universities, right here in Connecticut, I'll be bound."

They decided, privately, that age had at last turned Judith Oakes more than a little queer. "What school have you in mind for them?"

She was well past sixty now: thin, straight, vital, and strong as steel.

"The Moravian school conducted by the Countess Benigna Zinzendorf, in Pennsylvania."

She therewith, in triumph, produced a letter and a neatly worded pamphlet stating that, besides book learning and manners, young ladies were instructed in the art of making lovely embroidered pictures on cream-colored satin pillows. And off went her oldest girl grandchildren, the Misses Clarissa and Judith, to the Moravian boarding school founded by the Countess Benigna Zinzendorf. It was the first school for young ladies in the Colonies.

Before their education was completed—before, in fact, they had so much as finished a flock of the cream-colored hand-painted satin pillows, old Judith was wearing a widow's cap, and Captain Orrange Oakes lay in the Oakes family plot in the Oakesfield cemetery, an imposing edifice over him, in form a canopy that was like a marble table on which seraphim wrestled with cherubim, and urns and wreaths vied with each other. In later centuries lovers found it a convenient seat for loitering, and it was slyly whispered that that chaste white slab had been put to an even more unholy use.

Judith Oakes' garments of woe were monumental. Her widow's cap, in the mode of the day, towered half a foot high, with its insets of finest white plaited muslin, stiffened, tier on tier, with wire. She wore with this, in the meeting house, when she visited her husband's grave, or on the other rare occasions when she left her winter fireside, her great cloak of Russian sable—the one sable cloak in all the Colonies.

The Oakes family, magnificent Colonists though they were, remained forever English. When the Revolution broke, the Orrange Oakes of that time refused naturally to take part in it and calmly removed himself and his family to Nova Scotia until the unpleasantness should be over. His Connecticut neighbors seemed not to take this amiss. Many, indeed, followed suit, loyal to royalty. Indeed, one of the distinctions that marked the old Oakes house was that it, alone among the fine dwellings of the Connecticut colony, had never been slept in by General George Washington. Oakes women, later of course, looked down upon the Daughters of the American Revolution as upstarts.

And now the unrest that had brought these people or their forebears to Connecticut from Massachusetts, and to Massachusetts from England, had them again by the throat. By temperament and inclination they never had been farmers, really. They were restless, neurotic, great movers, irked by monotony, impatient of strait-laced convention. Primness and order and commonplace middle-class rigidity of conduct had established itself in Connecticut as prim, commonplace middle-class people flocked more thickly into the state. The truth was that they were not farmers at all, these early settlers and their offspring. They had a practical—an almost Teutonic—ambition for trade and enterprise. They were adaptable. They had learned from the Indians how to raise corn and tobacco and to store these in bins and cribs. They had learned the uses of wood and of clay and of rock. From the Indians they had got the knowledge of strange medicines—valuable febrifuges, purgatives, astringents, balsams, and stimulants. They employed witch hazel, corn poultices, lobelia, sweat baths, cascara. And into their too rigid Elizabethan vocabulary had crept the tang and bite of strange Indian words, quickening it. Indian summer—woodchuck—mugwump—chipmunk—toboggan—moccasin—squash—skunk—Tammany—pale-face —hatchet—fire water. Bury the hatchet, they said, when they patched up a quarrel with a friend. Smoke the pipe of peace. It gave a raciness and spice to their speech.

Judith Oakes' grandsons and their young friends were muttering now. Their restlessness grew, and their complaints mounted. The novelty was past. The fields were ungrateful, the winters long and hard. "There's no end to the stones in these fields," they protested. "The soil spews them up. No sooner do you get a field cleared of them than within another year a new layer has somehow worked its way to the surface. It's my opinion they boil up from hell, those stones, cooling on the way."

One by one, at first, and then in groups, they packed up their wives and daughters, the married men, or alone if single, and were off to the mellow lands of Ohio or the rich wastes of Texas. The mercantile minded drifted to the cities and engaged in trade or in manufacture. The sons of tin peddlers began to manufacture things of tin.

and the second or third generation of cap and cloth sellers settled in near-by Stonefield and turned out hats and caps in wholesale. They left behind them the old, the incompetent, the sick, the unadventurous, the contented. To their brothers tied to the farm, to their spinster sisters, to their mothers and fathers anguished at parting they said, blithely, "We'll send for you." But the stay-at-home brothers tilled the rocky fields, and the spinster sisters sat by the fire and spun, and the old people began to fill the little hillside cemeteries.

They lived terribly long, those old people, in that bracing climate. And even when they were gone they left behind them, inscribed on their gravestones, a note of resentment or a grisly warning like a bony forefinger shaken from beyond the grave.

ZEBULON TUTHILL
Life at the longest is a dream
How few our days how short our years

AE 90 yrs 10 mo 26 ds

GERSHOM PYNCHON
AE 87 yrs and 4 mo

Be Ye Also Ready

Or, confidently:

JARED DIBBLE
Gone to Heaven

Like a sign on an office door. Out for lunch. Back at two.

The living old ones became whiter, drier, more tranparent. All winter long they stayed indoors, hugging the fires in the low-ceilinged, boxlike rooms, enduring continual colds and aches and pains of age. February was torture, March a gray specter; but with the first pale yellow rays of the early spring sun you saw these old ones creeping timidly out of doors to sit creakingly on the doorstep, or to move for a grateful moment, very bleached and brittle, about the yard, like old slugs.

Thin blood intermarried with thin blood or married not at all. The wedded seemed to breed daughters, for the countryside was now almost denuded of men. Or perhaps it was only the daughters who remained locked, perforce, in the cold and stony embrace of this New England soil.

Time and weather began to take their toll even of the graceful and romantic names on the sandstone or marble of the old burying ground. Indeed, the elements seemed to find a malicious pleasure in first obliterating those names, leaving the unavailing epitaphs to the last. You could barely decipher some of them—others not at all. Cynthia. Amaryllis. Challons. Godfrey. Oliver. Malvern. Orrange. Judith. Coarser names shone out now as their neighbors. George. Jennie. Fred. Annie.

The houses, uninhabited, fell into decay. Ruined houses, eyeless, their windows destroyed by mischievous boys, or by time or weather. The empty gaping doors hung open-mouthed. Sometimes, on a deserted hillock, there was left standing, of a sturdy house that once had teemed with life, only a crazy chimney, like a gaunt and spectral sentinel.

The Puritan decline that had set in almost two centuries before, in early Massachusetts, was now complete. Restraint in England, and revolt. Restraint in Massachusetts, and revolt. A longing for possessions. A vain attempt to stifle this. Revolt again, and away for good and all. Away to the cities for these merchants and traders. No barren, rocky land for them. Let the pinched and poor-spirited have it and welcome. Let them stay on this hateful flinty soil and live on it if they could; and die on it.

So the gay splendid company of 1700 passed like a parade. You heard the faint ghostly echoes of their music, saw the last flash of their color, their glow, their vitality. Then their splendor vanished forever. The ghost of it sometimes haunted an attic chest, with its musty silks and satins and velvets, or grinned at you from a gravestone.

Then the landscape settled into the rigor of death. Only the orchards persisted in the spring, masses of delirious color and scent; and the old stone fences, erected in sweat and blood; and the ancient houses, neglected, stricken, gray. They took on the color of the land itself, and the land settled down, grimly content, and folded its drab garments upon its stony bosom, for it had had its revenge upon a people who had taken it without love.

IV
1890

B Y THE time Tamar Pring was fifteen and came, like a stray puppy, forlorn and alone, to live with her spinster aunt Judith Oakes, there wasn't a man in Oakesfield or for miles around. That is to say, a real man. There were the spring-halted hired men, native to the region, withered twigs of once-fine family trees. And there were the Poles, of course. But the Polacks didn't count. For that matter, queerly enough, the very week that had brought Temmie to live on her aunt's farm had seen Ondia Olszak installed there as hired man. Jude Oakes, brusque, and considered more than a little queer, had speedily had her way with the names of both these newcomers.

"Ondia?" she had snapped at Olszak when she had hired him. "What kind of a name's that?"

"Ondia is name," he had replied, with his charming frank smile. His eyes were very blue, his shoulders broad, his figure medium and stocky, his hands powerful, well shaped, with golden hair strong on the wrists. Jude Oakes felt a little queer as she looked at him; stirred. She resented this, fiercely, and doubled her brusqueness.

"Ondia is Pole name," he repeated, engagingly. This gaunt, bristling woman amused him and did not terrify. He had known the terrifying women of his own Poland. "Ondia Olszak."

"I'll call you Ondy," she had said. "I can't be bothered with these plaguy Polack names."

With her little niece, Tamar, she had been even more ruthless.

"Pring!" The name, as Jude uttered it, was a byword and a mocking. "There'll be no Prings under this roof. Bad enough that your mother should have taken the name—if she really did. Oakes—that'll be your name from now on, as long as you're in my care. Tamar Oakes. It's a name you'll do well to be proud of—Oakes."

The girl voiced a timid protest. "Mama always called me Temmie."

"Tamar," repeated Jude Oakes, as though steeling herself against the girl's touching youth. But Temmie she came to be, soon enough, to the household—to Jude, and to Jude's brother little Jotham Oakes, the dwarf; and to Ondy, and to the whole district of Oakesfield.

Oakesfield farmers of New England stock had been aghast at the news that Judith Oakes had taken on a Polack as hired man. It was known that she was hard to get on with—quarrelsome and domineering. She had had a long succession of hired men on her farm—native farm hands, and Swedish farm hands, and native again. She was considered a formidable woman, and hard. Once, in a particularly black fury, she had given out that she and her dwarf brother, Jot Oakes, would manage the work of the farm themselves and be forever rid of these hulking lazy louts—her words. But this was, of course, absurd and impossible, and lasted no longer than a day. Though the farm had dwindled, and much of it now was wild, there still were some four or five hundred acres.

Oakesfield resented the incoming Poles, though by now you found them employed on the manless farms all over this part of Connecticut, and up into Massachusetts. Here and there one of them even owned a small farm, paying for it dollar by dollar, usually, but sometimes buying it outright, astonishingly enough, with money saved by working a farm on shares; the entire family in the fields from dawn to dark. When first these alien people had drifted into Connecticut native Oakesfield had looked upon them distrustfully as a strange and even savage race. Much of that feeling still persisted. In an earlier day Puritan Connecticut and Massachusetts would no doubt have put them to death as evil beings who bewitched the farms and made them bloom by some black magic.

Now, more and more, into this desiccated community —into this unvital region with its manless households— came these foreign people in whom the blood of many countries combined to make the Slav. Blood of the Hungarian was in them, of the Austrian too, perhaps, of the Saracen, of the Pole, the Russian, the Bohemian. They came to this new country eager, humble, worshiping the dirt they plowed, the furrows into which they sowed the seed. They loved the land with the ardor of born farmers who come from a country where land has always been scarce and precious. Their passion went into it. They felt about it as men feel about women. It was their pastime, their emotional life, their dream of possession. Money they did not covet. They were land lovers.

These men were very male, too, the pulse pounding exultantly in their throats. Their ankles were strong and quick and flexible. The red blood was in their cheeks and the backs of their necks. You saw the sinews rippling beneath the cheap stuff of their sweaty shirts. Far, far too heady a draught for the digestion of this timorous New England remnant of a dying people. For the remaining native men of the region were stringy of withers, lean shanked, of vinegar blood and hard wrung. These Polacks, though, as they called them, did odd crazy things. A plume of lilac stuck into the hatband as they hauled a load of manure. They drank quantities of beer, made casks of hard, heady wine, fought fiercely among themselves; in field after field you saw the broad petticoated backsides of women bent over the tobacco plants. Razkows. Osniaks. Porzyckis.

John Veal, none too bright at best, hearing news of Jude Oakes' contemplated change, hurried, hotfoot, to warn her. He, in his day, had been one of the procession of hired men who had served under Jude's stormy reign.

He thought now, as he loped with his loose-limbed stride along the rutted country road from the crossroads store to Oakes Farm, that if she had not already hired this Polack she might give him another chance. He did not relish the idea of again working for Jude Oakes. No man of spirit could. But John Veal's virility had been none too glowing in his youth. Now, at fifty, he was a wattled and rickety pantaloon. But beneath his reluctance to face his former employer in the rôle of supplicant was a little anticipatory thrill that was made up of fear and hate and grudging admiration. While in her employ as hired man he and Jude had waged daily battle. He pictured her now as he trudged along. A ferocious woman, with smoldering eyes, her black hair heavily streaked with gray, but still strongly giving the effect of black. There was about her an intensity that somehow embarrassed men. There was a fixity in her gaze, a bite in her speech. Even when a girl of twenty she had been considered odd. Though Oakes Farm had got out of hand she made a great to-do about managing the place. It was accounted one of the worst-run farms in the district. Jude had a sort of office in the room off the main hall that in the old days of the great house had been known as the saddle room. Here she kept a mass of untidy books, papers, and files. Old catalogues were piled here, seed bags; out-dated calendars dangled crazily from the oaken pegs that once had held fine silver-mounted saddles. A musty gray shawl hung on one peg, at hand for Jude

to snatch up and throw over her head on a trip to barn
or field. A great copper basin that once had known
kitchen or buttery held dried bulbs. At one side of the
great desk was a lamp that had burned whale oil, and
the desk itself, could it have been seen beneath the ruck
of old papers, dust, ink spots, and canvas sacks smelling
of the barnyard, would have been found to be of finest
cherry wood, exquisitely inlaid and put together by the
loving hand of a master craftsman; scuffed now,
scratched, defaced by boot marks and stains.

It was here, John Veal thought, that he probably
would find her, as it was too early still for the midday
meal and too late for her morning chores. Many a stormy
session he had had with her in that room. A formidable
woman. Always frettin' an' frothin', John Veal thought,
an' raisin' Ned.

It was not easy to get into the Oakes house. It was
known that frequently Miss Judy pretended to be out
when she really was upstairs in her chamber, peering
down upon the departing visitor with a baleful eye
through the broken shutter. Certainly John Veal never
dreamed of considering the front door as a means of
entrance—that handsome old door with its fanlight that
looked like lace, and its gilded knocker. He went cautiously around to the rear, an eye out for the mean
mongrel dog, and hoping little Jot would answer his
knock instead of Jude. Jotham Oakes, the little man, the
dwarf, with his round red cheeks and his white thick hair,

and his china-blue eyes and his laugh that at first amused you and that later annoyed you to the point of frenzy.

John Veal glanced toward the barn and then beyond, to the dilapidated tobacco shed. But he decided to try the house, first. In his hand he carried a letter, and this he would make the excuse for his visit. The postmaster, who was also storekeeper at the crossroads, had given it to him for delivery to Miss Jude when Veal had announced his intention to call at Oakes Farm. The letter was bulky. It was postmarked New Orleans. John Veal was curious about it. Everyone in Oakesfield was inquisitive about his neighbor's business. Veal would have opened the letter if he safely could.

He rapped sharply at the kitchen door. Again. Again. No one answered. Softly he lifted the latch and peered into the kitchen. It was October, and cold. But the fire in the kitchen stove seemed to be almost out. A slovenly housekeeper, Jude Oakes. Evidently she had no one now to do for her in the house. Veal peered, listened, stepped in.

"Halloo!" Silence. In the little office, likely. He was determined to see her. The letter clutched in his hand would be his excuse if she started a tirade. Softly he tiptoed across the vast kitchen, opened a door, hallooed again, opened another, and thus alternately tiptoeing and hallooing came down the main hall and into the little musty office. It was empty. Again he called. Waited. He felt sure now that the house was empty. He tiptoed into the south sitting room, a place about which he always had had great curiosity and into which he had never before ventured. It was empty as the rest, but as he stood there, gaping eagerly about, his slow wits noted that a fire of hickory logs snapped and sparkled in the grate. His pale bulging eyes devoured the room. High ceilinged, graciously proportioned, it was now a welter of disorder. Papers and yellow-backed paper novels were strewn about. On the walls were French prints, delicate as pastels. The keys of the old piano, with its mother-of-pearl inlay, were yellow as a meerschaum. On a mahogany drop-leaf table was a miscellany of objects—a cut-glass luster candelabrum, a rare china bowl filled with a jumble of spools, nails, and buttons; a half-smoked cheroot. John Veal grinned at that. It was well known that Jude Oakes smoked little light cigars that she herself carelessly rolled. Along one wall was a broad couch covered in coarse brown denim. At one end was a crumpled mass of dusty brown cushions, stained and soiled and still bearing the indentation of the head that had nested there. At the foot, in a softly crumpled heap, lay a great cloak of fur, worn bare almost to the skin, but showing in spots here and there a deep luster, like a dark jewel. Mangy, moth-eaten, the coverlet that Jude Oakes sometimes used to keep off the night chill, it was nothing less than the sable cloak—the magnificent sable cloak—that Judith Oakes had had from Captain Orrange Oakes so long ago. Degraded now, sullied, degenerated like its owner, but somehow still bearing, like her, marks of a past splendor.

John Veal heard quick footsteps. He turned, took a lunging step forward, as though to escape. Too late. He gulped, grotesquely, so that his Adam's apple bobbed up and down. The letter trembled in his bony hand. But it was not Judith, in her long loose black gown.

A tiny man trotted in. He was rubbing his little hands with the cold. When he saw John Veal he came forward, enormously cordial. He chuckled and bubbled with laughter. He was like a happy child.

"Why, how-do, John Veal! How are you, John? Glad to see you. Sit down, sit down. Well, how are you? Glad to see you. It's cold. It's kind of cold."

He usually said everything twice, but was so sprightly about it that the repetition was not too irksome. Jot Oakes was exactly like one of those jolly little dwarfs you see in German gardens—a gnome, stepped out of Rip Van Winkle's long sleep. He was not deformed but very small, round, red cheeked. Usually he was merry, but occasionally he fell into strange black moods. At such time he would crouch behind the stove in the kitchen, refusing to talk, refusing to eat with his sister Jude. She sometimes left a plate of food there behind the stove for him, as though he were a little dog, or a naughty child to be punished. Certainly his pink cheeks and his round blue meaningless eyes and his thick shock of white hair gave him the look of a chubby old baby. He was now nearly fifty and could do the work of a man about the farm, but only if told to do it. Of initiative he had absolutely none.

"Come to see Miss Jude," John Veal gulped, awkwardly, but relieved.

Jot frisked into the big rocking chair by the fire and began to rock violently to and fro, his little round legs sticking straight out before him. It seemed as though he might momentarily pitch into the fire. "She isn't home. She's upstairs. She isn't home. She's upstairs."

Unlike the rest of the community Jude and Jotham Oakes spoke a colloquial but grammatical English. There was the making of a school teacher in Jude, and this emerged in her correct speech and had been transmitted to Jot.

"I got a letter for her," Veal persisted. "Come all the way up from the store to bring it."

Jot jumped out of his chair, leaving it cavorting, heel and toe, behind him.

"Give it to me. I'll bring it to her. She doesn't like you."

Veal clutched the letter more tightly. "Heard tell down to the postoffice she got shut of her Swede help, the whole caboodle of them, Swenson and his women and the boy, and was looking to hire another man. I guess she might be glad if I was to come and work for her again, hired man. She's upset, looks like." He glanced about the disorderly room.

"Oh, it always looks like this in here. Jude comes down here nights when she can't sleep, and lies on the couch and looks at the fire. She reads, too. Then, when morning comes, she goes upstairs and sleeps, sometimes. That's what she's doing now, I bet." He laughed, merrily. "Pret' near dinner time, too."

"Upset, is she?"

"My, yes. Judy gets into one of her tantrums, I tell you it's worse than a wildcat. Packed off Swenson and Huldy before you could say Jack Robinson, and the cows to be milked and all the chores, and no one to do it but me. Judy helped, but the cows don't like Judy because she's nervous and she hurts them, milking, being jerky, and they won't give down, and that made her madder than ever. Nobody to get the meals, either, but Judy. She's a terrible cook. She either burns things or doesn't cook them enough. So I cooked, too, but it's hard for me to reach. I had to stand on a chair."

At the memory of this he burst into a great roar of laughter, slapping his thighs with his tiny hands. Suddenly he became thoughtful, folded his hands across his stomach, and stood looking at John Veal with his bright blue eyes. He sighed, dolorously.

"What you need around this place is a proper man, like me. I come special to see Miss Judy about it. Place'll be gone to rack and ruin in another week. 'Tis as 'tis, pret' near."

"That's just what we've got, John Veal. But it isn't you."

Veal stared. "What isn't me?"

But before Jot could answer there came a rush of foot-steps down the stairway, light as a girl's. John Veal knew that step. He cringed. The tall gangling man and the little chubby one turned to face the woman in the door-way.

"What's this noise and clatter and row-de-dow so a body can't rest? And I'll thank you, John Veal, to tell me what you're doing in my sitting room, unbidden? D'you think this is a barn?" She did not even favor him with the full blaze of her glance. She fixed her scornful gaze on the spot where his Adam's apple was again work-ing convulsively.

In his panic he forgot about the letter. "Well, say, Miss Jude, heard tell down to the store you was looking around for a hired man, and thought I'd just step by on my way———"

"Could have saved your breath and shoe leather. I've got a man."

"Who you got?"

"None of your business. But I don't mind telling you it's Ondy Olszak, from out Fenwick way."

"The Polack, you mean!"

"A Pole, certainly." She was relishing her triumph.

John Veal suddenly jerked back two hundred years into the days of the pillory and the stocks. His bony fingers clenched. His pale eyes protruded. He stretched his neck forward menacingly, so that he looked like an enraged gander.

"Don't you dast! You'll have the whole of Oakesfield talking. They're savages, I tell ye!" His voice rose to a squeak. Jot laughed delightedly. "Wild savages. I seen 'em. They make human sacrifices, like in the Bible. They offer blood and human flesh up. They yell and make music nights and Sabbath, and the women folks are fierce as wild beasts."

Jude Oakes smiled disdainfully: a shabby Portia in her tobacco-stained black stuff gown that hung straight and long and forbidding about her tall frame. She wore steel-rimmed spectacles. Through these her cold eyes stared at the agitated Veal, with his mouthings, his falsetto voice. She looked with intense disfavor at his gnarled and fumbling hands, his rickety legs. Into her mind there came the picture of the man now at work in the tobacco shed—Ondy Olszak, with his firm, good-natured face, his quiet, strong hands, his powerful thighs. Something in her flamed warm. She felt strong, assured.

"You're a fool, Veal. Always were. Not as big a zany as I was, though, ever to have had you as hired help around the place."

John Veal had come of artisan stock, subservient doubt-less, in the old days, to the Oakes aristocracy. Something of this showed, now, in his bearing. His shoulders sagged.

"Don't say I didn't warn you, fair, that's all. You'll

be murdered in your beds, and they'll have your farm in less time than it takes to tell it."

Jot Oakes' face puckered like that of an alarmed baby just before it bursts into a wail. He trotted to his sister's side and took hold of her black robe with one tiny hand —a hand whose toil-worn palm and roughened back were as surprising and pitiful as they would have been in a little child. He looked up at her. "Judy, let's send him away. Let's send Ondy away. I'm scared."

As she looked down at him—at this withered offspring of a degenerate clan—all the tenderness of which her twisted soul was capable showed in her lined and sallow face.

"Stuff and nonsense, Jotham. Ondy's kind. Remember how he showed you how to rig up a back rest when you stood on the box and stripped tobacco, so it wouldn't tire you? And recollect how funny he was, and made you laugh, his talk was so odd? You like Ondy."

The dwarf's face cleared. "Do I?"

"Yes." She laid one of her hands, with its dry, brown-spotted skin, on his silver head. "Remember he told us his little boy in Poland is almost six, and that when he comes with his mother he'll be able to help on the farm, too. And when we said that couldn't be he said, 'Sure t'ing my kid Stas he six year big like you he strip tobacco I betcha like son of gun.'"

The round pink face now broke into laughter.

With a snort of righteous anger, John Veal shambled

[79]

to the door. Jot, all smiles, ran to bid him farewell. "Well, good-bye, John Veal. Come again, won't you? Come again." He grasped his hand. He saw the forgotten letter. "Judy, he's got a letter. John Veal's got a letter for you."

She snatched it from him. "What are you doing, tromping the country round with letters belonging to me, John Veal?"

He looked guilty and aggrieved. "Postmaster give it to me. I brung it along a favor. Thanks I get."

"Get along with you," snapped Jude. She looked down at the letter. She turned it round and round, examined the envelope closely, made no move to open it. With a sigh of chagrin John Veal disappeared kitchenward. A moment later his shuffling step was heard as he passed around the side path to the road.

New Orleans. She knew no one in New Orleans. Letters sometimes came to her from far-off places, because of her farm ownership. Catalogues of plants or seeds; new ideas on tobacco growing; circulars displaying farm implements or seedlings or poultry or cattle. She paid little enough heed to these, for she had practically no money. The farm was run in such a slovenly way that the money it made must go back into it. There was no new machinery, for the old always needed repair. Tobacco prices were so low this year that they swallowed the profit of last. Though Jude Oakes gave the effect of being shrewd and keen she was really as incompetent as Mrs. Jellaby, and as mad.

She knew this letter was different. It had about it a personal look. She got few letters of that sort. While little Jot stood staring up at her she slit it deftly with an old case knife that she surprisingly took out of the deep pocket at the side of her skirt. She read. The round blue eyes were on her, as though he sensed something important. They grew rounder and more shining as they beheld the change in the woman's face. She had flushed, slowly, to a dull thick red, all over her face and down to her throat. Then this purplish tinge receded and a putty colored pallor came to take its place. Her breath came quickly, and her lean hand shook, so that the paper fluttered as in a breeze. Her eyes, behind the steel-rimmed spectacles, were blazing, enormous. Her hand fell to her side, the cheap paper crackling. She stared, unseeing, at Jot. He laughed gleefully up at her, amused at this interesting proceeding.

"Well," he said, and scratched his gray head ruefully with his little paw. "I've got to be getting back to the barn. What was it I was doing?"

She spoke in a faraway voice, like someone talking in her sleep. "You were working in the tobacco shed with Ondy, likely." Then, in another tone—a tone full of terrible energy and resolve, "Listen, Jot. I've got to go and see Big Bella right away. Now. I've got to talk to her about something important. Now you get your dinner if it may be that I can't get back. There's cold pork, and turnips, and half an apple pie, and you can fry yourself up some potatoes all sliced in the brown crock if you want something hot, but be careful about the stove when you stand on the chair, and don't tip." She straightened out the crumpled letter in her hand, carefully, her lips compressed into a white line. "Let Ondy do it. I forgot about Ondy. Let him."

His lower lip trembled. "No. Me." Like a child.

"All right." She looked fixedly at him a moment, as though considering imparting to him the information that had so stirred her. The urge to confide quickly in someone was almost overwhelming. But as she stared at him the idea left her. Of what use?

She ran up the broad mahogany stairs like a girl, light and quick, moving with the speed of one who is energized by panic and excitement. She was down again in a moment cloaked and bonneted, her reticule on her arm. She went to the barn herself and hitched the old mare to the buggy. She looked alive and almost young, with the blaze of excitement in her, and the urge of news to impart.

As she careened into the road she cut old Nance smartly over the rump with her frayed buggy whip. Nance gave a rheumatic prance and a galumph like a cloth horse in a pantomime, rolled an eye, and subsided again into her accustomed clop-clop.

V

JUDE OAKES was bound for the house of her cousin,
Arabella Mossop. Big Bella lived two miles down
the road, on Pequot Ridge, in the fine old mansion that
had been built by her great-great-great-great-grandfather,
Big Noel Champion. Arabella had married her hired
man, little Hen Mossop, but no one in Oakesfield ever
called her Mrs. Mossop or Arabella Mossop. She was
Big Bella, or Arabella Champion.

Hope to merciful Providence she'll be in her senses,
Jude thought, and not gone with liquor and squatting
drunk in her chair like a heathen Buddha. I've got to
unburden to somebody.

Oakesfield folk frequently sought advice and consola-
tion and healing from Big Bella Champion, with her
clear and innocent eyes, and her knowledge of healing
herbs and ointments. An enormous woman, not fat so
much as huge, with the body of a giantess, the bones of
a behemoth. She must have weighed almost three hundred pounds, but at this time she did not appear repulsive,
for the layers of fat that came with later years and
alcoholism had not yet completely shrouded the magnificent structure.

Big Bella had lived in the handsome old Champion house from the day of her birth, and had never left it except for one mysterious month during her girlhood when she had gone to a place to which she referred as Lake Pomperaug. No one had ever heard of it. She had gone there, she said, to learn to be an herb doctor—yarb doctor, they called it about Oakesfield. Summoned home by the death of her only brother, Hal Champion, she never again left it. She had returned to Oakesfield with her hair cut short, a sight which so scandalized the entire district that there was talk of taking it up in church meeting. She had been only a young girl then—perhaps twenty-two—vast, breath-taking, with the high color and the terrific vitality of the glandularly fat. No young male (few enough the county boasted) would look at her. The eye of desire had never turned its hot glow upon her. So she had buried her brother, the last of the male Champions in the county, and had married her hired man, the wizened Hen Mossop, who reached scarcely halfway to her shoulder.

Hen Mossop had always had the appearance of an old man, though he really was not more than ten years her senior. A Daniel Quilp of a man, cruel, foxlike, sapless, with little mean eyes and a sharp-pointed scanty beard that waggled as he talked and seemed to stab and prick you as it waggled. It was openly avowed in the neighborhood that this pygmy beat Big Bella cruelly. Certainly she was terribly afraid of him; cringed when he spoke. Away from him she was a different person, with superb courage, and the decision and intelligence of a man. For that matter, she had to send away to the city for her shoes, which were men's shoes built to hold her huge weight. Big Bella drank, too, like a man, terribly. She drank hard cider as if it were water; and whisky, and home-made wine—anything. She herself made mead, of honey and water, fermented, from an ancient English family recipe. This mess she kept in a huge yellow crock on the kitchen shelf, with a long spoon in it. As she moved ponderously at her tasks about the vast raftered room she would pause, from time to time, and dip into this sticky stuff and spoon up a great mouthful, and another, swallowing them at a gargantuan gulp.

Yet the face and head of this unfortunate woman were strangely at variance with her body. Her fine eyes were gray, long lashed, and guileless as a child's. Her skin was marvelously fresh and clear, her color pink and white as a Kentish country girl's. This somehow persisted, in spite of drink and neglect. These limpid innocent eyes, this skin, so miraculously fresh and dewy, gave to the vast hulk a paradoxical girlishness and virginity.

Freakish as were her looks, it was for her deep knowledge of herbs that she was known. She knew herbs for healing, herbs for cooking, herbs to tie into a bouquet to give it spice and tang, herbs to steep with wine to give flavor and zest. Neighbors came to her from miles around for healing brews and salves and purges. Especially in the winter and spring she did a thriving business, but she always refused money for these things unless Mossop happened to be about. He tried to screw a dime or even two bits from these supplicants, much to Big Bella's chagrin. Certainly she never had money. The great farm had long ago fallen into ruin. She cared only for her drink, and her herbs and her flowers. She called flowers by their Latin names. The yokels stared, open-mouthed. *Viola cucullata,* she would say. *Kalmia latifolia.* They did not dream she was speaking of common wood violets, or mountain laurel, which they called spoon wood.

They only knew, gratefully, without consciously knowing, that about this vast ruin of a woman there was a sort of healing beneficence. When you asked her aid for ills of body or spirit her great gray eyes would become so pure, so mystic, so other-world as to cause you to feel a little embarrassment, as when a child's limpid gaze is suddenly turned on your adult nakedness. The grossness, the slovenliness, the almost obscene mass that was her body seemed then to fall away from her like a foul cloak, leaving only the spirit burning clear.

Hope that rat of a Mossop's taken the drink away from her, Jude Oakes reflected, as she drove along. It was common knowledge that though Hen Mossop drank, too, and that drink made him meaner and crueler than ever, he liked to hide the cider and the whisky and the blackberry wine and cherry cordial out of Big Bella's reach. No easy task, this. He would sneak up to the attic with it, and nail the big attic door tight, leaving only the tiny trapdoor that was approached by a spindling ladder. Big Bella could no more have crawled through this infinitesimal aperture than an elephant through a knot hole, even if the frail ladder could have sustained the weight of her body. Yet somehow she managed to get hold of the stuff. Strong as ten men when aroused, it was rumored that she had once pounded down the great oaken attic door with her fists and shoulders, a human battering ram. One wondered why, one day, she did not pick up the yellow withered little Mossop between thumb and finger and throw him into the manure heap in the barnyard.

Jude Oakes had great disrespect for Big Bella, and no love; was ashamed of her for the scandal she was in the countryside round. But between the two women there was the Oakes clannishness. In a way, too, Jude needed her. And she was bitterly jealous and resentful of her, though she never admitted this even to herself. It was not of Bella's herb knowledge that she was jealous, nor her exquisite skin, her fine eyes, her sage and human intelligence. Big Bella had married. True, her husband was a poor thing: small, mean, cruel. A common hired man, of no family, no money, no ability, given to drink. But a man. Bella had, in the desperation of that male-impoverished district, married him. They had bred no children, but she had known, surely, in these years, one moment of love, of ecstasy, of pain such as Jude had

never known. With this man Big Bella had lain. Jude
Oakes, the thwarted, hated her. Hated her as she had
hated her younger sister, Amaryllis, who had run off with
the peddler and been swallowed up in the silence of years
—almost twenty years, now.

The Champion house came into view against the blazing October background of the Ridge. Its dignity and
beauty of line and proportions remained in spite of time
and neglect. The clapboards had begun to fall off, and
Hen Mossop's sacrilegious hand had pasted up heavy
red paper on the outside of the grand old mansion, and
had secured the paper with laths nailed tight. As paper
and laths came under the influence of the mercurial
Connecticut seasons the house took on a rosy, faded
southern Italian look, like a painted old grande dame
gone gay. Mossop had managed to shingle it, too, with
cedar shingles, so that the weather did not actually enter
the house and destroy it. The structure had, in distant
view, its original beauty. Above it the great chimneys
rose, majestically.

Jude Oakes stepped from the buggy, light and agile
as a girl, tied Nance to the oak hitching post, walked
swiftly around the path to the rear of the house. Everyone went round to the back, as they did nowadays at the
old Oakes place. The neglected garden was at this side.
The hens had scratched it into a dust patch by now, but
every spring the daffodils and the narcissus bravely
bloomed again. Once there had been a double row of

beehives, too, there beyond in the orchard. But now the bees buzzed and swarmed and bred untended. No one even took the trouble to remove the honey.

Jude stepped quickly to the kitchen doorstep, rapped smartly, lifted the latch at once. Her skirts brushed the enormous cucumbers at the side of the step, turning yellow, ripening for seed. After the brilliance of the October noonday sun blazing on autumn foliage, Big Bella's kitchen seemed dim and deserted to her peering eyes. It extended across the entire back of the house—an enormous room, pine paneled, with many cupboards. Panels, cupboards, ceiling, and walls were almost black with smoke and age and dirt and grease. On the long kitchen table was a piece of yellow oilcloth, faded now and worn, a high note of color amidst the blacks and browns. From the rafters hung ears of yellow corn and festoons of peppers, red and green. Yellow cucumbers lay on the window sills, and tomatoes, too. And from every hook and hinge and wooden peg were suspended bouquets and sheaves of herbs, pungent, aromatic, spicy. Piled on the table were unwashed heaps of early Sandwich glass and yellow crockery, reminiscent of dead meals. Yet about the whole room with its yellows, its browns, its black, its red, its gold, there was the somber beauty of a Rembrandt.

Big Bella was sitting behind the stove in the kitchen, weeping silently, like a man. It was a strange hour for weeping, noon. As her cousin entered she did not start, or wipe her eyes hastily, or show any other evidence of embarrassment at being thus discovered, wallowing in grief. She looked up at Jude. The tears ran a rill down her plump pink cheeks and dropped on her enormous bosom. Her face was not distorted. She wept great pearly drops, like a heroine in a novel.

"What's ailing you, Bella?" Jude demanded in her hard, belligerent tone. "Sitting a figure of woe."

"I'm sick." Big Bella's voice was sweet, clear, high, like a boy soprano's.

"What's the matter with your plaguy herbs you're forever dosing other folks with?"

"I'm not crying because I'm sick. I'm crying because nobody cares that I'm sick."

Jude snorted contemptuously at this and strode over to the stove. She lifted the stove lid, peered at the dying embers. The great room was chill in the sharp October air. She reached into the wood box, making a great clatter with wood and lid and poker. "Talk like a fool. What ails you?"

"My stomach. I can't relish my vittles."

Jude was not a lady of reticence. "Small wonder. Lining of your stomach's all eaten away with alcohol by now, likely as not."

"Why, Jude Oakes, I never touch a drop, except for medicinal purposes. I know what it is. It's this salt pork and fried potatoes and yellow turnips, year in year out. My stomach's coated with grease. If I didn't take a little something now and then to cut the grease I'd be caked with it, same's a pig."

"Fix yourself a mess of greens now and then, the way other folks do, you wouldn't feel so lumpish." Jude cast a withering glance about the kitchen—a glance altogether unjustified, for her own kitchen, when she was left to manage it, was as slovenly as this one.

"How can I get down to gather greens? It's all I can do to bend to my herb garden and gather the herbs folks need that come to me, let alone skipping in the field and garden patch like a kitten in catnip."

The feat of associating this ponderous mass with so playful a figure of speech was too much for Jude's patience, never too long enduring at best. She snatched up her reticule from the kitchen table where she had flung it and made great pretense of drawing her cloak about her. "If you're as sick as all that there's no good my staying. I'm in sore straits, too, for help and some-one to talk to."

Big Bella's tears ceased with the abruptness of a fountain whose spigot is closed. Her great gray eyes grew soft with sympathy. With astonishing lightness she rose and emerged from behind the stove. "Do tell me, Jude. I'm feeling better now I've told you my complaint. I made sure you'd only come to scold me." For earlier in the week, as she had come unsteadily across the south meadow from her herb gathering, more than a little gone in liquor, some Polish boys, new to the neighborhood, had hooted at her, and even thrown stones at her. She thought this had come to Jude's ears. Now she was relieved, buoyant again.

Jude, still annoyed because the first glow of her entrance had been dashed, was not to be won over thus lightly. "Oh, I doubt you're in any state to hear a word I say, let alone advise."

Big Bella came over to the table and drew up a chair opposite Jude. Her face took on its look of rapt attention. Her innocent gray eyes regarded the saturnine Jude with the beneficent glow of an angel's. Her cheeks bloomed like a tea rose. She was again the sibyl.

"Just you unburden yourself, Jude. I'm listening. Take your time and relate."

Abruptly Jude dived into her reticule and brought forth the letter with the New Orleans postmark. The dull red flush came again to her face as she opened the envelope. Two separate letters were disclosed. She slapped them down on the table.

"Rilly's dead."

"Rilly?" The childlike blue eyes stared.

"Don't gawp like a zany, as if you'd never heard of my sister Amaryllis. Two weeks she's been dead. Here's a letter came this morning from New Orleens."

"New Orleens! Why, that's other end of the world, or nearly. What in time's Rilly doing down in New Orleens!"

"Nothing!" snapped Jude, with the fury of the frantic.

"She's doing nothing down there. Rilly's dead, I'm telling you. And that's not all." Big Bella held out her hand for the letters. But Jude snatched them away. She must know the harrowing pleasure of telling it; of watching the placid pink face take on an expression of wonder and dismay.

"The letter—one of them—is from some kind of town committee—selectmen, or the like. As if she hadn't caused disgrace enough. Seems he left her. There's a letter of hers along of theirs. And now she's to be sent up here to me, if you please, and I'm to take care of her the rest of her life. As if I hadn't enough trouble and to spare, with a new Polack hired man on my hands, and Jotham the care he is, and all."

"But, Jude, why in time do you have to take care of poor Rilly the rest of her life if she's dead? You said she was dead, didn't you?"

Jude Oakes shook the sheets of the letter in Bella's bewildered face. "Not Rilly. Tamar! Temmie, she calls her."

But this was too much for the sibyl. She descended to the plane of ordinary humans. "Judy Oakes, I can't make a mite of sense out of any word you say. First it's Rilly that's dead, and then she's coming here to live. Then it's somebody named Temmie. Temmie! Who's Temmie?"

By a superhuman effort Jude Oakes gathered her faculties together and told the details of the letter, talking mincingly, as though to a child.

"Listen, Bella. And try to understand. Land knows I'm tried enough as 'tis, without having you to bear with. Rilly's dead. Dead in New Orleens, and don't ask me how she got there, because I don't know any more than fly. The peddler left her, as anyone could have told her, and saved her the trouble of running away from a good home and breaking her mother's heart and leaving me alone on the farm with Jot to take care of the rest of my life."

"But, Judy," put in Big Bella, mildly, "she fell in love with that man, that's the way 'tis when you fall in love, you don't take any account of what you're doing or how it will affect other folks. You set everything by a man, and it's like you were bewitched."

The other woman's face grew dark with venom. "Bewitched! Bewitched by love! You sit there, looking a figure of fun, and talk to me about bewitched by love!"

The great childlike eyes grew soft with pity. "You don't know, Judy. You just don't know."

"This much I do know, Bella Champion. I know better than to marry any tramping peddler or tippling hired man that comes by. 'Tain't knowing kind of cattle that's caught with mouldy corn. And furthermore, I'll be saddled with no child of a peddler and a wanton woman— for that's what Amaryllis was, sister or no sister. And so I tell you."

She was breathing fast. The unlovely red of bitterness and frustration dyed her sallow cheek. Big Bella regarded her with a look so full of understanding that Jude Oakes would have had fresh cause for rage had she sensed it.

But her mind was full of the two letters, both of which now lay on the yellow oilcloth under her hand.

"Read me the letter, won't you, Jude?"

"No, I'll not read it to you. Read it yourself, if you like." She could not trust herself to read it aloud, was afraid that some note of pity, of relenting, might creep into her voice were she to read the epistle.

Bella reached for it, opened it, and, instead of perusing it in silence, began to read it aloud in her singularly fresh young voice.

"DEAR SISTER JUDE:

"It may be that you are not alive. It has been so long. Sometimes I used to think it had never been true—that I could see out from my bedroom window and look at Pequot Ridge, and the river, and those mists rising in the early morning off the meadows. But now I remember them more plainly than ever. I suppose that is because it is all finished now, for me. Jude, I am dying. Sometimes, when things were so bad that I thought I couldn't stand it, I used to write to you and ask you to help me, but I never mailed the letters. Are you still there in Oakesfield, dear Judy, and have you been there all this time? It isn't possible, though. Not when so many things have happened to me. So many things. Now these little knives are stabbing and stabbing inside of me deeper and deeper so that pretty soon one of them will stab deep enough, and then I shall be able to sleep. Judy, will you take care of Temmie? She is fifteen. She is a real Oakes. Judy, she is like that other Tamar they used to tell us about when we were little girls. The one whose ashes lie under the hearthstone in the dining room. All her ways, so different from most little girls, and so full of courage, and her nose powdered with little tiny golden freckles, so sweet. Oh, Judy, please take her and take care of her. They will bury me here, but sometime, if you have a great deal of money and want to do something wonderful, will you have my body brought there to Oakesfield and buried in the old cemetery where Orrange Oakes lies, and Judith his amiable consort? You remember? But of course you do. Isn't it funny, Judy, that all the things that have happened to me in the last few years seem far away and unlikely, as if they had happened to somebody else, and not real? And the things of long ago, in Oakesfield, seem so near and real. I guess that is the way it is when you are dying.

"Well, Jude, no more. It will be soon now. Then they will send you this letter. Oh, Jude dear, please. She is so sweet and has seen so much trouble, a little girl of fifteen. Perhaps you are worrying about him. He is dead. He left me two years ago. I send you these papers to prove it."

Big Bella let the letter drop to the table. Then she shoved it across the table toward Jude Oakes and stood up, gathering a kind of majesty about her. Her tears of a brief half hour ago, shed for her own miseries, were quite forgotten now. On her plump cheeks were tears for another woman's woes.

"Why, Jude Oakes, just you run along about your business and don't you give it another thought. She shall come here, and welcome, the poor forlorn thing. I've always pined for a child, and Mossop's thrown it up to me."

"Who shall come—where?" Jude Oakes rose, too, gathering her black robes about her.

"Temmie, the little one, that's in such dreadful woe, and only a child of fifteen." She reached for the letter again. "Where does it say to send?" She peered at the letter. "Maybe I ought to send a dispatch instead of a letter."

"You'll do nothing of the kind, Bella Champion. And so I tell you. Rilly's my sister, not yours. I'd admire to tend to my own family."

The pink face crumpled like a great dismayed roseleaf. "But you said——"

"I'll thank you to mind your own business and leave mine to me."

With which astounding about-face Miss Judith Oakes prepared to take her leave. Big Bella, a ponderous mountain of injury, essayed one last bewildered gesture. "But you're stopping for a bite to eat, I make sure, before you go. There's cold pork and fried potatoes and yellow turnips, and I can heat up some coffee, and a slice of apple pie from last night's supper."

But Jude Oakes was already moving toward the door. "I couldn't choke down a morsel. I've too much to see to."

Big Bella had the good-nature of the very fat, but now even she was moved to protest. "Well, I must say, Judith Oakes——"

But what she must say was never said. The black-garbed figure swept out of the room, down the path, scattering hens, squawking, as she went. She unhitched the mare, climbed into the buggy with acrobatic swiftness. But swift as she was Big Bella, more surprising still in her swiftness, was down the path like a charging rhinoceros.

"Your letters," she cried, waving the papers high in

her hand. "You're forgetting the letters and won't know where to send."

Jude calmly gathered up the reins from where they were wound around the buggy whip in its socket. Negligently she held out a hand for the forgotten letters, never dreaming how significant was her forgetting them.

"You didn't read the New Orleens men's letter. They'd made inquiry here at the postoffice by telegraph for my whereabouts before ever they wrote. Thought Nat Tuthill was looking at me queerly when I was in a fortnight past. I don't need to know where to send for her. She's sent." With which final dart she was off, leaving Big Bella agape.

She was conscious, as she drove down the road, that it was autumn; and perhaps something of the mad splendor of the landscape served to add to the excitement under which she was laboring. The hillsides were a conflagration. The black birch had turned brilliant yellow, the sugar maples red, the soft maples scarlet, and sumac was massed in magenta. The whole made a dazzling carpet flung across hill and valley. The hemlocks, black, only served to accentuate the tongues of color that licked up the landscape like flames. She saw this, though not with her conscious eye. It was an old enough story for this frustrated woman who had seen it for more than forty years. Her gaze was, doubtless, lackluster as she beheld it now, but the very glow and excitement of the blaze must have excited her as she looked, helpless to reject it entirely, as one cannot but be affected by music, by flame, by perfume, by beauty, no matter how atrophied the senses.

Here she was, in middle age, saddled with a great hulking girl of fifteen, daughter of a peddler and a runaway girl. A runaway girl who had been her sister, and who had gone her way and left her, Jude, alone in the big brick house with the jealous mother and the dwarf brother, to spend the rest of her life eaten up with bitterness and longing and pride. Pride. She'd show them what the Oakes stuff was made of. She would run the farm alone. She would have none of those louts who were, in her girlhood, all that the countryside had boasted. She remembered one, especially, with his great calf eyes always staring at her in church and when she passed him on the road or in the village. What was his name?—Baldwin. Baldwin. The old farm. She heard that Poles had bought it, or were buying it, after working it on shares. The boy had run away. Some said he had gone West and got rich. Likely story. A lout. How he had looked at her. True, his name was. True Baldwin.

She was too far gone in bitterness for much resentment of the past. She brooded, now, on the future. Another woman in the house. Another mouth to feed. Clothes. She had her ways. She dreaded interference—fiercely fought it. She liked to prowl the house late at night, a restless, tortured figure, black garbed. Sometimes, on brilliant starlit nights, she would wander out into the dusty ruins of what once had been a garden, or down to the old glass wing with its broken panes that old Orrange Oakes had built for his wife, Judith, and there she would look at the stars, for they fascinated her, wheeling through space. She had found some old books on astronomy—books that had been dumped in the attic by careless generations of Oakes. On the flyleaf, in the neatest of copper-plate hands, faded now, was written—Judith Oakes. 1710.

Judith Oakes. Judith Oakes. She, Jude Oakes, was here, driving the buggy down the road toward Oakesfield, troubled in mind and spirit, seething and rebelling, because this woman, this other Judith Oakes, had borne children, centuries ago.

The faded brick of the old house came into view. She turned into the barn. She was home. She would leave the horse for Jot or Ondy to unhitch. Emotion had given her an appetite. She was glad she hadn't eaten at Bella's. There would be something left. She could cook some eggs if they had done with dinner. A cup of hot black coffee.

She hurried around the side path to the kitchen door. She had left a good fire in the kitchen stove. Jot would have kept it up, or Ondy. Ondy. Ondy Olszak. That story he had started to tell her last evening when he had brought in the wood at supper time, and laid it high in the sitting-room fireplace.

Laughter. Laughter. A man's deep-throated laughter. Ondy Olszak. Male laughter, but not quite like a man's—

like a boy's. Jot. Another laugh, soprano, rippling, gay, high—a girl's delighted laughter.

Jude Oakes leaped to the great oaken kitchen door, threw it wide, almost stumbled into the vast kitchen.

Ondy Olszak sat at the table, cluttered with the remains of their dinner. He sat back, at ease, a Connecticut cigar in his hand, his handsome head thrown back, his face content, alive, gay. She had not seen him look like that, spirited. Her eye leaped from him—she took in the scene, really, at a single glance—to where little Jot was performing his favorite trick—the trick with which he liked to send shivers of terror and delight up and down the spines of the children of the district. The midget stood bent double, his legs apart and his head between his legs, his back to the others in the room, and his face in the frame of his legs engaged in making the most fantastic and blood-curdling contortions, upside down. And in the center of the room, poised on one foot, the other leg stretched out behind her, was a young girl in the costume of a story-book Indian maiden—beaded doeskin dress, head band, moccasins; a bow and arrow actually held in position in her two hands. She was posed as though for an audience. A small slight creature, "skinny," the New Englanders would have called her, with a little pointed face, clear gray eyes, and golden freckles powdering her cheeks and the bridge of her little nose. She had very thick, long chestnut hair, too heavy for her small head. It was fine, and blew about her face a little.

And in her high clear voice, between shrieks of laughter, she was saying:

"Step up, ladies and gents, and try this magic wonder-working Housa-tonic, the Great Indian Remedy, the Elixir discovered two centuries ago by the historical Chief Waramaug himself, of the friendly Weantinock Tribe of old Con-nect-ticut! And revealed as a her-i-tage to Captain Orrange Oakes of Puritan fame. Enriches the buh-lood! Brightens the eye! Makes the pulse leap with health. Strengthens the heart. Eases and ul-ti-mately *cures* all ailments of the lungs, liver, *and* kidneys, ladies and gents."

All about the floor lay the contents of two open satchels, evidently rifled for the Indian costume. Gay silk dresses, hats, bits of lace, and her small shoes lay all about in confusion.

Into this scene of high merriment Jude Oakes burst like a black cloud at a picnic. Her deep voice thundered, her eyes flashed, her whole presence was a cold douche.

"What's this screaming and yelling till I wonder the people in the road don't come in? Olszak! Jot! Who's this girl?"

But as she looked, she knew. She knew before the girl's voice said, tremulously now, the bravado of the showman all gone, "Oh, you're—but you—you're Aunt Judy!"

The girl's face was so stricken, so blighted suddenly with disappointment. It was as though the frost had nipped a flower. "I'm Temmie."

"Oh, so you're Tamar, are you? And what's this screeching?"

"We were playing medicine show. The way Father used to do it, evenings, on the corner, or at the fairs, selling Pring's Cure-all Indian Remedy."

"What's that dress you've got on? That Indian dress?"

"Well, you see, I always stood up beside Father on the cart, after Mother was too—too sick—and I'd be the Indian maiden, descendant of old Waramaug, of the Weantinock tribe, of Connecticut——" At the look on the woman's face the girl's voice faltered, broke, died away.

Jude Oakes' face was terrible to see. She threw off her cloak and hat and cast them on a chair. She pointed with one long bony forefinger.

"If you've finished lolling there with your cigar, Ondy Olszak, like a nabob, I'll thank you to get to work in the tobacco shed, where you belong. . . . Jotham Oakes, get along out of here. . . . Don't let me have to tell you twice." It was almost as though she would strike him, like a naughty child. "You, young lady, off with that dress, and don't you ever let me see it on you again, or I'll burn it in the fire, sure as my name's Oakes."

Then, at the look in the white pinched face—the tiny pointed face with its golden dusting of freckles, twenty years rolled back, and the girl of fifteen was another girl, frightened, desperate, trapped, before she made her dash for life and freedom with the peddler, Joel Pring. "There," said Jude Oakes, almost gently. "Don't look so struck. Nobody'll harm you here. You're right welcome, Temmie. It was just—coming in on you like that—and all laughing—and you standing there, in that dress, looking for all the world like—— Oh, my God, she an Oakes woman, standing at the tail of a cart in an Indian dress for loafers to hoot at!"

Suddenly the hard, sallow face was distorted. Her two hands covered the working face. A dreadful sob, hard and dry, shook the lean shoulders. And so it was the girl who comforted the older woman, coming over to her and putting a hand timidly, and yet as one who is accustomed to the gesture, on the convulsed shoulder.

"There, Aunt Judy, it's all right. She didn't mind. She didn't mind a bit, really, because I was always there, too, with her."

VI

IN ALL her vagrant life Tamar had never seen the inside of a house like this, much less dwelt in one. But she knew about it. It was uncanny, her knowledge of the old house. In her wanderings from Louisiana to Minnesota with Pring's Indian Miracle Medicine Show she had looked at fine houses, an outsider; had known that people lived in them. She had seen the galleried and crumbling old mansions of the South, the Spanish haciendas of the Southwest, the solid, ugly dwellings of the Middle West, with their glittering new windows, and their prim green yards, and their vulgar front porches on which their owners sat and rocked and stared and were stared at in turn.

Tamar and her mother, drifters, used to wonder about these houses, speculate about the people who occupied them, stroll past them, sometimes, in the early evening, before it was yet time to join Joel Pring on the gas-flare medicine cart. But whether handsome, picturesque, vulgar, or stately, not one of these mansions but received a disdainful shrug from Amaryllis.

"If you think that's fine you just ought to see Oakes House, Temmie."

"Finer even than that, Mama?"

"Oh, much. And not just square, like that, and no elegance to it. It seems to have been there always, Oakes
House, like the land around it—it has, really, when you
come to think of it, because your great-great-great-great-
grandfather, Orrange Oakes, built it of bricks made from
the clay of the land the Indians granted him."

Temmie had heard the story a hundred times—a
thousand. It was the child's lullaby, her romance, her
picture of permanent beauty in their gypsy life.

"Tell me about black Esau . . . tell me about old
Waramaug—not Papa's story on the cart, but really, I
mean . . . the time little Temmie ran off to see the
Indians and they found her dead . . . the hearthstone
in the dining room . . . the glass house . . . the attic
with chests full of old silks and satins and high-heeled
shoes . . . the oak leaves carved around the top . . .
Orrange Oakes the Younger, who came into collision
with Cromwell . . . the ovens . . . my picture in the
big chamber holding the fan and the rose—well, not me,
of course, but the other Tamar . . . here lies Judith
Oakes, amiable consort . . ."

There was nothing she did not know about it. She
never tired of hearing it; Amaryllis Oakes never tired
telling.

Joel Pring, overhearing, would laugh his dry, barking
laugh.

"What a spieler you'd make, Rilly. I guess I'll let you
take the hayseeds to-night. Anybody could make that old

tumble-down pile of bricks look like what you make it look when you talk could sell a cartload of Pring's Elixir to Samson the Strong Man over in Mac's side show."

"What do you know about it!"

"Seen it, ain't I? Sold notions to that hell-cat ma and old maid sister of yours time I was courtin' you on the sly. Don't you believe a word of all that taradiddle, Temmie. A run-down old Yankee farmhouse, and land so poor you couldn't raise skunk cabbage on it."

Rilly Oakes had learned the futility of combating this thin-lipped man with his shifty eyes and his laugh that cut you like a cough. But little Temmie was a fury aroused.

"It is true! It's as big as a castle in the fairy tales. Twenty rooms and twenty fireplaces and a hundred slaves and thousands of acres and silks and satins and silver spoons and two big oak trees like soldiers on guard——"

And now, at last, she saw it. She saw it with the eyes of a child of fifteen who has known the seamy, disillusioned life of a woman of fifty. Those gray eyes, with the golden flecks in them, saw the dirt, and the enduring beauty, and the squalor and the magnificence and the ruin and the glory that was Oakes House.

Jude Oakes felt something like fright at the girl's sure knowledge of every turn, every corner, every closet and chimney and panel.

"Here's the saddle room." A silence. A sinking of the heart. "Oh." Then, with fresh courage, fresh interest,

"This is Tamar's room. My room? My room? Please, Aunt Judy!"

Jude Oakes resented it—this chit's taking possession of the house in spirit. "How does it come you know so much, Miss Smart?"

"Mama told me. . . . Oh, you've moved it, haven't you?"

"Moved what?" tartly.

"The chest used to be there, and the high-boy there, and the mahogany chess table with the crack right through the middle—yes, there it is." Triumph. She found enormous satisfaction in the crack.

The child had a kind of fierce energy born of nerves, and alone she tried to bring forth some sort of neatness out of the dirt and disorder of years. It was evident that she had been the housekeeper in that strange wandering life of the circus, the side show, and the county fair, while the sick woman, her mother, was slowly dying of the knives that stabbed deeper and deeper. That autumn Temmie attacked the old house with fury: mop, pail, broom, and rag. She actually did most of the housework, in an unorganized way. Her aunt Jude often stayed in her chill room upstairs until noon—a strange habit for a woman of her New England breeding. She had, too, sudden fits of energy when she raged about the house, the barns, the fields, lashing Ondy, Jot, Temmie, with her pitiless tongue. At other times she would hitch up old Nancy and drive to Stonefield to be gone all day. As the top of the old black buggy disappeared below the slope of Gallows Hill the whole household would relax with a sigh of relief that was almost a groan.

Temmie cooked. She concocted strange messes picked up in the tents and the jolting wagons in which they had lived. She made chili con carne and tamales learned in Mexico, and spoon bread she had eaten in the South; and took the curse off the everlasting fried pork by smothering it in cream gravy.

When Jude's back was turned Temmie and Ondy and little Jot would feel swelling within them the exhilaration of freedom. The noonday meal, usually eaten under the shadow of Jude's blighting black brows, would become a thing of almost Roman ease. They would sit, lolling and replete, long after the food had been dispatched; talking, laughing. Sometimes Ondy would cook. Temmie would tie a calico kitchen apron round his waist, and he would prepare queer Polish dishes. He made Polish potato pancakes as he had often seen his mother and his wife Polcia make them in Poland. He would grate the potatoes, Temmie would beat the eggs, Jot would run for a spoonful of flour. Ondy would fry them in deep lard, the other two standing by, rapt, to see them emerge sizzling, with crisp brown edges, to be eaten with a spoonful of apple butter or a dab of jelly, or even a sprinkling of sugar. He told them about cabbage balls. But cabbage balls were difficult to make; besides, they needed chopped beef, and that was out of the question without Jude's knowledge. There was very little butcher's meat in that household, or in any other in Oakesfield. But he promised they should have this delicacy when his wife Polcia arrived, and little Stas.

The girl Tamar accepted Jot, the dwarf, and Big Bella, the giantess, and Olszak, the Pole, and Jude, the shrew, with the cheerful tolerance of one who all her life had mingled with the twisted, the odd, the misshapen, the outlandish. Pring's Indian Miracle Medicine Show had, perforce, kept strange company. Hard, tough men; bold-faced women. Pring followed the tent shows, mostly, or played the county fairs—any place where the yokelry gathered with its dimes and quarters jingling in its pockets. Jo-Jo, the Dog-Faced Boy; Franko, the Living Skeleton; Mlle. Maude, the Fattest Woman on Earth; Major Hop-o'-My-Thumb, the Smallest Living Man; Haj, the Armless Hindoo Wonder—he writes with his toes; Bonita, the Bearded Lady. All these the public knew in their professional capacity, but Temmie knew them in their hours of ease. They gave her dainties, bought her little gifts, petted her, told her stories, mended her torn frock if Amaryllis was too ill. They were more real to her than the gaping, pop-eyed people who stared at them outside the tent, or filed foolishly in to stare again for a dime. In Temmie's eyes these men and women of the side show were normal, friendly; those others of the outside world it was who were strange, frightening.

Her acceptance of the bizarre household in which she

now found herself was immediate and complete. Jot and Ondy loved to hear stories of her nomad life. To Ondy they were an American fairy tale; to Jot, who all his life had known nothing but the acres of Oakes Farm, it was a saga of which he never tired.

"Temmie, tell about the time you were in Kansas when the cyclone struck the tents and the boa constrictor got loose and the fat lady ran way down to the main street in her tights and the jail blew down and the old drunken tramp who had been locked up saw the snake coming toward him . . ."

These were gaudy Arabian Nights tales that Jot's simple mind, and Ondy's, could readily appreciate. Ondy would throw back his handsome head and roar with laughter. "By golly, Temmie, you got fun when you was little girl!"

Jot, always an easy laugher, would grow a dangerous scarlet with mirth; his tiny hands would wave the air, he would stamp his little feet, slap his thighs, roll about in a paroxysm of glee.

There were sad tales, too. Stories of the tents when business was bad, the rainy season endless, illness and death and mishap stalking the wagon shows. There was the story of the death of Bonita, the Bearded Lady, and how they had to leave her to be buried in the lonely little Nebraska prairie town in which she had died while the rest of the show moved on, perforce, to play the county fair engagement in the next town. Strange morbid eyes

had stared ghoulishly down at the hirsute face of this unfortunate woman lying so pitifully unprotected beneath
the glass of her cheap coffin.

"Bonita sewed beautifully, too," Temmie said, recall-
ing the many charming qualities of her departed friend.
"She showed me how to embroider. Bonita always had an
embroidery hoop in her hands and made the loveliest
doylies and lunch cloths—wild-rose patterns with petals
and leaves scattered over them just as if they'd been
thrown, they were so natural. And strawberry patterns,
too, and yellow daisies with brown centers, perfectly darling. Wait. I'll show you. She gave me one."

She was off to rifle her little tin trunk—her treasure
trove. Ondy touched the square of linen and gay embroidery with one rough brown forefinger. "How you
called this cloth?"

"It's a lunch cloth."

"For eat on?"

"Yes, of course. Bonita was a lovely cook. She taught
me, sometimes. That's how I learned. She would cook
dinner on Sundays and invite her dearest friends. Mama
and Franko and Mamselle Maude and Major Hop-o'-
My-Thumb—his real name was Oscar Schmaltz . . ."

Ondy was tremendously impressed. He listened,
gravely interested. There seemed to him nothing ridiculous in the picture of this bizarre company gathered about
Bonita's festive lunch cloth, while she herself bustled between gasoline stove and table, her kindly bearded face,

above the homely apron, flushed with heat and hostess fever.

Some of these strange doings in this America Ondy tried to put into his letters written to his family in far-off Poland. He was, as are all Poles, an inveterate letter writer. He wrote his wife, Polcia, and his boy, Stas, and his mother and his father and his sisters and his brothers and his aunts and his uncles and his cousins.

"When it comes to writing letters you do beat all, Ols-zak," Miss Jude said. "I never saw such a hand for it. Wonder you have any strength left for lifting a forkful of hay or milking."

He would get out the pencil and soft tablet paper, blue-lined, and with his tongue protruding now from this corner of his mouth, now from that, would write and write and write. Between times he refreshed himself with a pull at his Connecticut cigar, gazing contemplatively up through the clouds of smoke, his face rapt, smiling. He was very content. They did not know that this letter writing was a social duty of a ceremonial character.

Always his letters began the same, as was proper in a Pole.

Praised be Jesus Christus. And I hope you will answer: For centuries of centuries. Amen.

He wrote, too, the "bowing" letter.

So now I bow to you, beloved wife, and to you, beloved sister Frania, and to you, beloved brother-in-law, and I wish you happiness and health and good success—what you yourselves wish for from God, this same I wish you. So now I bow to Aunt Doruta and to my brother Aleksander and to Jozef and to you, my grandmother. Now I bow to brother-in-law Moscenski. Now I send the lowest bow to the Doborkowskis and to their children . . .

It went on like this, through the whole prescribed ceremony, for Ondy was of good peasant stock and knew what was mannerly and right. His mother and father had been manor servants years ago and had learned some gentle ways and neat. Ondy and his brothers had learned to read and write.

He tried to describe some of the people at Oakesfield and his life here. Of little Jot, after some physical description, he wrote, simply, "He lacks the fifth stave." On Jude he wasted little time. He knew women like her in his own Poland, fierce, shrewish, formidable. He wrote of Temmie; of the farm. He wrote most fully of the farm.

We eat here every day what you get only for Easter in our country. I send you $50. It is a great deal of money, I know. Here I get $30 a month. Later it will be more. This woman will not let me manage the farm on shares, so I do not work so hard. What is the use? If I could manage this farm on shares I would work all day and all night like a horse, like an ox, and raise fine big crops of tobacco and hay and potatoes, and we would soon be rich. It is like a manor house, and there are many hundreds of morgs of land. The woman is a fool. She sits and reads out of books and stares at the fire, and here are hundreds of morgs of land. She never lifts hand or foot to work in the fields. She cannot even milk a cow. She cannot cook a meal for a man who works all day in the fields. Only the little dwarf works, and the girl who is nearly sixteen and goes to school. The Americans are all fools. I inform you now that it is cold here, and no planting or sowing is done at this time, but there is always a good fire and plenty to eat.

Well, I say farewell to you in English. I speak English very well. *Gud Baj.*

With which airy salutation he would close.

Sometimes Temmie helped him with his letters if he wanted to make a showing of his English. She would even guide his hand to form a sentence of English words wherewith to impress his family in Poland. Jude soon put a stop to that. Coming into the kitchen one evening after supper she had found Ondy seated at the table, the lamp casting a mellow glow about his great shoulders humped over the sheet of writing paper, his head on one side, his face fixed in a grin of mingled agony and joy of achievement. The pencil was clutched between his fingers, and over his broad hand was Temmie's little hand, guiding him. She was leaning over him, pressed close in her earnestness. Her fine long hair brushed his cheek.

"I send you love and kisses. These crosses are the kisses I send you. See, Ondy, you make a whole lot of criss-crosses, like this. Each one means a kiss."

"Sure," said Ondy. "That is fine. I make fifty criss-cross kiss." He smacked his lips. "I am Yankee American now, you betcha."

On this scene Miss Jude descended with blighting effect. "You'd much better learn to read and write properly yourself, let alone trying to teach others. No more schooling than a baby."

"Why, Aunt Judy, you oughtn't to say that. Mama taught me every day, when she felt well, and Franko taught me arithmetic because Mama wasn't so very good at arithmetic———"

"Franko?"

"Franko is living skeleton," Ondy explained, graciously.

"God A'mighty!"

"He was smart as a whip," Temmie went on. "Everybody said so. He used to keep accounts for the show. He could add up two columns of figures at once, like lightning."

"Franko or no Franko, you'll do a little more adding up of figures yourself, young lady, in November. School starts in November, when the tobacco's all hung. You'll march off and learn something in decent civilization. Living skeletons, indeed! And how does it come you're up this hour and not off to bed, where you belong!"

"But I'm not a bit sleepy, Aunt Judy. Please."

"March!"

But Temmie was accustomed to the easy informalities of the wagon and the lot, to the roving life, the shifting crowds. She had gone to sleep when the gas flares were dimmed, the crowd dispersed, the shouting and clamor quieted, and the silence broken only by the stamp of the horses' feet on sod, the whining and bickering and snarling of the mangy animals captive in their cages, or the peevish cheeping of rural birds, alarmed at these strange nocturnal noises.

Jude herself was given to late hours. A night prowler, she wandered about the house. A week after Temmie's coming she had padded softly into the south sitting room long after midnight in her long-sleeved high-necked flannel nightgown and her flannel dressing gown. There usually were embers glowing in the fireplace, remains of the one decent fire the house afforded. She would burrow into the dusty brown welter of the couch, draw the old sable cloak about her lean knees, and read the yellow-backed novels of lurid romance wherein handsome heroes had their way with cream and roses. Toward morning she would doze off. Usually daylight found her again up in her own bedroom, the stuffy south sitting room deserted.

This night she had come upon a little round ball on the floor before the fireplace. Temmie had stolen downstairs, had wrapped the dilapidated remains of the sable cloak about her, and had curled up on the floor like a little animal. It was plain that she had sat staring at the fire until sleep overcame her. Jude's first impulse was to rouse the child. Shrill words rose to her lips, but as she looked down they stopped there, unuttered. Temmie was turned half away from the dying glow of the hickory log fire. The little heart-shaped face was serene, almost smiling, very childish and defenseless in sleep, and on her cheeks the bitter salt tears had not yet dried.

Jude stood a moment, her strong black brows knit. Then she stooped and picked up the child, fur cover and all, in her arms and laid her on the couch, a pillow beneath her head. The girl stirred, murmured drowsily, drugged with sleep, emotionally exhausted with the strain of the week's strangeness. "Go sleep," she said, in an anxious, almost maternal, voice. "Take your sleep medicine. Go sleep."

She herself slept again, her long silky hair half covering her cheek.

Sleep medicine. Sleep medicine. Jude Oakes pulled a chair in front of the fire and sat there gazing into the embers, a gaunt, unlovely figure in her grotesque dishabille. Rilly had taken sleep medicine, then, for the little sharp knives. White powders, probably, or little pellets with a bitter taste to them, but a sweet forgetfulness within that bitterness.

For the most part Temmie kept to the kitchen or her own chill bedroom. Jude resented intrusion into the south sitting room. She wanted it to herself, as she had had it before the days of Temmie's coming. She did her haphazard accounts there, for the dusty little saddle room off the main hall was far too cold in the winter.

Dusty and disordered though it generally was, this south sitting room was, besides the kitchen, the only really habitable room in the house. During the sharp days of the Connecticut autumn and spring, and throughout the bitter winters, there always was a bright fire of hickory logs snapping and crackling there.

Ondy would come in with an armload of wood for the fire to find her sitting there in her shapeless black robe. At his approach she would look up with her sharp glance through her steel-rimmed spectacles. Her grim face would relax into something very nearly resembling a smile. It was curious when Jude Oakes smiled. You saw then, startled, that her mouth was full and sensual, her teeth very good for a farm woman—strong, yellow, sound. When she turned her head and glanced round at Ondy, standing there with his armload of hickory logs, it was almost as if she had been waiting for him.

He would free one hand to knock with his knuckles on the door which was closed to keep out the cutting draught that swept through the wide lower hall.

"Come in, Ondy!"

He would enter, smiling. He had about him genuine charm and an indefinable sweetness and inherent gayety. He was, probably, more Austrian than Pole; the western Pole, not dour, harsh, with the streak of brutality that characterized many of the more northern and eastern Poles of the neighborhood.

He came in with a little half-bow—a bending of the knee, fruit of his manor training.

"Is cold, by golly!" He would place the logs, deftly, quietly, stir up the fire, turn, glancing at Miss Jude with his bright merry glance.

"What do you hear from your wife and little boy?" Jude might ask, primly.

A little frown would cloud his serenity. "She is here quick now, she is got ship ticket. First she say she not come, little Stas sick; then she say she sick; now she say she come quick like anything. Crazy woman, my woman Polcia."

"Crazy, is she!" Miss Jude exclaimed, in alarm. "Well, if she's coming here to cook and keep house—though I don't really know's I need her now Temmie's so handy and all—but if she's coming she can't be crazy around here. Enough crazy people in this house as 'tis."

"Oh, my woman Polcia she no crazy like you say. No." He laughed, tolerantly. "Polsky womans is all time funny how they make."

He never presumed to sit in her presence—at least, not here. But it came to be true that he sometimes stayed there with her an hour at a time in the little warm stuffy room, talking in his broken English while she listened. She never asked him to sit in a chair. He knew better than to do so. But after he had placed the wood and tended the fire he would squat on his haunches at the side of the fireplace. They would talk, at first, of the farm, like two men—the tobacco crop, tobacco prices, the buyers who were making their rounds of the local sheds, the lateness of the needed November rains so that the tobacco leaves should become moist and soft and limp as they hung on laths in the sheds. They would talk of the live stock, of winter work on fences and outhouses and cold frames. Ondy was not a very good farmer. He was too light-hearted, too careless. He liked a good time; to drink and eat and talk with the other neighborhood Poles Sundays and even on weekday evenings. Then, too, the Oakes farm implements were antiquated, insufficient. Jude would not dream of spending money for more modern equipment, Ondy had known no better in his life in Poland. But he loved the vastness of the land; the sense of acres and acres and acres under his hand. That was fine.

He would begin to talk of Poland, of his tiny farm there. She would question him. Sometimes he told her of strange Slavic habits and customs. She listened, hungrily. About these people there seemed to be a mingled ferocity and simplicity. Some of the tales were childish, some terrible.

As Ondy talked in his halting English he omitted the article, the conjunction. Usually all tenses were thrown to the wind except the present. Pronouns feminine might be used with a masculine noun, or vice versa.

"In Poland is not much land, not like here, no. Two morgs—three—is much. In Poland no farmer has enough. To live, that is all. Many children, five, eight, nine, more. There is not enough land for all, and Pole, he like land. He like land more than anything. So one woman she have old husband, one woman she have sick husband, one woman she mother is old, father is old. So pretty soon they go to Aunt Susi. Aunt Susi is midwife. She has medicine in bottle. Strong medicine. She take fly paper and she soak fly paper in water and make medicine. Then she put medicine in bottle, and Pole womans pay money. They make a fine feast—duck soup and meat and potatoes and onions and brandy, fine, I tell you. Then husband he eat, and old mother and old father, and pretty quick cry loud with pain, and the women smile behind their faces. Then they walk to the cemetery and place wreath on grave. Soon husbands begin to wonder why woman is whisper so much behind shawl and always talk, talk with each other and with Aunt Susi. So they watch and listen, and one day is Peter Paul Day the twenty-nine of June, they eat cake and dance and drink is festival, then the soldiers come and take Aunt Susi and forty-two women of village. Some tell, but not Aunt Susi. Is all kind of people at trial—magistrate and doctor and lawyer and rich lady and gentleman from manor, and even from Warsaw people come. And Pole farmer come in sheepskin coat and embroidery leather, and women in bright shawl and fine handkerchief around head. So Aunt Susi she say she midwife, she do nothing, so they let her go home, they know they not got all women have killed husband and father and mother. So Aunt Susi go home but police they follow, and she go quick here and there in village, and then too late she see they follow her and take to prison women she visit. So she go home, and when she see sun flash on bayonets behind hedge in front of house Aunt Susi put bottle of medicine to mouth, she have it hide under apron, and quick she is dead. She is sixty-nine, Aunt Susi. She is a woman!"

"God A'mighty!" exclaimed Jude, half in horror, half in admiration, which was, after all, the mood in which the story had been told.

Then there was the legend of Prince Stefan. "Prince Stefan was a fine prince, I can tell you. He want to know how country people live, his subjects, so he put on poor clothes, and ash stick in his hand, and go about the country. He go to farm and ask to sleep for night in barn, and piece of bread to eat. Well, my mother come to the door, and she see beggar with poor clothes and ash stick and she know him right away she know it was Prince Stefan. Well, of course anybody know that beggar will bring you luck if you treat him kindly and give him something. It is a religious duty. But my mother she know. So she give this beggar sheets to sleep on from her cupboard and soup and cabbage out of the kettle, and in the morning he is gone. But it is the Prince Stefan, all right."

At this Jude sniffed, scornfully.

"Prince Stefan—my foot! The beggars must have had a high time of it in your country. Well, good luck or no good luck, don't you expect any Prince Stefans to come around Oakes Farm. They'll get no sheets from me, or cabbage, but a dog bite in the seat of their pantaloons."

Ondy looked at her pityingly. Even the hard fierce women of his country would not treat a beggar like that.

"Your Polcia, or whatever it is you call her—an outland‑
ish name—she won't be up to any poison tricks, with
medicine in a bottle?"

He smiled at that. This strange woman, this Miss
Oakes, an old girl, with a big farm like this, and no hus‑
band.

He wrote Polcia a little of this strange one, and per‑
haps that decided her, and hastened her coming, though
after the first year she had been strangely reluctant to
join her husband. Truth to tell, Ondy seemed not too
impatient to have her. But now no boat was quick enough
for Polcia.

There was much that Jude Oakes did not know about
Ondy, with his frank merry eyes, and his engaging smile,
and his strong flexible hands, and his muscular legs, as
hard as steel.

Ondy's cousin Feliks Smentkowski had first come to
America, with Aunt and Uncle Smentkowski. He had
sent letters beginning, "Praised be Jesus Christus. And I
hope in the name of God you will answer: For centuries
of centuries. Amen." Then he had launched out into a
description of this America and this other place that they
could not pronounce. Connecticut. In Connecticut, Feliks
had written, there was land and land—morgs and morgs
of it—to be had almost for the taking. With houses on it,
too. Not huts, like the Polish farmhouses, but big fine
houses, and barns to them, apart from the houses, in
themselves big enough to make fine houses.

The letter had worked like a fever in Ondy's brain. "I receive here eighteen dollars a month, pretty soon I will get a dollar a day."

These sums, translated into terms of Polish currency, made Ondy's brain reel. But more than money or food he thought of the land, rich black land to be had for the taking, morgs and morgs of it.

Then Feliks came back to Poland on a visit. Ondy had married in the meantime, but when he saw Feliks he knew that he must come to this America and send for Polcia later, when he could. Feliks was a sensation in the village, certainly. He had come home for his visit wearing shiny leather shoes so fine that your feet danced just to put them on, and they glittered like a mirror. You could see your face in them. And a bright blue suit, and a watch and a real gold chain, and he smoked cigars. Ondy reeled with envy as he looked at him. He implored Feliks to use his influence with Uncle and Aunt Smentkowski so that they would send him money for a ship ticket. He would work to pay it back, once in America. He would even pay back more than the cost of the ship ticket.

On the ship he was sick and apprehensive and more than a little frightened, but it had been fine, just the same. He had watched the ship cutting through the gray-green water, and he thought it was like a plowed field, with its furrows. He had come to Fenwick, near Oakesfield, where the Smentkowskis were. His first meal had been of pork and greens and potatoes and a thing called apple pie, which Aunt Smentkowski had learned to make—an American dish. It was like a big tart, with fruit inside. And there was hard cider, and whisky too. Ondy Olszak thought he was in heaven.

After three years in Fenwick he spoke English well enough, being intelligent and quick and young. He had not yet sent for Polcia. Polcia, by now, seemed very far away and unnecessary. But he meant to send for her and for the boy, Stas. It took years, though, to earn enough money to pay the debt of his own ship ticket, and another for his wife and boy. Sometimes he longed to see the boy, Stas. He rarely had a longing for Polcia.

After almost four years he came to Oakes Farm as hired man. Cousin Feliks had married. He had married an old girl. When one married an old girl it was understood that it was for money and because one did not want many children. There was no pretense about it. The Polish women who had married young rather looked down their noses at these old girls. They felt very comfortable indeed—fat and shapeless though they now were—at the remembrance that they had been married for their charms alone.

Feliks' wife, Julka, had brought him a handsome dowry. She was a city girl who had worked as servant in the household of a hat manufacturer in Stonefield. But after their marriage her city ways and the assurance that went with her dowry were a source of amazement and disgust to the jovial Ondia Olszak.

She was forever ordering her husband about, this old girl, and acting the grand lady as she had seen the hat manufacturer's wife in Stonefield do it.

"Feliks, will you bring me my shawl? . . . Feliks, will you hand me that water, dear?" . . . It turned Ondy's stomach to see his own blood cousin thus humbled by a woman. In a mincing voice and an attitude of swooning languor he imitated her. "Feliks dear, will you kiss my backside?"

This witticism was considered very choice and went the length and breadth of the Polish settlement.

When Ondy went to work for Jude Oakes there was much coarse jesting. Perhaps Ondy himself had speculated a little about this woman who owned hundreds of acres of land, all her own, and the finest house for miles around. But when he saw her, tight of lip, black of brow, bony of hip, flat of bosom—the hard-bitten New England spinster—he thought of the Polcia he had married, plump, juicy, broad hipped, full bosomed. His masculine eye soon saw that here before him was that cosmic comic—the middle-aged virgin.

He had been twenty-six when he came to America. He was thirty now, with a steady blue eye, but merry too; a brow less thoughtful than it looked, for he had wrinkled it during the years in the effort to speak and think in English. His mouth was firm and full and sweet. Women's eyes rested on it, and their own lips curved and opened a little. He was of medium height, stocky, with broad powerful shoulders and well formed, strong hands. Women liked to look at his hands, too.

They got on well enough, these two, though they were miles apart in their ways of thinking. Ondy accepted her as he accepted everything in America, cheerfully. Perhaps this Jude Oakes had been born out of her time, as had that other Judith of an earlier day. She hated the farm, and farming, yet she was jealous of anyone who attempted to lay proprietary hands on it. It was this that kept her from allowing a hired man to work it on shares. Born two decades later, she might have been one of those emancipated spinsters who, going in for suffrage, feminism, or prohibition, worked off their emotional energy from the platform, or by marching in parades, or in picketing for a Cause. She would have loved to be hauled off to jail for a Cause. Having none of these outlets, she became more acid of tongue, quicker of temper, harsher, more and more eccentric of habit and mind. There was in this woman much of the iron of her ancestors; but it had corroded with the years, so that now everything she touched was stained with rust.

VII

IN NOVEMBER Temmie was sent off to the district
school, protesting. Her protests, in fact, assumed the
proportions of what her aunt called a tantrum. From a
gentle and wistful little sprig of the Oakes tree she suddenly seemed to stem directly from that other Temmie of
centuries ago. She cried, kicked, screamed, stamped, and
ended by running out of the house and down the road two
miles, to the house of Big Bella. Already she had learned
that in Big Bella she had a staunch ally. Here she was
always certain of sympathy and understanding. And sure
enough, there was Big Bella in her kitchen in the late
afternoon dusk. She seemed to be doing nothing there.
The lamp was not lighted. There were no preparations
for supper. The fire was low in the kitchen stove. Even as
she sobbed out her story of persecution and revolt some
small voice within Temmie reproached her for coming.

"There, there, my pet, my posset. You stay here with
me. You stay here and live with your cousin Bella, and
we'll have a regular King George's time."

She stuffed her with such grubby dainties as the poor
larder afforded, soothed the overwrought child, held her
on her enormous lap, and murmured her to sleep with

soft whisky-laden breaths of tenderness. She put her to
bed in a queer tumbled room off the kitchen, smelling of
yarrow and elder and camomile and licorice and pepper-
wort and rue. Big Bella gave her a steaming cup of some
hot aromatic brew. Temmie shuddered away from it, but
at Big Bella's insistent coaxing she gulped it, dutifully.
When she awoke two hours later there were sounds of
high, angry altercation in the kitchen. Shivering with
chill, and her sudden awakening, and the strangeness of
her surroundings, Temmie pulled on her shoes and crept
into the kitchen. The lamp was lighted, the stove was
glowing, supper was in progress, but no homely atmosphere of peace and plenty pervaded the room. Hen Mossop was there, snarling. Big Bella was moving ponderously between stove and table, her every step an earth-
quake. She gathered Temmie in her elephantine embrace.
But by this time Temmie, refreshed and physicked, did
not crave the solace of Big Bella's capacious bosom. It
was a kindly haven, but undoubtedly it did smell
strangely of various conflicting things, all unpleasant. Big
Bella smoked big cigars—not little cheroots, like Aunt
Jude, but big cigars, such as Ondy smoked on Sundays,
or after his noonday meal. The women of Temmie's
Medicine Show days would have been shocked at that.
Bonita, the Bearded Lady, had coughed delicately when
the showmen smoked pipes or cigarettes in her vicinity.
Then, too, Temmie had an instinctive dislike for Hen
Mossop. He looked at her with little furtive foxlike eyes

hard and hot. He pinched her cheek between index and middle finger, holding it as in a vise and twisting it until she screamed with pain.

"Have done, Mossop, you vermin!" Big Bella protested in her high clear voice like that of an indignant boy.

"Slut!" His voice was squeaky. His little pointed, scraggy beard waggled. This was, evidently, the continuation of a quarrel begun while Temmie slept. "Ye great drunken slut! Screeching at me like an Indian with the toothache!"

"Drunk yourself, and with the drink I brewed, else where'd you get it? You haven't a penny to bless yourself with, but that you steal off my land and my farm."

Names vile, obscene. He advanced on her, actually struck her on the breast with his fist. She cowered pitiably, burst into tears.

Temmie felt physically nauseated. She thought she was going to be sick, there in Big Bella's dreadful kitchen. She looked this way and that, like a trapped wild thing. A knock at the kitchen door, and then the door latch lifted, a rush of cold November night air.

Ondy Olszak stood in the doorway. He was smiling. His cheeks were red with the cold, his kind blue eyes looked at her. She rushed to him. She threw her arms about him. "Ondy, Ondy, Ondy! Take me home. I'll be good. I'll go to school. Take me home."

"Sure. I come for take you home. Miss Judy say, no,

let her stay, she be glad come home next morning, but I say little girl like Temmie sleep home in own bed, Miss Judy say no buggy, no horse. I walk. You can walk home, Temmie?"

She had her coat, her warm hood; she buttoned and tied feverishly. "Oh, yes, yes. Good-bye, Cousin Bella. Good-bye, Mr. Mossop." She was at the door, frantic to be gone. Then, remembering her manners, "Thank you. I'm afraid I must be going now." With a prim, grown-up air.

"How did you know I was there? Ondy, how did you know?"

"Oh, Ondy he smart fella. He know."

She put her hand in his big warm grasp. She trotted the two cold miles down the road, content.

Ondy, little Jot, even Aunt Jude seemed dear and altogether desirable; Oakes House was home, the great kitchen heaven, her own bare cold bedroom a haven of rest.

Aunt Jude, on her return, had shrugged indifferent shoulders.

"I made sure you'd come back when you were good and ready. I reckon you know by this time where your bread's buttered. Go and live with that great lump of lard and welcome, if you're a mind."

Temmie's eyes grew enormous, grew starry, in her pointed little face. "Oh, don't say that, Aunt Jude. I like it here. Please say you're glad I'm back." The child was starved for love, for warm approval. The older woman was starved, too, but the process had gone on too long. She could not **speak** the words of love. The fount was dry.

In penance Temmie was up before daybreak next morning. She scrubbed, she scoured. She even tried to bring some order out of Jude's welter of papers, books, and old files.

"Drat the girl!" Jude protested, in wrath. "Take your hands off my private belongings and keep them off. I'm not dead yet, no, nor nearly, that you should come snooping around my papers."

Temmie, grubby as Dick Swiveller's Marchioness, went to the kitchen to prepare the morning meal. Ondy stamped in, ruddy, cold, smelling of the outdoors, of the barnyard. Jot trotted in, his round blue eyes staring. "Hello, Temmie. Hello, Temmie. Temmie, don't go away again. I like you here, Temmie. Don't go away again." He came up to her, put his tiny toil-worn hand in hers. In a rush of gratitude she stooped suddenly and kissed his cheek. He leaped back, frightened. He rubbed his cheek with his fist, hard. "Don't do that!" he shrilled. He ran to the cracked mirror on the kitchen wall, its fine old mahogany frame warped, blistered, grease-stained. Nimbly he scrambled up on a chair before it and peered in. He surveyed his reflection in the wavering mirror, intent on his cheek as though he expected to find some brand on it. Then, suddenly, he began to laugh, ho-ho and ha-ha, his great meaningless laugh.

Instinctively Temmie knew that never before in all his life had anyone kissed the dwarf.

Tamar went to school that first winter and loathed it. She was never a good student, but it was not that. The school house was a one-room cottage by the roadside, two miles from Oakes Farm. In it were huddled a score of children of varying ages ranging from five to fifteen, and of these Temmie was the oldest. She was almost as old as the nineteen-year-old school teacher, a young lady with weak eyes, and a bad complexion born of a régime of pork and pie and bad air. It was curious how the character of the school had changed. It had been a school of perhaps eight or nine children. You heard familiar names. Pete Leere. Johnny Tuthill. Sarah Dibble. But in the last two or three years the roll call had undergone a transformation.

"Will Vaine?"

"Present."

"Victor Pawlak."

"Present."

"Hannah Brown. Max Konstanty. Katy Wroblewski. Sophie Markiewicz. Joseph Krupa. Paulina Borek. Nathanial Brown."

Present. Present. Present. Present. Scuffle. Sniff. Scrape. Cough. Giggle. Squeal. Sniff.

Temmie hated it. Her little pointed face grew more pointed still. The schoolroom smelled of chalk and mice and ashes and unwashed bodies. The logs crackled in the big wood stove. The air of the room was close and stale. The two-mile walk in the brilliant Connecticut air each morning and back in the late afternoon probably saved Temmie from serious illness, accustomed as she had always been, in her nomad life, to following the sun, the easy life of the Southern towns in the winter, of the Middle West and Northern small towns in the summer; out of doors on the show lot, or walking about in the dull quiet streets, tree shaded.

Until the time of Polcia's arrival Temmie rose in the blackness of the early winter morning, prepared breakfast, did a hundred hurried household tasks before she donned her rough coat, wound her muffler about her throat and lower face, pulled on her wool cap and mittens, and prepared for the plunge down the road to the school house. When the roads were snow packed, as they were for weeks on end, she would pull a pair of heavy coarse black wool stockings over her boots. Yet even with this double protection of wool her feet were always numb as they stumbled up the school-house step.

Chilblains. Itch. Snuffle. Cough. Scrape.

Ondy's wife, Polcia, and Stas, his boy, arrived at Oakes Farm one snowy December afternoon while Temmie was at school. Maks Kusak, one of Ondy's far-flung family connections, a Polish tailor living somewhere in the twisted streets of downtown New York, had obligingly met the bewildered woman and the child when the sea had spewed them forth, a frightened, bedraggled, sour-smelling boatload of immigrants. He had managed to put them on the right train for Connecticut. Ondy had met them at the station with the farm team. And now, as Temmie came running home in the dusk, her breath freezing on the air, her thoughts anticipating the warm, pleasant old kitchen, there they were. The vast room seemed full of strange noises, strange smells, strange people. There were the hard, explosive consonants of the Polish tongue spoken rapidly and in excitement; Polcia's big bulk; the weary screams and whines of the little boy Stas; Ondy's steady flow of conversation.

"Temmie, look, my boy Stas! Look. Is big, huh, like twelve year! He work like son of gun, I betcha." He tossed him up in his arms. He gave him a great slap behind. The boy was a bullet-headed stocky little fellow and perhaps less ill favored than he now seemed; tired, bewildered. He scowled at Temmie beneath dark brows, stuck out a lower lip, jabbed his father with a sharp elbow and aimed a kick at him with his queer, foreign-looking boots. "My woman," Ondy went on, but he did not touch Polcia. "See what a fine woman I got." But his heart was not in it, that was plain. He turned to the silent Polcia. "Temmie is little girl I tell you in letters. Ain't she nice little girl!" Then, at the look in his wife's face, he realized that he was talking to her in English. Quickly he translated into Polish, but her grim look did not relax.

"How-do," said Temmie, politely, and put out her

slim little hand, chapped and rough. Polcia looked at it a moment. Then she dropped a sort of curtsey and kissed the hand extended to her.

"Oh," cried Temmie, sharply, and blushed to the roots of her hair.

The woman was large, unlovely, and sullen looking. Her skin was a peculiar gray, as though she were ill, her hair, very thick and light brown in color, was tumbled and untidy, with wisps stringing down the back of her neck. Her bosom was large and pendulous. "Well," thought Temmie, "dear me, if this is the wife he has been waiting for all these years, and saving and working!" She smiled sweetly and put a hand on Ondy's arm, with her natural inclination to comfort and reassure. "It's lovely, Ondy," she said, "and now you'll be happy, with your wife and little boy here." She looked at the woman and smiled, but Polcia glared at her, glared at her hand on Ondy's arm. Her face was fierce, almost menacing. Involuntarily Temmie snatched her hand away.

"Tem-mie!" shrilled a voice from the front of the house. "Ta-mar!"

"Yes," answered Temmie. She picked up her school bag from the kitchen table and ran in the direction of that summoning voice. Its tone demanded haste.

Jude Oakes was sitting in her chair by the fire in the south room. She was sitting there, doing nothing, yet she had the effect of being tremendously busy. The air was electric with her mental activity.

She wasted no time; opened fire at once, her fine eyes blazing behind her glasses.

"What do you think of that!" Then, before Temmie had time to answer, "She'll not stay in this house, and so I tell you. She's a murderess. It's in her face. Hulda Swenson was no great shakes for looks, God knows, but it didn't give a body a turn just to see her. There she was, kissing my hand, slick as grease, and we'll like as not find ourselves murdered in our beds by to-morrow. Ill-favored, she is, and with a look in her eye that gave me a feeling I'd got a knife in my ribs. I wouldn't eat a morsel she cooked—not a morsel. They soak fly paper in water and feed it to you on the sly, and next thing you know you're screaming in knots and dead."

Temmie could make nothing of this. "Fly paper! But, Aunt Jude, it's December."

By supper time the woman, tired and bewildered though she must have been after days of anxiety and sea sickness and improper food, had got herself washed, had combed her untidy hair. She had tidied the boy, too, and now he and Jot were having a fine time, though neither spoke the language of the other. Jot had given him delicious thrills by performing his favorite trick of bending double and making horrible faces between his legs. The boy had responded with squeals of delighted terror. Supper was late, but soon tantalizing smells came from the kitchen. Temmie, who had done most of the cooking in the last few weeks, sniffed ecstatically. Ondy had brought in a rabbit from the woods the Sunday before, and this turned out to be rabbit pie, baked in the oven with salt pork and onions and water, so that it emerged brown, crusty, with a rich gravy, smoking hot. Even Jude risked the writhing death she had predicted for all of them, and ate a second helping of the savory dish.

After supper she called Ondy and the weary Polcia into the south sitting room. She sat, a grim Portia in her black gown, by the fire. Polcia looked about her, pricked to a temporary wakefulness by the splendor of her strange surroundings, but it was plain that the hot fire, the rich supper, the excitement, the trip, had brought her to a kind of stupefaction.

"Listen, Olszak. If I die, this farm goes to Jot. If he dies it goes to Temmie. If we all three die it goes to Big Bella Champion. If she dies it goes to her husband. If he dies it goes to a hundred next of kin living scattered all the way from England to Texas. And now you know. Nobody but Oakes kin can ever have it."

"Sure thing," said Ondy, bewildered but agreeable. "Is fine." He was weary, too. What was the matter with this strange woman now?

"Tell your wife." Then, as he stared, perplexed, "Tell her right this minute, before me. And I understand a word or two of Polish myself, so don't think you can make a fool of me, Ondy Olszak. I'll have no arsenic and fly paper in this house."

The light of understanding came into Ondy's face. He

roared with delight. This was a fine joke. This was the American woman boss's way of making a joke. Grinning and spluttering he turned to Polcia with a fireworks display of Polish. At the end she smiled, too, wanly. She did not understand this American woman. Perhaps tomorrow morning. She was too spent for jokes.

The Olszaks were to have dwelt in the loom house. Ondy had lived there in solitary state. It was not uncomfortable, the one large raftered room, and a small one off it, with its enormous fireplace, a big double bed, its ladder-backed chairs for which a collector would have given his soul, the old loom itself, broken now and useless, as were the old hatchel and the carding comb. But it was found inconvenient, this plan of living out of the main house, and finally the Olszaks were installed in the north wing and had the run of the kitchen.

Polcia turned out to be what Jude pronounced, sniffily, no great shakes of a housekeeper. She was slovenly and dirty, and she seemed to prefer the rough work of the field and barns to the less difficult tasks of the house. She actually appeared to like hard manual outdoor labor. She grasped a pitchfork with a kind of frenzy, pitched hay to the cattle like a man; a forkful that many a man, indeed, would have staggered under. In the house she was forever moving heavy pieces of furniture that required no moving; lifting loads that might better have stayed where they were.

"What ails the woman?" Jude demanded. "She's like

a wild bull in the house, ramping and pawing and stomping."

Lacking though she was in most household graces, this
Polcia fed them fairly well. She was, as a matter of fact,
bewildered by the plenty she found all about her. To an
American the farm, the house, the meager provender
would have seemed wretched enough, but to this Polish
Polcia, coming from a land where everyone lived scantily,
it was marvelous, it was unbelievable, to have, at last, so
much. Land, and land, and land. Live stock—not one
cow, but three. Not one pig, but a half dozen, and a
litter to come. Horses for plowing and another that ate
its head off in the barn and, so Ondia told her, was used
by this Miss Jude just for driving around the country
when she pleased. There was food, too. So much food.
Salt pork, chickens, even beef; eggs, potatoes, cabbage,
apples, turnips, any day. Not just at Easter. Every day.

The furtive, secret look still lurked often in Polcia's
pale eyes, but as she padded heavily about the house,
about the barnyard, Polcia sang a song of plenty, hanging out the clothes in the knife-like morning air, looking
almost pretty with a dark shawl pinned tight under her
chin, peasant fashion. Ondy, though, did not seem happy.
He who had been cheerful, joking, gay was now moody,
scowling. His eyes dwelt on Polcia with suspicion and
actual distaste. On the boy, Stas, he lavished his affection. At night one heard voices loud in altercation.

Temmie was content enough. There was a kind of

ominous disquiet in the house, a current of something dark and secret, but at any rate there was life in abundance. Clatter, voices, Jot's foolish hearty laugh ringing out; Ondy's pleasant voice, very male and reassuring; the high childish treble of the boy Stas.

Polcia turned out queer, heavy, rich dishes for them in the Polish style. Jude scorned them or appeared to, but they were delicious to Temmie's more cosmopolitan palate, used to strange foods in odd out-of-the-way places.

Polcia would thump a steaming dish down on the table. "Cabbage balls," Ondy would explain, pointing with his knife. "Is good." Little Jot smacked his lips over the cabbage and chopped beef and rice and rich gravy. He grew more rounded than ever, so that his width almost equalled his length. Polcia gave them rye bread with caraway, which she baked herself. She gave them raisin bread, too, baked with raisins and real butter and eggs. It was like a cake. She gave them cheese with the rye bread, made from sour milk that stood warming by the stove until it thickened to curd. She gave them the delicacy of prune soup, like a pudding, sweet and thick, made of strained prunes and meal boiled together into a kind of thin pudding and served, strangely enough, at the beginning of the meal; but this even Jot did not relish. It was too sickly sweet, and came at the wrong end of dinner.

Jude's bristling antagonism, which must fasten on

something, now was transferred to Polcia. She sought
to enlist Temmie against the woman. Polcia bore the
nagging and fault-finding without resentment, humbly.
As for Temmie, she pitied Polcia, tried to defend her,
but felt strangely light-hearted and refreshed, as though
a load had been lifted from her shoulders.

Little Stas was sent off to school with Temmie, though
he spoke no word of English. Within a week he had
picked up seven dirty words, and had whipped in battle
(boots, teeth, nails, and head all admitted as weapons)
a boy two years older than he. The child did a surprising
lot of work about the barns and sheds. He actually
worked on the rebuilding of the old stone fences, cut
brush, fed the chickens, carried slops to the pigs. If Big
Bella, as sometimes happened, dropped by in the midst
of such Saturday morning activity, the effect to an outsider would have been frightening. Polcia and Big Bella
in the kitchen, Stas and little Jot performing feats of
labor in the barnyard, would have convinced the onlooker
that he had strayed nightmarishly into the land of the
Lilliputians and the Brobdingnagians.

To Tamar the winter seemed terribly cold, unbearably
long. It was endless. Spring would never come to this
Connecticut country. When, finally, it drew near, she
was not patient with the slow unfolding of its beauty;
but at each fresh sign of the breaking up of winter she
held her breath, as though the miracle might vanish. By
very early spring even the skunk cabbage, that noisome

and most despised of growing things, took on loveliness in her eyes because it was the first green thing to show above the encrusted snow and ice. Then followed the arbutus, with its tough fibrous stems. It was Big Bella, of all people, who showed Temmie how to brush aside the snow in the woods to discover the starlike beauty and ravishing scent of the tiny pink and mauve blossoms. Then the little wild pear trees suddenly were abloom in the dim woods, all white, like young brides in a cathedral. The school children began to bring to school tight moist bunches of hepaticas, depositing the lovely wilted things on Miss Mapes' desk. Then, in a delirious burst of bloom, came the apple blossoms, and that was a kind of madness sweeping over the countryside. The ridges, the valleys, the hills, the flat farm lands, the slopes—wherever you looked your eyes were dazzled with the tossing tumult of land clouds, pink and white, and your senses swooned with the perfume. After that came the lilacs, not bushes, but huge lilac trees a century old, bearing plumes of purple a foot in diameter. Then the white lilacs, more delicate than the purple; then the aristocratic Persian lilacs, brought originally, no doubt, by some New England sea captain of the old days who had sailed in his trading vessel to Far Eastern ports, and had carried back the slip or seedling. Its plumes were feathery, frothy, and its leaves a more delicate green than those of its hardier relations. Then, last, came the roses. Old rose trees, high as a man's head, with single blossoms, deep red, that turned fainter and fainter with each successive blooming as the weeks passed, until they were pale pink. And then the Connecticut valley knew that the miracle of spring was at an end. Summer was here.

Long before the roses bloomed it was easy to see what was wrong with Polcia. Jude had predicted that the kitchen would be overrun, after her coming, with Polish relatives—the Smentkowskis, the aunts and uncles and cousins. But Polcia kept aloof from them. It was odd. Ondy went to see them sometimes, on Sunday afternoons, taking little Stas with him. Polcia stayed home. Now it was plain.

"Out she goes!" shouted Jude, when the indications of what was happening beneath Polcia's apron were unmistakable. "When her time comes, and before, she'll leave."

"Oh, Aunt Judy, Ondy too? Do you mean Ondy's going, too?"

"He can stay, if he's a mind. She'll live elsewhere."

"But where?"

"Plenty of her kin hereabouts. I'll have no Polack brat squalling around my place. The very idea! So that's why she's been doing all that lifting and hoisting and tromping and pitching hay in the barn." For a lady of austere habits and secluded mode of living, Miss Jude Oakes seemed to have a broad knowledge of obstetrics. She now began counting on her fingers. "End of August, the earliest. Must be. She didn't get here till December. And

God A'mighty, end of August we'll be pressed with haying, and all the tobacco to be cut. I declare, it's enough
to rile a body into a fever."

"Maybe," suggested Temmie, very earnestly, "if you
tell Polcia about the haying, and the tobacco to be cut
in August, she'll wait a while."

"Oh, my land sakes alive!"

She put her blunt questions to Ondy, but he shrugged
evasive shoulders. Polcia went about her work as usual,
but she was putty-colored, drawn, and haggard. "She's
a sight now," Miss Jude confided to Big Bella, "and
here 'tis only April. She's a long row to hoe till her time
comes. Heaven alone knows what she'll look like by
then. I'll not have her around, that's certain."

"I've some herbs will help her," Big Bella suggested,
mildly. "After all, it's natural. Hear you go on, a body'd
think the woman had done a crime."

"Oh, you and your miserable weeds. Ondy's to take
her to Dr. Waite, in Stonefield. She's ailing and scarcely
able to do the work."

But Polcia would not see a doctor. Ondy, questioned,
said sullenly, for him, "Polcia, she no want to see doctor.
She all right. Pole woman is not like American woman."

Jude knew that the Polish farm women of the district
brought forth their children without medical assistance,
"Like wild Indians," Jude commented. Mrs. Krupa, living up near Pequot Ridge, mother of seven, had nearly
died with her eighth. Dr. Waite, summoned after it was

almost too late, demanded wrathfully, "Why didn't you send sooner? A woman of your age, in your condition!"

Mrs. Krupa had rolled her eyes toward Krupa crouching bewildered by the bedside. Krupa, unaided, had delivered his first seven offspring.

"He put um in," Mrs. Krupa explained, simply. "He take um out."

It was on a late afternoon early in April that Temmie, in the kitchen, caught a glimpse of Polcia's face. What she saw terrified her. A sharp New England spring day, the beads of sweat stood out on Polcia's upper lip and on her clammy brow. But her face was not flushed. It was a curious gray, and her eyes seemed sunk far back in her head so that the Slavic cheek bones, always prominent, now stood out like ridges. She was an old, old woman.

"Polcia! What's the matter? Are you sick?"

Some childhood memory stirred in Temmie. One of the women, wife of a sword swallower in a wagon show, had looked like that, one morning. When Temmie asked why, they had evaded the question, and next day there was a new baby, very tiny. It had come in the night.

"Naw, naw!" Polcia replied, hastily, through her teeth. "No sick, no sick." She moved ponderously across the room, busied herself at the stove to prove her words. Temmie heard her groan. She turned quickly to find Polcia bent double. But at Temmie's cry of concern she straightened as though by a superhuman effort and

[*147*]

turned on her a distorted smile that was a hideous grimace of agony.

That night a girl was born to Polcia. It was not born before its time. A full-sized child, perfectly formed, weighing eight pounds, and over. The night in the north wing of the old house, so remote from the other sleeping occupants, was a grisly thing. Finally, in the dark of early morning Ondy went to fetch Miss Jude. The child was not his. He had known all this time, since Polcia had first come to America with another man's child in her womb. But now, in her agony, he had tried to do what he could for her, in his clumsy way. During the dreadful hours of the night he had looked at the gray writhing mask that was her face, and his kind heart was wrung with pity and shot through with alarm. Polcia had tried, gaspingly, to tell him what to do. And now the child lay, a wriggling bundle, on the bed. It seemed well enough. "Rozia. Rozia." Polcia had gasped the name, between groans, while she still could speak.

Jude came, in dressing gown and shuffling slippers. At sight of the woman on the bed the words that were on her lips remained unuttered. Polcia was a big woman, taller than the average, and plump in health. But this woman was gaunt, wasted. Her face that had been round was long. Her piquant snub nose was long. Her temples were hollow. It was as though her face, turned to rubber, had been pulled to a fantastic length by fiendish, inhuman hands. Her eyes were half closed, and only the whites showed. Her hands wandered over the tumbled bed covers. They, too, had undergone the change. The nails were blue, the skin strangely shriveled. She was groaning, not like a human thing but like an animal; it was a bleating, a lowing, like a heifer in agony.

"Quick. The doctor," commanded Miss Jude between white lips. "No, not you. You're to stay here, Ondy, case anything—you're to stay here, with her. I'll hitch up. Jot'll go." She roused Jot. "The doctor. Drive to the store and wake them and use their telephone. Stop at Big Bella's. Tell her to come quick's ever she can."

Dr. Waite arrived as promptly as might be, which was hours later. Big Bella came, calm and efficient, bearing purges, ointments, salves, physics made of her most potent herbs. She looked once at the tortured face on the pillow and put her bottles and her jars to one side.

"It's no use frettin' and frothin'," she said. "The poor creature's beyond our help."

They buried Polcia in the new little Polish cemetery that had suddenly sprung up not far from the old burying ground where lay Orrange Oakes, and Judith, his amiable consort, and Big Noel Champion, and all the others whose fine-sounding names were showing fainter and more faintly on the gravestones that now leaned crazily this way and that.

The Smentkowskis were sent for, but before Julka arrived Temmie had taken charge of the baby Rozia. The child was amazingly fine. It was plain that its eyes would be dark, its hair dark, its skin olive. It resembled the dead Polcia not at all, and most certainly not Ondy. Polcia had evidently gone far afield in the old country for her new love.

"Howdy-do," Jude said severely, in greeting, to Julka Smentkowski and Feliks, on their arrival. "Ondy's willing to pay you to take the child till something can be decided, if it's agreeable to you. I'm told you've none of your own, nor likely to have."

She stared coldly at Julka. Julka, the erstwhile old girl, bridled, flushed, bit her lip. "You're no judge of that," she said, pertly. She had not lived in Stonefield, a city girl, for nothing.

"That's as may be. At any rate, it'll not stay here in my house, and so I tell you." She stood up, the interview, so far as she was concerned, at an end. "Where's Temmie? She's got it. Tell her to bring it here. Tell her the Smentkowskis are here to take it." This to Ondy.

He went. They waited. Jude tapped an impatient toe. Jude's patience, small enough at best, was soon exhausted. She raised her powerful voice. "Tam-ar! Tamar Oakes! Come bring that child this minute."

Quick footsteps down the winding mahogany stairway, but careful, too. Temmie entered the south room, the child in her arms. Her eyes were enormous in her flushed little face. Burdened, she nervously brushed the soft wisps of hair off her cheek with one shrugging shoulder. Some odd and very long garment trailed from the bundle and reached almost to the floor, covering the entire front of Temmie's dark wool frock.

"What in time've you got there?" Miss Jude demanded. "What's that stuff hanging down?"

With one hand Temmie laid aside a corner of a moth-eaten old shawl—a soft flannel thing, brown now with age and decay, but a fine embroidered garment in its day. And the Smentkowskis, and Jude, and Ondy, staring, saw the puckered red and care-worn face of the new-born infant, Rozia Olszak, in a nest of tucks, embroideries, flutings, ruffles, and pleatings of a by-gone era. Yards of muslin, yards of fluting, yards of tucking. Out of the dust and decay of the old chests in the attic Temmie had filched the fine hand-made garments worn centuries ago by Oakes infants in the day of their splendor.

"Tamar Oakes, I vow I'll thrash you for this, big as you are."

But Temmie was sixteen now. She had not her first awe of this formidable female, her aunt. Her face tender, her eyes pleading, she came close to the bristling woman, the bundle held tight in her arms, as though fearful that the brisk Julka would snatch it from her.

"Aunt Jude, let me keep her. Please. Please, Aunt Jude."

"What's the girl driving at?"

"She's so darling. Please, please, Aunt Jude, let me keep her. I can take care of her. She won't be a bit of trouble to you. You'll never even hear her unless you want to, or see her. I've always wanted a baby of my own. Please! Please! She knows me already. Look! She holds my finger just as tight."

Something of the girl's terrible earnestness and longing seemed to penetrate even Jude Oakes' defenses. Certainly her tone, as she took the infant forcibly from Temmie's clinging arms and placed it on Julka's barren bosom, was less scathing than it might have been.

"Oakes Farm will soon be an orphan asylum, no less. I vow, if you weren't my own flesh and blood, Tamar Oakes, I'd turn you out with the child." Then, at the stricken and bereft look on the girl's face, "There, there, don't take on as if she belonged to you. Be ashamed of yourself, a young girl like you. You can go see the baby, sometimes, maybe. Can't she, Mrs. Smentkowski?"

"Why, sure," said Julka Smentkowski, graciously.

"And off with that dress, miss. That's an heirloom. I'll have no Oakes dresses on an Olszak—or whatever she is."

But, "You're—you're holding her wrong, Mrs. Smentkowski—her head," was all that Temmie said as the little procession moved toward the kitchen.

VIII

SPRING, in Connecticut, made fair false promises which summer was called upon to keep. It was not until June arrived that Temmie felt certain spring would not change her fickle mind and fly back to her lingering old lover. There was that chill moment of panic when, coming out of the school house one April afternoon, Temmie had beheld the countryside covered with great patches of white as far as the eye could see. Her heart sank. She thought the winter snows had come again to nip the first green growing things. But it was only the protecting white cheesecloth which the tobacco farmers all through the valley had stretched tightly over the wooden frames of the hotbeds to protect the young seed-lings before transplanting.

Summer, Temmie decided, was a fine thing in Con-necticut. She had arrived in the last blaze of October splendor, soon faded. That first winter had been bitter, strange, often lonely, more than a little frightening. The spring had been blighted by the tragedy of Polcia. But now here was summer, hot, sweet-smelling, with fresh early morning breezes dispelling the mists that hung low on the pastures and over the Housatonic, creeping along the meadow brooks in curling wisps. The dews were heavy, so that it was like walking through water to cross the early morning fields. In the cool of the evening the shadows lengthened across Pequot Ridge and stalked, long-legged giants, into the valley.

Polcia's brief American interlude was almost forgotten. When Temmie or Ondy went to the Smentkowskis to see the dark-eyed Rozia, they somehow did not associate her with the bewildered and desperate woman whose life had ended when hers began.

Temmie was sixteen and over; she was healthy, the sun shone, there was work, there was food, there were friendly human beings to talk to, and young; Ondy, strong, genial, kind; Jot, running about, with his short-legged rolling gait, like a jolly little pirate; stocky Stas, a serious, stolid child. With these at home, and the red-cheeked Rozia to be visited at the Smentkowskis, life at Oakes Farm was not so bad, in spite of the caustic and fault-finding Jude. The farm itself was going well enough—better, surely, than it had in fifty years and more. Ondy's feeling for the land was too inherent not to serve it well, even though no clod of it belonged to him. He made no secret of his determination to buy a piece of land for himself somewhere in the valley as soon as he had money enough put by. Other Poles of longer standing in the community were buying, acre by acre. Under their slavish tending the valley was taking on a second youth; blooming like a widow wooed.

Jude and Ondy were forever bickering about the way

in which the farm should be run. Jude seemed to enjoy these tiffs.

"And I'll thank you to remember I'm boss here," she was always saying. Her sallow cheeks would be flushed, her eyes bright behind the glasses. She was pleasantly stimulated by these emotional battles with one of the opposite sex.

"Sure Miss Oakes is boss. Ondy he know to run farm."

"If you're so all-fired smart at it, why didn't you run your own farm in Poland?"

"Is big here, is fine here, is land for everybody. Ondy he make Oakes Farm rich like anything. You see you have more fine tobacco November as in your life, I betcha."

"I'm not complaining about the way you work. But you've got such crazy notions. I never heard anything so crazy. Speak about the water and the land and the very fire in the stove as if they were folks. And the cows in the barn."

"Sure is like folks. Cow he is know things peoples not know."

Just the day before, Jude had come to Temmie in considerable agitation. "I stepped into the barn, unbeknownst, and there was Ondy with the red heifer that's sick, and talking to the animal as polite as a pair of sugar tongs. Not just so-bossy, so-bossy, as a body sometimes does, to soothe, but talking. It gave me a turn."

Temmie did not seem surprised at this. "Ondy is like

that, Aunt Jude. He told me. He says all Polack farmers are like that. He says the fire and the water and the earth and the animals aren't just things. They're like people, only better."

"Don't you ever let me catch you talking such nonsense. I'm beginning to believe John Veal was right. They're heathen, those Polacks."

Certainly Ondy, and all the other Poles of the region, had outlandish customs and beliefs connected with the business of plowing, planting, sowing, reaping. Earth, fire, water, plants, animals—all were associated with Old World myths in Ondy's mind.

When the red heifer fell sick Jude was for using such customary methods as she and Big Bella and the other farmers of the neighborhood had always relied upon.

Ondy shook his head. "I fix him." He spent half a day searching in the woods and fields for a certain plant. He tried to explain to Big Bella what it was he sought. When he came upon it he bent it down, fastened its top to the ground with a stone, and said aloud, in Polish, "I will release you when you make my cow well."

"To-night," he told Miss Jude, on his return, "cow he is well. You wait. You see."

Next morning, sure enough, the cow had recovered. Ondy hastened to the spot, three miles away, where he had found the plant, removed the stone, released the plant; for if he failed to do this the cow would fall sick again, and die.

Ondy was for planting in the dark of the moon all seed whose fruit is under the ground—potatoes, onions, turnips, and the like—and in the full of the moon the others—beans, tomatoes, pumpkins, cucumbers, peas. Beans, especially, were planted on Good Friday. There was simply no moving him in that.

"The man's daft as a loon."

Hail, in the sudden cold of late spring, is the great terror of the tobacco grower, when the tender young plants may be battered to death in a few brief minutes. Ondy assured the scoffing Miss Jude that a furrow drawn around a field by a pair of twin oxen would insure that field against hail.

"You're safe enough saying that, Olszak. Go find your-self a pair of twin oxen in all the county, to prove it." Still, to Temmie or to Big Bella she sometimes admitted, with grudging admiration, "He's a knowing kind of cattle, that Olszak."

Temmie, brought up on the superstitions and childish beliefs common to the wagon shows and the carnival companies, accepted, wide-eyed, all that Ondy told her. Jot believed him, too, like a simple child.

Once, when Jude Oakes, in anger against Ondy, had confided to Temmie her suspicion that Olszak was schem-ing to get her land away from her, Temmie denied the accusation earnestly. "Oh, no, Aunt Jude. He wouldn't. He couldn't, you see. Even if he wanted to, he wouldn't."

"Why not, I'd like to know!"

"Because every field knows its real owner, and if somebody else tries to take it away it won't yield any crops."

Temmie understood now why Ondy loved the land. She, too, began to love Oakes Farm and all that was on it. Not the house alone, but all that was on the farm and of it. She heard and believed—or thought she did, because she wanted to.

Water should never be wantonly dirtied or dried up. Nothing bad should be said or done near it, because it knows, and can betray. Swallows and lizards know herbs that can revive the dead. Fires lighted on the Eve of St. John—June 24th—make the crops succeed. There are all about us witches, goblins, devils, vampires, water spirits, earth spirits, giants, dwarfs, invisible. A *potudnica,* the midday woman, strangles anyone who sleeps in a field at noon. Water spirits, *boginki,* have human bodies but can become invisible at will. They often try to change their children for human ones, stealing a child from a household and putting their own in its place. A child changed thus can be recognized by its bad temper, its growing ugliness, and its enormous appetite. Sometimes Ondy, jestingly, called little Stas a *boginka's* child, and Stas, at this, stuck out a tremulous lower lip in protest. Cloud beings, *planetniki,* dwell in the clouds and bring rain, hail, thunderstorms. Bees will never stay with a thief. The swallows will leave a farm where some evil deed has been committed. If fruit trees grow well, if crops succeed, it is not the result of man's activity; the

plants and trees are conscious of being well treated
and show their gratitude. Fire is a superior being. Ondy
blessed it when he lighted it in the morning; when he
covered it with ashes at night. Snakes and wild birds
are the most knowing of creatures, but all four-footed
animals understand some things better than men.

Now Temmie understood Ondy's way with the cattle.
On cold, bright winter noondays he would turn the cows
out of the dark, noisome barn, and they would stand
gratefully in the barnyard, their nostrils smoking. He
would put his strong gentle hand on their flanks, on their
necks, and they would turn their soft eyes on him. Every
day he gave each cow two ears of corn, lovingly, tenderly.
Good corn, he seemed to be saying. Kind corn.

During that summer a certain peace and contentment
settled down upon Oakes Farm. Even into Jude's face
there came a kind of nipped blooming. Ondy throve with
the crops. He had had the baby, Rozia, baptized by
Father Scully, the handsome young Irish priest of the
big church at Fenwick. There were now so many Poles
settling throughout the valley that they had sent him—a
student priest—to Warsaw, and there at school for three
years he had learned the language, so that now, when
he addressed the Irish-born members of the thriving
congregation in English, or the Polish members in Polish,
it was with a trace of the brogue in both tongues. Whenever she could get away Temmie would be off to the
Smentkowskis to see the child. Julka Smentkowski

[*159*]

actually kept Rozia more neatly dressed and better fed than she otherwise might have done, merely because she never knew when Temmie would appear, pounce upon the baby, and examine her from head to toe for possible signs of neglect.

"If you had a hunderd dollars," Julka said one day, jestingly, as Temmie was bathing the baby in a deep pan in the warm, bustling Smentkowski kitchen, "you could buy Rozia off of Ondia and me and Feliks and then you got her for yourself."

Temmie, kneeling before the tub, had a protecting towel over the front of her dress, for Rozia, during her ablutions, was a splasher. She looked up at Julka now, startled, dazzled, but she remembered to hold Rozia's round dark head well out of the water. "I could! Julka! Could I? Really, you mean! Oh, Julka!"

At the glow in the little heart-shaped face, at the look in her eyes, Julka felt a little abashed. "Well, maybe not now, you couldn't. But time you're eighteen and got a hundred dollars you can do what you want to. It is the law. Nobody is your boss time you are eighteen."

Rozia, temporarily on her own, made a terrific to-do with legs and arms, so that Temmie sat in quite a shower, unheeding. Temmie looked down at the plump wet morsel in the crude tub. Rozia wriggled, slippery as an eel. "But I haven't got a hundred dollars. Where—how could I get a hundred dollars?"

"Work for it. I did."

"But I do work. Only——"

"Not for that aunt of yours. I wouldn't work for her, not for a hunderd dollars a month, even, I wouldn't. For somebody else, why don't you? Ondy says you do all the work, mostly, and cook good. For nothing."

"An Oakes," Temmie said, and unconsciously her voice took on something of Jude's tone, "doesn't work for other people."

"Oakeses is no better than other people."

"Oh, yes, they are, Julka," Temmie said, quite simply, as though stating a fact.

A hundred dollars by the time she was eighteen. Temmie dwelt on this as she lifted and carried and scrubbed and baked, washed dishes, made beds, at Oakes House. She would not be seventeen until the end of October. She would not be eighteen until a whole year after that. But by that time Rozia would be a year and a half old.

There was work enough, and to spare, in the regular course of the day's routine. But every now and then Temmie, in a frenzy of orderliness, would attack one of the closed and shuttered rooms which lay in a perpetual twilight of disuse. There was something touching in the sight of this diminutive creature armed with mop and pail and rag and broom against one of the high-ceilinged, somber, dusty chambers. Temmie's angular lines had filled out a little. The pointed face was a shade rounder in contour; the sharp elbows, the immature arms had taken on softer curves. But she was still very thin, very small for her age. With her bright soft hair bound up in an old towel against the flying dust she was like a little girl playing at housewife.

Sometimes Jude Oakes took a hand in one of these cleaning orgies. But she was more nuisance than help, Temmie discovered. She would always leave unfinished any task she started. If she began tidying the welter of a bureau drawer she would leave it when garments were scattered all about the floor, and never return to it; or, impatient and bored, she would stuff the objects back into the drawers in a disorder worse than that with which she had begun. If she happened to be washing woodwork she would rise suddenly, brush down her skirts, and say, "I've got to tend to something downstairs. Look, Tamar. I've done from here to here. You finish." And off she would stalk, not to return.

Temmie liked to clean the big front chamber wherein there still hung the portrait of that other Tamar Oakes. It was not, perhaps, a very good example of portrait painting. This Dutchman, Van Oogstraat, had been an admirer and emulator of the early Dutch masters, without their mastery. Generations of Oakes had dealt harshly with the old house and its treasures. Many possessions —pictures, silver, furniture—had disappeared. But Jude Oakes had never parted with so much as a pewter spoon or a hand-made kitchen chair, though by now it was well known that city people were snooping all about the valley, prepared to pay fantastic prices for such things—for quite common things, in fact, such as Jude would not give attic room. The Tamar Oakes picture had survived, and still hung on the wall above the fireplace, facing the great four-poster. And in the dim wide lower hall Sir Orrange Oakes, who had died for freedom, looked sadly down upon the ruin which his descendants had wrought.

Temmie, in her calico work dress, her head bound turban fashion, loved to stand gazing at the portrait of this other Temmie in the rich overdress of rose-flowered brocade chiné, pinked over a pale blue satin petticoat. Her eyes, hungry for beauty, dwelt on the delicate tracery of the point lace collar, on the massive jeweled stomacher, so absurd on that childish bosom; on the fan, the rose, the little buckled shoes, the curls that hung over each shoulder. The portrait had a kind of stiff charm. In the girl's little pointed face, in the gray eyes with the gold flecks in them, in her slim elegance, the Dutchman had managed to catch something half mocking, half serious, as though this Tamar had been quite well aware of her own importance, even while she thought the whole business slightly silly.

"Stand there gawping like a zany."

"What? Oh. Do you think I look like her, Aunt Jude?"

"Likely," sneered Aunt Jude; a withering glance at the calico dress, the towel-turbaned head.

"Not the dress, I mean. Me. Do you suppose that dress is up in one of the chests in the attic?"

"There's a ruck of things up there. Rubbish. Moths and dust and rats, too, you'll find, so keep your hands off what isn't yours."

But she persisted. "It might be, though. Mightn't it?"

"Are you going to finish that bed you're polishing, or aren't you?"

Temmie fell to rubbing the great posts of the enormous bed that was in itself as big as a room. The wood had the rich patina that comes of hundreds of years of polishing. From the heavy framework there still hung suspended in remarkable preservation the crimson satin damask of the seventeen hundreds.

"Why don't you sleep in this room, Aunt Jude, instead of yours?"

"Me! Sleep here!"

"I should think you'd love it, mornings. You'd wake up and look out there across the valley, to the river. And the bed's lovely and soft."

In proof of this she plumped herself into the middle of it and bounced up and down.

"Off that bed this instant, Tamar Oakes!"

Temmie scrambled off, obediently, after a last jounce.

"I'll make it up for you, shall I? It's all been sunned —the bedding—in the yard. Why don't you, Aunt Jude?"

"Because," snapped Jude Oakes, "none but a wedded Oakes couple sleeps in that bed, or ever has. No single person has slept in it—not since it was built into the house in the day of Captain Orrange Oakes himself."

"And his amiable consort Judith?"

"Yes, stupid. Who else?"

Temmie surveyed the vast conjugal couch with new interest. "What wedded Oakes couple slept in it last?"

"Oh, my sakes alive, I don't know. My mother and father, I suppose." Jude banged cupboard doors and dresser drawers.

Temmie passed one work-stained palm gently over the once splendid brocade counterpane. Then, suddenly, she stooped and laid her fresh young cheek on the pillow. "I wonder if I'll ever be an amiable consort and a wedded Oakes and sleep in this bed, Aunt Jude?"

The banging grew in sound and fury. "Wedded! You've brought your pigs to a fine market for that, coming to Oakesfield." She laughed, high and sharp and dry.

Temmie already had invaded the attic, had surreptitiously tried on such ancient gewgaws and fripperies as could be hastily donned while Jude was busy elsewhere. But she had never come upon the dress of the Tamar portrait. It might well be there, in one of the great oak chests looming dark in this corner or that, covered with great rolls of dusty stuffs, piled with broken furniture cast off by generations of Oakes. Her childish arms could not hope to move these. She wondered if Ondy, one day, would not move them for her, in one of Jude's rare absences. She loved to dress up. The slim little figure had a certain elegance, even in the workaday calico. She begged to be allowed to go to church sometimes, on Sunday, because this gave her an opportunity to wear one of the dresses she had brought to Oakesfield on her arrival in October. Miss Jude never went to church. She had quarreled with the minister, naturally, as she quarreled, ultimately, with everyone with whom she came in contact. The church was a clear-cut little gem of a building, with an authentic Wren cupola and steeple, and a jewel-like window of stained glass that had been ordered from England by Captain Orrange Oakes and set up, bit by bit, to glow down upon a once colorful congregation, now grown primmer and sparser and more pinched with the passing of the years. Temmie's best dress was a cashmere bluet, with fine shirrings at the waist and wrists, and further enhanced with a white muslin guimpe at the top. That deft needlewoman, Mlle. Bonita, the Bearded Lady, had made it for her from a pattern out of *Harper's Bazaar*. With this she had originally worn her figaro jacket of velvet, making a most romantic effect. But Aunt Jude, after one look, had forbidden it.

"You'll not wear that monkey jacket to church, Tamar Oakes, and so I tell you. Nor that outlandish coat, either."

The coat in question was of Jacqueminot red, warm and woolly, and Tamar's dearest possession. She had, too, an apron made of Roman striped silk which she longed to wear afternoons, when the housework was done, but this, too, Jude would not countenance.

"I never saw such a hand for dressing up. No, sir, I

never saw the beat in all my born days. Like a play actress. You'll be painting your face next, I shouldn't wonder. Well, just let me catch you, that's all, miss."

Jude would have been still more horrified had she known that Temmie had often been allowed to paint her face in the days of Pring's Miracle Medicine Show. On dull mornings, or rainy days, Temmie had been allowed to dress up to her heart's content, under the amiable supervision of the tent and wagon-show ladies. Here were gaudy tinsel and spangles and tarleton and cotton-back satin. Her slim little shanks had pirouetted in pink tights. It had been lovely. Amaryllis, hearing Tamar's breathless accounts of the morning's delights, would look a little frightened.

"It's all right—just for dressing up, darling. But Mama doesn't want you—when you are grown up it would be nice to live in Oakesfield, at Oakes Farm, and be a young lady, wouldn't it?"

Temmie had said yes, dutifully, but privately she had thought it would be dull compared with the world of the wagon shows.

In the face of Temmie's tears and protests Jude Oakes had dyed the Jacqueminot red cloak a sad and snuffy brown. But she could not spoil the cut and line; and Tamar's Sunday hat was undeniably chic. Bought in New Orleans, it had been made by a wizened little side-street milliner with a dusty fringe and beady black eyes and withered clawlike hands that had a French trick with a bow of ribbon and a feather. Temmie, sitting straight and alone on Sunday in the high-backed Oakes pew, was the only figure of elegance in that clammy little church, with its fusty and desiccated congregation, to the women of which a hat was only a covering for the head. Her clear-cut face, aglow in that dim pew—the stained-glass window, aglow on the south wall—seemed akin; and alien to the drab ghosts that sparsely dotted the pews of lesser Oakesfield worshipers.

Small wonder that Temmie thought the attic of Oakes House a maze of mystery and enchantment. It was a vast, oak-raftered place, with a vaulted roof, cross-beamed like a cathedral. Under Jude's eagle-eyed supervision she had been able to steal little time for visits to this store-house of wonders. But such ecstatic moments as she had spent in its dim and spidery atmosphere had yielded breath-taking treasures; unheard of possibilities for the pastime of dressing up. Moths and mice and dust and the imminent danger of Jude's menacing step had no terrors for Tamar as she saw revealed old pelisses of camelot, scarlet cloaks, satin-flowered mantles, shoes with fine silver buckles, tarnished now to black; dresses of velvet and satin trimmed with silver galloon, white hoods tricked out with lace; handkerchiefs, aprons, fans, quilted petticoats, even wigs and silk wig bags.

Somewhere, she felt, she would come upon the rose-flowered brocade, with the edges pinked over a petticoat of blue satin, and the point-lace collar, and the fan, and the—but of course not the rose, silly, she said to herself. When she found the dress, as she knew she must, the rose could come from the huge old rose tree still wanly abloom in the south yard.

Tamar's chance came in July. The second week in July Great-aunt Charry Minot, of New Kent, died, aged a tidy ninety; and on a convenient Friday, so that the funeral could be held on Sunday.

"Aunt Charry Minot was always a great hand for things being just so," Tamar overheard Jude confiding to Big Bella. Temmie looked at Jude's face to see if this were not a grim joke, but Aunt Jude seemed quite serious. Jude went on, in an annoyed tone, "Well, there's nothing for it, I'll have to go, I s'pose."

They were in conference in the south sitting room, the faded green blinds half shut against the heat of the day. Big Bella had mysteriously been sent for, and was now seated on the brown couch as the only piece of furniture able to contain her great bulk. Her vast knees were spread apart—she could not bring them together when she sat, Temmie had discovered, fascinated—and her enormous feet, in their men's boots, were planted firmly on the floor. Her great paunch rested comfortably in her lap, and surmounting this mass of her body her bland pink face glowed like a sunset on a mountain top.

"I don't know's I can go, Judy," she said. "I don't know's I'm really able, with my stomach feeling so poorly."

"Certainly you're not to go," Jude retorted, with asperity. "One's enough to represent the Oakesfield branch."

Temmie was mystified by all this. Her knowledge of death, heretofore, had been accompanied by genuine sorrow. When her mother had died, when Mlle. Bonita had been so suddenly stricken, there had been a storm of weeping. The women on the lot had been red-eyed for days, beneath their powder.

"Were you fond of Great-aunt Charry Minot?" Temmie now asked.

"Fond of her! I haven't seen her in twenty years and over. A more spiteful, cantankerous old woman never breathed, and stayed so to the very end."

"Oh. But then, why do you go to her funeral?"

"There! Did a body ever hear anything so uncivilized! It just shows what your bringing up must have been. When an Oakes kin dies you go to the funeral, I hope. The last respect you can show." Jude turned from Tamar's bewildered face to Big Bella's placid one. "I know for a fact she had a tidy bit put by, what with never spending a penny, year in, year out, and living on Phebe, though it's well known Uncle Manasseh left her comfortable, and if Phebe Minot thinks she can keep those four silver candlesticks from me, when everyone knows they belonged to Oakes House in the beginning, as I can prove from Captain Orrange's will that that miserable Peter Leere sold before my time, and it's now in the library at Stonefield."

Tamar's head was ringing with the strangeness of this conversation, with the venomous relish in Aunt Jude's tone, with Big Bella's placid acceptance of it all.

"I'll leave Saturday morning," Jude went on, "and back Sunday night, the latest."

Tamar felt her own heart leap for joy in her breast. Aunt Jude would be gone two days. Two whole days. This was Friday. She would leave to-morrow, then. She turned to quit the room. She must find Ondy, Jot, Stas, and tell them the joyful, the unbelievable news. But at Jude's next words she paused, dismayed.

"You'll stop here while I'm gone, Bella."

"Course I could, Judy. But I don't see's it's called for, with Temmie such a hand for cooking and all. And Mossop won't hear to my being gone overnight and acts like possessed."

Temmie could bear it no longer. "But why, Aunt Jude? I'll do everything just the same as if you were here. Saturday pies, and the kitchen floor, and all."

"Don't you like your Cousin Bella?" said that sentimental lady, reproachfully, in her lovely clear voice.

"Oh, I do, Cousin Bella. I do. Only I thought it would be such fun keeping house all alone, like a grown-up person, just as if it was my own house——"

"Likely I'd leave you here alone with that man." Jude's tone was pure horror.

"What man?"

"Olszak."

"Alone! But what—and anyway—why there's Jot and Stas—and anyway, what——"

"Never you mind, young lady. You'll do as I say."

Big Bella stayed. Jot was sent surreptitiously to fetch her vast flappy bed slippers and her vaster nightgown, for she vowed if she herself went for them the possessive Mossop would never permit her return.

Early Saturday morning, sure enough, Jude Oakes departed for New Kent and the silver candlesticks and Aunt Charry Minot's last rites. Though she was to be gone two days, Jude made clear that her bony hand should be felt in her absence. She left behind a string of instructions which, if carried out, would have taken two weeks.

"There's burdock and milkweed enough in the greens to choke them, so's a body is put to it to tell whether we're raising garden truck or weeds, and that's a fact. . . . Stas didn't get those hop vines near out of the ground. They've got to come out, roots and all, or they'll choke the corn black by August. . . . Tamar, see you get those flour sacks hemmed for dish towels Saturday afternoon, and no running to those Smentkowskis like possessed. . . . Jot, the fence south end the east meadow looks as if the Hessians had tromped through it, and if I've been at you to mend it once I've been at you a hundred times, and the cattle could get in easy as stepping over a twig, and will, too. . . . Olszak, I hear the watering cart is going the rounds, and I s'pose you haven't spoken for it, and the tobacco dry as ashes with no decent rain since June. But I'll pay no fancy prices, remember. . . . Tamar . . . Jothom . . . Olszak . . . Stas . . . cook . . . cattle . . . shed . . . fence . . . pies . . . milk . . ."

She was gone. A sigh that was almost a groan of relief went up from the very vitals of those left behind.

Saturday morning passed peacefully enough. They ate dinner in mellow content, seated about the big kitchen table. Big Bella took little of the bountiful meal that Temmie had prepared. She had rather mysteriously retired to the comparative coolness of the south room almost immediately after Jude's departure, and Temmie had with difficulty awakened her for the noonday dinner. But Jot, Ondy, Stas ate heartily enough. About the relaxed group there was a pleasant soaring of the spirits, as though something long suppressed had been released.

Flour sacks. Hop weeds. Burdocks. South fence. Defiance sat on each glowing face. She can't any more than kill me, Temmie thought, tossing her head.

She did the dinner dishes with lightning speed. Her pies, baked that morning, were cooling in the pantry. Big Bella sat, breathing stertorously, in one of the ladder-backed chairs by the open window. It creaked beneath her breathing.

"So close a body can't catch their breath, scarcely," Big Bella complained. She lifted herself ponderously from the chair and went toward the front of the house, along

[*173*]

the central hall. "Come on in the south room and talk
to your cousin Bella, there's a good girl."

"I've so much to do."

"Stuff and nonsense. That Jude, with her do-this, do-
that. Come sit and cool off and talk to your cousin Bella,
that never sees you, hardly." When Temmie joined her
in the south sitting room Big Bella was wiping her mouth
with the back of her hand, and something heavy sagged
and swung in the capacious pocket at the side of her
voluminous skirt. "There," breathed Cousin Bella, and
the air was suddenly pungent, "that's better."

She sat down on the broad old couch. Her lids closed
over her beautiful eyes, misted now and strangely blank.
Temmie, seeing this, essayed to tiptoe from the room.
The eyes came open. "Stay here with Cousin Bella." The
woman began to weep, gently, great pearly tears that
rolled down her pink cheeks and fell on the vast plateau
of her bosom. Temmie moved restlessly about the room.
She picked up one of Aunt Jude's paper-backed books,
laid it down. She wandered over to the table in the
corner on which reposed a huge tattered volume. She
opened it. The flyleaf read:

The Holy Bible. Containing the Old and New Testaments with
Arguments prefixed to the different books, and Moral and Theo-
logical Observations illustrating each chapter. Compiled by the
Reverend Medad Skelton.

Temmie glanced at Big Bella. The eyes were closed.
She stole toward the door. The glazed eyes flew open.

Oh, dear, thought Temmie. Oh, dear, oh dear. Gibbon's Roman Empire. The Last Days of Pompeii. The London Encyclopedia in tattered yellow leather dated 1845, printed by Thomas Tegg, 73 Cheapside.

"Don't you want to lie down, Cousin Bella, and be comfortable?"

"No, child." Whereupon Cousin Bella leaned back and toppled, a mountainous heap, onto the dusty brown cushions. Temmie waited yet another moment. The innocent gray eyes remained closed. The pink cheeks glowed like those of a child, dewy in sleep.

The attic. She was up there as though wafted by the winds. It was stifling, but Temmie did not mind. She lifted pieces of furniture as though they were light as eggshells. She scrambled over dusty heaps of piled-up rubbish. She opened chests and cupboards in dim corners to which she had never yet penetrated. Out came caps and cloaks and bits of silk and cloth stuff, old boots, yellowed gloves, bustles, hoops. Bluebeard's wife never poked and pryed with greater surge of forbidden joy.

It will be at the very bottom, she told herself. At the very bottom, somewhere, because it was so long ago. And in a small box, alone, because that is the way Judith amiable consort would want it. And led thus by her intuitive feeling for that other Tamar Oakes, she came upon it just as she had thought, in a cherry-wood box that was like a little exquisite coffin. Perhaps Judith Oakes, cheated of the comfort of a coffin for her beloved daughter, had ordered it made thus for the repose of Tamar's earthly garments, for that her earthly body, reduced to ashes, reposed in the white jade box beneath the sandstone slab in front of the fireplace.

Tamar opened it with fingers that shook. The stiff little gown with its satin hooped petticoat, the rosy over-skirt faded now almost to buff, elbow sleeves, low-cut neck, little silken slippers, the fan—where was the fan? —this bit of yellowed ivory and tattered lace. Yes. Temmie rolled it all into a bundle, but gently, and sped down the attic stairs to the front chamber, closed, dark, breathless. She placed her precious bundle on the bed, sped to the windows, opened one, then another, in a series of superhuman tugs, unfastened the shutters, threw them wide. The hot sweet July day streamed into the musty room.

Off came the calico workday dress. Her comb. She flew, in petticoat and shirt, to her own bedroom for her comb wherewith to make ringlets over each shoulder. Back again, her cheeks scarlet, she tossed the dress, a great balloon of dusty silk, over her head, let it settle on her shoulders. She thrust her feet into the stiff frayed high-heeled silken slippers, never heeding the discomfort they gave. Now, then, the fan. The rose. Oh, my gracious sakes alive, she had forgotten the rose. She was down into the desolate garden in a moment. She plucked a pink rose from the old rose tree and was up again, breath-less. She would not look in the swimmy old mirror—

the long mirror in the gold frame—until all was finished. She combed her hair loosely back from her forehead, as it was in the portrait. Her eyes were on the portrait as she dressed. Curls—loose ringlets—over each shoulder. Now straighten the revers so that the waist looks tiny, like that in the portrait. Now the fan. Now the rose.

A last look at the mocking girl of the Van Oogstraat portrait. She walked deliberately over to the long mirror opposite it and looked at herself.

She looked at herself. She looked at the portrait behind her. She looked at herself. Tamar Oakes. Which Tamar Oakes? They were the same. They were one.

"Oh, my goodness, it's scary! It's kind of scary!" She stood again, surveying the likeness between these two girls. It was as though the dust in the white jade box had gathered itself together and pushed aside the sandstone slab and risen to take form.

"How do you do?" Temmie said, aloud, to the girl in the mirror and the girl in the portrait. "How do you do to-day, Tamar Oakes? How is your mother Judith amiable consort, and your father, Captain Orrange Oakes, and how is black Esau, and Big Noel, and old Chief Waramaug?"

She laughed, a high, hysterical laugh. It was too lovely. It was too perfect. That was it. She must share it with someone. She lifted the full rustling skirts, she clattered down the winding stairway in her rickety high heels.

"Cousin Bella, Cousin Bella!" But Cousin Bella, a mound on the couch, snorted, groaned, rolled ponderously on her side, slept again. Ondy. Ondy would be topping tobacco in the field, or he'd be in the barn, perhaps, this being Saturday afternoon. She stood in the kitchen doorway and hallooed. Ondy! Ondy! Yoo-hoo! A voice answered from the dim recesses of the barn. She lifted her silken skirts and sped toward the voice. She stood in the barn doorway, taking care not to sully her cracked silken shoes.

"Ondy, Ondy, come here, quick."

At the urgent quality in her tone Olszak emerged from the barn, a pitchfork in his hand, smelling of manure. He wiped his forehead with the back of one bare arm. His blue eyes blinked in the strong sunlight after the darkness of the barn. "Whew, is hot!"

"Look! Look at me!"

She stood, in her silken dress, the skirts outspread, the fan in one hand, the rose in the other.

Ondy stared. She smiled up at him, impudent, important. "By golly, Temmie, is pretty how you look!"

"It's the picture. I look like the picture, don't you see? In the big bedroom, over the fireplace. Tamar."

But Oakes family portraits played no part in Ondia Olszak's life.

"Sure," he said, amiably. He looked down at the girl, and his eyes were brighter and bluer, Temmie thought, than she had ever seen them before. They rested on her

slim young arms in the elbow sleeves, on her white virginal
bosom in the low-cut dress. Slowly, gently, he put out
one forefinger and touched the curl that lay on her
shoulder. His finger touched the curl, touched her throat,
gently. She swayed forward a little, then away. She
stepped back. He stepped forward.

"Ondy," she said, quickly, "Ondy, let's have a show."
Queerly enough she had not thought of it until then. She
thought of it quite suddenly, in that moment.

"Show?" He was frowning, as though displeased.

"You know—a show—a regular show, like those I've
told you about, when I was with Papa and Mama and we
followed the carnivals."

"Who is make the show?"

"All of us. Jot can hitch up and go round and tell
people it's to-night—anyone—at the store and around—
and we'll charge maybe five cents, because you've got to
charge for a show, or people will think it's no good. And
besides, I've got to make a hundred dollars by the time
I'm eighteen, so I may as well start."

"Show? Who makes show?" He was bewildered but
smiling as he looked down at the eager, flushed girl.

"Don't you see, Ondy dear? All of us. I thought of it
all in a minute. Jot'll be Major Hop-o'-My-Thumb, the
Smallest Living Man. Cousin Bella can be the Fattest
Woman on Earth. She is, really. I'll be living pictures.
I'll be Mlle. Tamar, the Living Picture."

"Me. What I am?" Ondy looked a trifle apprehensive.

"Well, you'll have to give the ballyhoo, I guess, and take money at the door. You know. Tell what there is to see at the show. I'll teach you."

The thing grew, swelled, became reality. Ondy had a cousin Wiktor, who played the accordion. It was Ondy, too, who, entering into the spirit of the thing, suggested that they get Zeb Biglow, the idiot, to play Jo-Jo, the Dog-Faced Boy. It was he who suggested that they sell hard cider at five cents a glass, with Temmie's fresh-baked doughnuts. He had been at fairs in his own Poland. He had attended a county fair or two here in the district. This was going to be fine, by golly. He was gay as a boy, and resourceful beyond Temmie's dreams.

Big Bella was a problem. Big Bella was still a mountain on the surface of the couch in the south room. "She can't be the Fattest Woman on Earth if she won't sit up," Temmie wailed.

"Coffee," Ondy suggested, from the depths of his masculine wisdom. "She feel fine quick."

Supper was the sketchiest kind of cold meal. They had decided to give the show in the small bare tobacco shed, near the house. Every lantern about the house or barns was hung ready for lighting. Every lamp in the house was placed on an upturned box. There were terrific problems to be solved before eight o'clock, the hour set for the show. They worked with a kind of frenzy. Big Bella was still quite drunk but amenable. She even seemed to understand, vaguely, what was going on, and to enter into the spirit of the thing with a childish enthusiasm. She let them remove her bodice, tugging and pulling, and swathe her upper body in a sheet, fold on fold, leaving her great column of a throat, her chest, and her enormous arms bare. Temmie powdered her pink cheeks generously with flour.

"Mlle. Maude always wore tights," Temmie said, as she worked. "But of course we couldn't do that, I suppose, being it's Cousin Bella, really. Anyway," suddenly practical, "we haven't any tights."

The picture of that other Tamar Oakes was taken from its place on the wall in the big chamber, carried down to the shed, and mounted on a tobacco box. "I stand in front of it, you see," Temmie explained, "because I'm the living picture. And the lighted lantern just there, over me, so folks'll see how much alike we are." She was, certainly, with a true showman's instinct, giving herself a place of vantage. Still, Big Bella loomed up very well, and little Jot had been decked out in a pair of satin breeches and a hat with a plume that Temmie had found in the attic. The knee breeches were much too large, and Temmie had tucked them up as best she could with safety pins. The effect created by Major Hop-o'-My-Thumb, while not chic, was undeniably arresting.

"There! Now, Ondy, listen. You say, 'Step this way, ladies and gents. The greatest show on earth. See Jo-Jo, the Dog-Faced Boy! Mlle. Bella, the Fattest Woman on Earth. Mlle. Tamar, the Living Picture.' Like that. And watch Stas so that people won't try to pass him without paying the money at the door. Five cents."

Ondy's cousin, Wiktor, worked away at his accordion, head, hands, and feet. Passers-by were few along this quiet by-road. One or two, hearing the music, the shouting, stopped their teams on their way to this or that Saturday-night country revel, to listen in amazement. Curious, three or four ventured round to the shed to see what could be happening about the old Oakes place, usually so somber, so silent, brooding in the shelter of the giant oak trees. But the Poles had their own Saturday-night diversions. The native New Englanders stirred out little after nightfall. By half-past eight, though Wiktor's accordion squealed and grunted, and Ondy shouted his gibberish, there were few besides the neighborhood children staring open-mouthed at the spectacle of the decorous old Oakes place gone mad. By nine Ondy proved the chief patron of the hard cider. Thus befuddled, though things were not going very well, he put his whole heart into his work. Lacking this stimulant, his adult common sense would doubtless have cautioned him to cease this nonsense.

"Step up, step up, step up! Is greatest show on earth. Only nickel-half-dime! Look Tamar Living Picture! Look Jo-Jo is Dog-Face' Boy! Look smallest living man in world! Come, come, come! Show is begin! Step up, step up! See Madam Bella, she is fattest woman on earth, I betcha."

He knew his part by now. When his energy flagged he had another glass of the hard, heady cider.

Giggling, open-mouthed, wondering, the straggling yokelry, though few enough in number, made up their lack by their appreciation. They stared, only half believing what they saw, while the lanterns guttered, the lamps smoked dangerously in the old shed.

Temmie, rose in one hand, fan in the other, one foot advanced a little, tried to smile mockingly in exact imitation of the Tamar in the portrait just behind her. She was beginning to weary a little. The smile was a trifle wooden by now. This was not like the days of Pring's Miracle Medicine Show, when the crowds had milled round the figure in the Indian dress, while Joel Pring held them with his slick ballyhoo. Ondy had stopped his shouting. They would never get a crowd at this rate.

Suddenly, as she turned her gaze toward Ondy in the doorway, the smile on her face became fixed, glazed, as though it, too, were painted there, like that of the other Tamar.

From the black of the Connecticut night there appeared in the shed doorway a white-faced woman in black. To Tamar, in that first flash of horror, it seemed that this woman, standing there in the doorway, was taller than any woman in the world, her face whiter, her dress blacker, her eyes more terrible.

It was her aunt, Jude Oakes, come home before her time.

Jude Oakes had quarreled with the New Kent Minots as soon as she stepped foot in the house of mourning. The quarrel grew to bitter proportions. Staying there became an impossibility. In a rage she had packed her valise and had, that very evening, taken the train for Oakesfield and home.

The motley little gathering in the tobacco shed seemed to sense tragedy in the air. Heads began to turn without knowing why they turned. The woman said nothing. It was as though she had been struck dumb. Her eye fell on Big Bella in the white swathings of the sheet, her great arms and bosom bare. Her face showed girlishly pink through the coating of flour. Jude Oakes raised an arm and pointed a finger at Big Bella, her hand shaking crazily as she pointed. Her finger, in its shabby black glove, looked endless, and the tip of the glove, Temmie noticed, was ripped at the seam, and the forefinger stuck out. Jude Oakes stared at Big Bella, and her lips moved, and she pointed, but no words came. Big Bella stared back at her, glassily, her head lolling coquettishly on one side. It lasted, perhaps, not more than three or four seconds. It seemed many minutes. Then, terrorized, Temmie gave a little cry. It was wrenched from her.

Jude Oakes turned her head, slowly, as though the muscles were stiff, and saw Tamar there on the box near the door under the lantern light. The portrait was behind her. She stood, transfixed, the mocking wooden smile on her lips, the fan still clutched in one hand, the rose in the other.

"You——" Jude Oakes began to speak, but her voice was a croak. She tried to swallow, opened her lips again. "You——"

Then a curious thing happened. She began to utter strange thick sounds, as though her tongue had become caught at the roof of her mouth. And her mouth itself was twisted all askew at one side of her face, so that she was wearing a fearful and crooked smile that was not a smile at all. Someone within the tent began to laugh, perhaps in nervousness or hysteria. The right side of Jude Oakes' face remained fixed in that dreadful crooked smile, but the right arm, that had been extended, suddenly dropped like an inanimate thing, and then her whole body sagged on the right side, and slowly the tall black figure, with the fearful smile frozen on its face, crumpled to the floor of the tobacco shed and lay there.

IX

AT SIXTEEN it is hard to be downcast for long. In the months that followed, when the old house became too clammy with ghosts, Tamar could run out into the summer sunshine to where Ondy was hoeing in the tobacco, or Jot was picking off the tiny budding tops, so that the growth of plant and leaf might not be retarded. Jot, busily topping, stood little higher than the thriving plants themselves. All through the Connecticut valleys, mile on mile, the rich green foliage stood thick as ferns in a tropical jungle. And where the green was richest and most abundant there you knew that a Polish farmer labored in the fields.

Jude Oakes, stricken with silence, was more terribly

eloquent than Jude Oakes of the bitter ready tongue.
Speech returned haltingly, after some weeks. During her
muted days and nights those baleful eyes, glaring out
from the frame of her sallow face, with the black hair,
streaked with gray, ever in wild disorder from the tortured tossing of the arrogant head brought low on the
pillow, spoke more plainly than her tongue ever had, of
frustration and hate. Those eyes, following Temmie
about the room as she ministered to the sick woman,
seemed to shrivel the soul within her. Sometimes the girl
would stand outside the invalid's door, before entering,
and pray a little silent, desperate prayer. Dear God I am
sorry I have told you so a hundred million times please
let the miracle happen the doctor said it might straighten
itself her face and she could talk again and even walk
maybe and let her not hate me so her eyes please dear
God amen.

She would push open the door and enter, tray in hand.

"Look, Aunt Jude, I made some pudding with apples
cooked in it. I found the recipe in a piece of old newspaper that was wrapped around the shoes Ondy brought
from the cobbler's."

But the bony finger would point, trembling, to the little
pitcher of cream that accompanied this dainty, and the
head would shake its negation. The parchment face
would go dull red with anger. The twisted tongue would
utter thick sounds of protest. Cream was not a thing to
be wasted on farmhouse food. To the Connecticut to-

bacco farmer, until the crop was in the sheds and the buyers had made their rounds of the countryside, the precious milk and cream spelled ready cash. The vegetables, too, were products to be disposed of in Stonefield. But this summer's drought promised to be an unprecedented one. The beans and peas and summer squash shriveled day by day, and the earth was like ashes under the hoe. The whole valley concentrated on keeping its tobacco moist and loose. The unsucculent greens were accepted grudgingly by Jude. "Just try the peas, Aunt Judy. I cooked them in a teeny bit of milk because they were kind of little and withered."

Little and withered, Jude's glance conveyed, because she was bedridden, and who but Temmie to blame.

Yes, certainly, Jude Oakes' silence was more terrifying than her spoken wrath had been. In health she had given the old house a kind of vitality, even though it had been the vitality of destruction.

It was strange and pitiful to watch little Jot. His disorderly mind would cause him to forget, from time to time, this thing that had come upon the forceful Jude. So long as he worked in the fields with Ondy or Stas he was right enough. But when he returned to the house he would scurry into the south sitting room. There, bewildered, he would stand looking about him like a lost puppy who seeks his mistress. "Judy! Judy! Where are you!" There had been little enough of warmth, of affection, in

the spinster's conduct toward her unfortunate brother.
Little as it was, it had been all that her repressed soul
would allow her to give. Even that emotion had, oftener
than not, taken the form of fault-finding. But sometimes
—rarely—one had seen her reach out and put a hand
on his white head, and there was in the gesture a paradoxically rough tenderness. He, in turn, would take hold
of her skirt or her hand with his little work-calloused
paw.

"Jude! Judy! Temmie, where's Jude? H'm? Temmie,
where's Jude?"

"She's upstairs, don't you remember, Jot? Jude isn't
feeling well."

His round red face would be overcast. The china-blue
eyes would stare wider. "That's so. I forgot. I guess I
won't go up and see how she is. I guess I won't go up."

"Oh, yes, do, Jot. She likes to have you come and sit
by her bed and visit."

The short legs laboriously mounting the great stairway. When he came down he would sometimes be moody,
almost unmanageable. He would sit in a far corner of the
big kitchen, his back to the room, refusing to eat. Or he
would trot into the south room, scramble up into the big
rocker, or burrow in the welter of dusty brown cushions
on the couch. Temmie would bring him a plate of food,
as Jude often had done. Sometimes he would consent to
eat it, the tears streaming down the round pink face;
sometimes he would push the plate away, and when Tem-

mie essayed to comfort him he would run off and hide, like a sick animal.

Worst of all, he frequently forgot the facial contortion which had come upon Jude. When he saw her, after an absence of a few hours in the fields, he would stare, and then burst into sudden laughter—rich hearty laughter, like that of a jovial man, amused. At such times the baleful eyes of the woman in the bed would grow somber, not with resentment, but with pity.

The Oakesfield neighbors came calling. News of the stroke which had laid Jude Oakes low was the talk of the district following that night of the show in the tobacco shed. For years the women round about had tried, on one pretext or another, to penetrate the secret and inhospitable fastnesses of the old Oakes House. For years the vitriolic Jude had waged triumphant war against them, resisting all their advances. Most of them had never seen so much as the kitchen doorway during her reign. Now they came to the front door (impregnable to them as the gates of heaven to the wicked) and to the back door with this or that home-made offering as excuse. They came with careful, genteel steps, in their hands a dish or pail covered over with a clean red-and-white napkin.

"How-do, miss. You're Tamar, ain't you? Tamar Pring?"

"Yes—I'm Temmie."

"I'm Miss Hannah Pynchon. Knew your ma, time she

was a girl." The eyes would dart this way and that, noting everything in the old kitchen, so long denied them. They would even try to penetrate the front of the house, but this Temmie barred successfully. Her fancy could not even picture her aunt's terrible rage if one of these were to set alien foot in the south room. Dr. Waite, summoned from Stonefield, and now in regular attendance, had warned Temmie against further shock or excitement.

"She's had a shock. And a stroke. She'll likely get over it and walk again and talk as lively as ever. But another shock, or any great excitement, and she might be helpless for life, or even die of it."

He looked with kindly eyes at Temmie. Temmie said only, "I'll be careful. I'll be careful."

"Who's to take care of her? Who's in charge here?"

"Me." Her two hands went to her breast in her earnestness.

"Well, my child, you're just a little girl. We've got to have——"

"I'm sixteen, going on seventeen."

"I'd have said fourteen."

"Oh, no. I can do everything, really. I always have."

"Have, eh? Always. H'm. Well, don't be overreaching yourself, child."

Fusty, old-fashioned, kind, with his pills and his little vials, underpaid if paid at all, overworked. He alone of those who came to Oakes House was allowed to enter by the magnificent front doorway, with its Adam knocker and its lacy fanlight. Jude had conveyed this order to her; as well as another to the effect that the minister, should he call, must not be allowed to enter, front or back.

Certainly here were social problems before which a much more experienced hostess would have quailed. Small wonder the heart-shaped face grew pinched and that bluish circles appeared under the eyes.

Confronted by one of the neighboring natives Tamar would stand, timorous yet determined.

"I heard your aunt Jude was real poorly and I thought she might relish a little of my floating island. It's real light and tasty." Or, "I'm Miss Urania Dibble. I baked to-day and I thought to myself there's nobody there but that child and likely as not couldn't bake a loaf of bread to save her life so I just stepped by with a batch of my biscuits light as a feather if I do say so, and some of my new currant jell."

Temmie, racked with apprehension and misgivings, would stammer her thanks. Through the great oak planks and beams that separated her, in the kitchen, from Jude in the chamber upstairs, she could almost feel the baleful eye upon her.

"Thanks, Miss Dibble. I'll tell her. She doesn't eat much. She——"

"Just lays there, does she? H'm? Tell me about her, dearie. Do you mind if I sit a spell? So hot and dry these weeks past, seems a body can't get their breath, scarcely."

"Oh, dear!" thought Temmie, listening for the pounding of the cane on the floor above her head. Jude's left arm was well enough, no matter how stricken the right. "There. That's Aunt Jude. She wants me. I'm sorry. You'll have to excuse me." Somehow she managed to shoo the unwelcome caller to the door.

Jude's hearing, always painfully acute, now amounted to a sixth sense. Up in her bedroom she could tell whenever a local buggy or light cart stopped before the door; she seemed even to know to whom they belonged. She refused to touch the dainties brought to her bedside, and on one dreadful occasion, when the offering had been that of Miss Tryphene Foote, with whom she had long waged a more than ordinarily bitter feud, she had seized the dish in her left hand, and with amazing swiftness and superb aim had hurled it through the open window so that it landed with a plop at the feet of the departing caller.

Big Bella begged to be allowed to see Jude—to sit with her—to administer such brews and lotions as she felt certain would benefit the sufferer. But Jude refused to see her, and became so overwrought at the suggestion of her presence that Temmie dared not allow her to mount the stairs.

The distorted twist of the lips remained; fixed in a clownish grin which made the eyes the more baleful in the livid face. But speech returned; at least, the thick sounds that came from the wry mouth were intelligible to one accustomed. And the right leg, though it dragged almost a dead weight, could, with the aid of a stout cane, achieve a painful step or two. Sometimes she hobbled from bed to bedside chair; a harrowing business. Though she had protested fiercely at first, she now submitted to being carried occasionally down to the south room, where she lay on the broad bosom of the old couch. It had been Ondy's suggestion, this; and the Pole had carried her in his strong arms down the great stairs. At first she had held her grizzled head stiffly away from his shoulder, but as time went on it lay there, gratefully. One might almost have said that it nestled on that strong breast as though to draw vitality from his abundant life force.

He would place her on the couch; adjust her skirts with clumsy gentle fingers. The somber eyes were fixed on his face. A curious deep red tinged her cheeks. "So. Miss Oakes is good now. Next mont' sure—maybe next week—is good like old times and come to field you see how Ondy make with tobacco. She grow like corn—so high. Is high like Stas. Is fine, by golly. Pretty soon November is good rain and Miss Oakes got plenty money. Is rich."

In August, under Dr. Waite's insistence, they got a wheel chair. Jude learned to get about in it unaided. It was fairly light, rubber tired, almost noiseless. In it Jude Oakes achieved the destructiveness of a Juggernaut. One never knew when the black-garbed figure with blazing eyes would come whirling in upon one, soundless as fate.

The household lived in daily fear of this helpless, half-dead woman. It was grotesque, it was macabre. Little Stas, especially, held her in terror. Stolid and round-headed though the boy was, he was conscious of this strange woman's antagonism, of Ondy's indifference; of the tired Temmie's impatience with his muddy boots and insatiable appetite and grubby hands and dirt-grimed face. To make matters worse, Jot had developed a consuming jealousy and resentment toward him. It was, doubtless, due to the fact that Stas had grown inches in the past eight or nine months. The child was now taller than the white-haired dwarf. Jot did not resent the height of the adults about him. But he now saw, with smoldering anger, the child who had been of his own height gaining upon him inch by inch. One could almost see him growing, like the tobacco plants in the fields. Jot's jealousy turned to active dislike. He tried to harass the child at every step; performed mischievous tricks; undid the work he had done; delighted in frightening him. Temmie or Ondy would look up from their plates at meal time to see Jot engaged in screwing his face into fearful contortions wherewith to scare Stas into tears.

"Jot, stop that this minute, or you'll leave the table, and no pie."

Sulks, broodings, tears, complaints to sister Jude; up-braidings.

This, then, was the life of the girl, Tamar. The

stricken bitter woman; the midget with his muscular body and the mind of a child; the stolid, unsmiling Stas; Ondia Olszak, the Pole, kind, fun-loving, crude as the earth itself. She had a keen zest for living, Tamar Oakes, though she did not think much about it. She only knew that she longed to be happy and to make happy the people about her. She was as ingenuous and lacking in guile as the flowers that grew in the fields. Of tenderness and affection she received almost nothing, so she gave lavishly of her own store. Luckily for her, she had a full and colorful background to draw upon. She had known romance and tragedy. Unconsciously, those years of her childhood with Pring's Miracle Medicine Show, haphazard, shifting, had taught her to take life as it came— the run of the mill.

She saw no young thing of her own age. Two hours away by train was New York of the early twentieth century; gay, brilliant, rich; its avenues clop-clopping to the beat of horses' hoofs, jingling with silver-trimmed harness, flashing with enameled barouches in which silk-clad women sat against plum-color cushions, while coachman and footman, liveried, stared superciliously down from the box. Delmonico's flower-trimmed windows framed the satin shoulders of women and the broadcloth backs of men, dining, supping. Shoppers flounced down Fifth Avenue with taffeta dust ruffles trailing the pavements; jewels smoldered in heavy gold settings all about the Diamond Horseshoe at the Metropolitan. And nearer—much nearer—only a few miles away, at New Haven, in Connecticut, a thousand young American males were attending Yale University, striding about in their tight trousers and jerseys and absurd little caps and bulldog pipes, laughing, running, studying, playing, loving. Less than an hour's ride would have brought them to Temmie, or Temmie to them. Never a young thing of her own class and kind was seen about Oakes Farm, or lingering in the green crypts of the near-by tree-shaded village. She had heard, vaguely, of New York as some far-off exotic place. She was never to see it.

For loving she had only the infant, Rozia, rarely seen. Remorse, and her sense of duty, made her a slave to the frustrated woman in the wheel chair. From the Polish laborer she had kindness, and a cheerful companionship of a sort.

But there was the sunshine, there were the fields, the woods. She was young. When life became too unbearable in the ominous house she could snatch her sunbonnet off the hook and skip out into the barnyard or across the fields to where one tall stocky figure and two strangely small ones moved rhythmically up and down the long green rows. All over the valley you saw similar figures moving, bending, nipping the tiny retarding buds off the tops of the cherished tobacco plants. The valley of the Housatonic and the Still rivers thought, talked, ate, slept, worked, only in terms of tobacco. Life, in the year to come, depended for comfort, for sustenance itself, upon the future of these broad green leaves. The tobacco farmers tended the plants like slaves. Twice in August the sucker shoots had to be broken off. Late in August the tobacco was ready for cutting. The tobacco hatchets laid the plants low. Then came the tedious task of stringing the thick green stalks on four-foot laths, the broad leaves hanging tip downward. Then the laths, heavyladen, were drawn to the tobacco sheds and hung suspended on poles. Temmie loved the sight of the dark green leaves hanging there in the shed, a forest of them. They filled the two sheds to the very rafters. Here little Jot was invaluable. His tiny arms and legs were very muscular, yet he was so light that he could climb like a monkey to heights and across beams on which a fullsized man could not venture. From the topmost crossbeams of the sheds down to where the broad leaf tips almost touched the dirt floor, the stalks hung, row on row, close-packed, a jungle of them. The loose side boards of the shed were opened or closed, according to the weather, for ventilation and humidity. Slowly, through September, the leaves wilted, dried, faded from brilliant green to darker green, then took on a rich brown tone that deepened day by day. Some were such a dark brown as to be almost black, some were tan, some golden, some nigger brown. The best of them, measuring from twenty-two to twenty-eight inches from stem to tip, were delicately marked with reddish veining.

Ondia showed these to Temmie, unrolling the softly

crumpled leaf. "Look, Temmie, how is little veins, like blood. That is fine leaf, make good cigar. Here is bad leaf make filler is got white vein, like sick person. See. Good leaf is like you." He took her hand in his strong brown fingers and touched the veins on her wrist with one forefinger, gently. "Good blood, young and good health. Here is white blood in other leaf like Miss Oakes, is sick."

And now the tobacco farmer could only sit and wait for the autumn rains; the abundant rains of late October and early November, without which the tobacco crop would be a failure. Already the summer drought had worked its havoc on the crop, stunting the leaves, desiccating them. But now, in September, the green must dry to brown, must curl and wither. By October they were brittle. By mid-October they crumbled to dust in the hand. The stalks, leaf-laden, rattled like skeletons as Ondy passed up and down the narrow aisles between the close-packed rows.

"By golly is no rain pretty soon I guess we eat tobacco leaves make soup." The valley scanned the brilliant blue skies; the faces of the Connecticut tobacco farmers were like one enormous beseeching face upturned, parched and pleading, toward the sky. The farmers were moody, restless. Neighbor quarreled with neighbor. Hired hands were sullen under constant nagging. Even the genial Ondy was irritable. As for Jude Oakes, helpless in her chair or on the couch, her restlessness and fault-finding were maddening, unbearable.

Now the slopes of Pequot Ridge, of Wepawaug, were blazing scarlet and orange and gold and magenta, as they had been on that first day of Temmie's coming, a year ago. The eye was dazzled by their brilliance. Temmie went a little mad with the searing beauty of the conflagration, as some people are excited by fire. She was forever going off into the woods, scrambling up the slopes, coming home with branches of dried sumac spears or orange bittersweet. In the house she was a frantic thing, feeling imprisoned, breathless, much as that other Temmie had felt on that day so many years ago when she had escaped to seek freedom in the woods and had come upon it in the form of death. Even her terror of Jude, and her sense of duty toward her, were powerless to keep her indoors. It was as though she dreaded the winter to come; as though she were getting her fill of sun and light and air before the bitter cloud-hung winter months closed in upon her, imprisoning her in the somber house with the sick woman.

The rains came late in October. Now that they had come they were unceasing. Day and night, day and night, the gray rains came down. Temmie had seen the hills turn from green to gold and crimson. Now they faded to maroon and brown. With November there were only the hemlocks massed black against the ridge, with here and there the dead leaves clinging tenaciously to a branch of oak or elm, rusty, the color of old dried blood. Winter was almost upon her. Temmie faced it, frightened.

Whenever she could leave the sick woman or her household tasks, she would escape to the tobacco sheds, where the men were stripping swiftly, methodically. There was something soothing and graceful about the gesture. She loved to watch it. With her shawl wrapped round her she would sit on an upturned tobacco box as the leafy stalks, hung on laths, were suspended for stripping between two looped ropes. Little Jot had to stand on a box to reach them, and so, too, did Stas. Stas had learned to strip tobacco like any full-grown farm hand.

"Sure my Stas he seven year old he strip like son of gun," Ondy boasted throughout the neighborhood. "He strip so good like man, by golly. Me I strip four hundred pound a day. Stas he strip two hundred pound a day. My Stas he smart feller."

It seemed very simple to the onlooker. Temmie tried it and found it was not easy to keep the stripped leaves well back in the palms of the hand while the fingers traveled down, down the stalk, stripping it clean, leaf by leaf. Once learned, the gesture was swift and smooth and graceful. Somewhere in the travels of her childhood she had seen a great golden harp being played. She thought, dreamily watching the men like one hypnotized, that this gesture, across and down, was like the plucking of harp strings.

Now the farmers who had prayed for rain prayed that it would stop. The downpour never ceased. The unstripped leaves were now not only limp, they were

clammy. The last of the crop was threatened with pole-
sweat. Ondy had to build small charcoal fires on the floor
of the tobacco shed to regulate the humidity. He worked
early and late. So did little Jot, and even Stas was kept
from school, as were most of the Polish children round
about, to help with the stripping and to tend the fires.
Temmie did what she could. She sent them off in the
morning with a vast New England breakfast of buckwheat cakes and sausage and coffee and fried bread, dispatched before Jude, who rose late, could intervene.
Ondy would eat his supper and go back to the sheds at
night.

In November the rains ceased for two days, the skies
remained overcast, but the air became strangely close.
"Is end of world, I betcha," Ondy said in the evening, at
supper. "Never in my life I see like this weather. Is
crazy." All the Slav in him was at the surface. He had
worked under strain for days. The rains had made him
moody, the charcoal fires had stifled him, he snarled at
Stas and cuffed him over the head, pushed back his plate,
stared with distaste at the yellow-faced Jude, rose and
stood a moment on the stone slab outside the kitchen
doorway, looking up at the leaden sky, drawing a deep
breath of the clammy air and expelling it as though he
had taken a mouthful of something unfit to swallow. He
needed, he knew, to go off and have a good time and get
roaring drunk with his Polish cronies.

Moodily he lounged off to the big tobacco shed almost a quarter of a mile across fields, looming dark red against the lowering November sky. Soon Stas, too, scuttled off across fields, and then Jot. Temmie cleared the table, washed the dishes, got the sick woman ensconced on the couch in the south room with pillows piled high behind her, a hickory log fire snapping in the grate, and a dog's-eared book in her hand.

At eight Jot and Stas came in, heavy-eyed. The fire in the south room had burned to red embers. Jude was tapping the floor with her cane until the sound rattled like shrapnel throughout the house.

"Where's Ondy?" she demanded in her thick tongue. "I want to be helped up to bed. Sit here and call. I could die, for all of you, and good riddance, I've no doubt."

"He's in the shed, Aunt Jude, with the fires."

"Off with some good-for-nothing Polack, or worse, more likely."

Among them, Temmie, Jot, and Stas managed to help her up the stairs, half carrying, half dragging her, for she made herself stiff as a poker and berated them at every step. Stas and Jot were off to bed without another word.

The sick woman sank back, a yellow mask, on the pillow. Now, then. Temmie this. Temmie that. Water in a glass. The little night lamp lighted. The old heavy hunting-case gold watch. Two little white pills. The cane hooked over the head of the great bed. They had tried to persuade her to sleep in one of the downstairs bed-

chambers. She would not. They had tried to coax her
into the vast comfort of the front bedroom with its view
across the valley by day and the luxury of its enormous
bed by night—the old master chamber wherein Orrange
Oakes and Judith had first slept. But at that she went
into such a fury that the subject never again was
broached. Now Temmie brought to her aunt a steaming
cup of camomile tea as her Cousin Big Bella Champion
had taught her to brew it.

Jude Oakes lipped it with the eager clumsy gulpings
of the sick, spurning Temmie's offer of aid.

"Never mind, miss. Never mind. I may be good as
dead up to my neck but I can swallow still and help myself. Have done with your reaching."

"I only wanted to help you, Aunt Jude."

"Help. Help. You'd like to help me into my grave, I
know. I don't let on, but I can smell a rat's far as the
next one."

Cup in hand, Temmie descended the great winding
stairway. She looked up at the picture of Sir Orrange
Oakes as she passed it in the hallway on her way to the
south sitting room. The haunting eyes followed her. She
walked quickly past and into the south room, but it was
close and airless; stifling with the smell of the sick woman
who had been crouching there all day.

Temmie fled gratefully back to the kitchen. She went
to the kitchen stove, added wood, sat down with some
sewing in her hand, to wait for Ondy. She was tired. But

she would wait. The thought of the cold clammy sheets upstairs did not tempt her to bed. She was waiting, though she did not know it, for a cheerful human word, for a friendly smile before her day was ended.

Now the wind, rising suddenly, blew around the house. A shutter banged like a pistol shot. She went to the hall door to hear if Jude, startled, had called out. Nothing. Floors creaked, boards groaned, blinds rattled with a sound like the dry cackling laughter of old bones long dead.

The kitchen, of all rooms in the house, had always seemed friendly, almost cosy, in spite of its vastness. To-night it looked gloomy with shadows. Temmie glanced around, nervously. She thought of the white jade box under the sandstone slab before the fireplace in the dining room. A shadow danced in a far corner. The girl, overwrought, gave a little scream and was frightened afresh by the sound.

She could stand it no longer. She went to the door and peered out. Perhaps Ondy's friendly lantern might even now be dancing across the fields like a huge lightning bug as he came clumping home over the wet furrows. She thought how warm and safe the old house would feel if Ondy were in it—Ondy, with his great shoulders, his slow, merry smile, his rough tender hands.

A gust of wind, sudden and sharp as a physical blow, slammed the door behind her. Close upon it came a flash of lightning, bitter, unseasonable. It showed a freakish

sky, green, ominous. Then came a rumble of thunder.
Every evil spirit of which Ondy had told her in his
stories of Polish folk myths now came swarming about
her—wind, thunder, clouds, earth, water. She saw them
as he had pictured them in his simple mind—claws, fangs,
poisonous breath.

In desperation she pushed open the great oak door,
snatched her shawl off the hook, ran out into the night,
across the fields, to Ondy. She could just see, in the blackness, the light of his fire and his lantern through the open
side doors of the great tobacco shed, almost a quarter of
a mile away. She sped across the wet furrows, the soft
loam clinging to her shoes as though to hold her. Yet the
outer darkness was less terrifying than the noisy silence
of the old house had been. Her carnival show days had
accustomed her to the out of doors after nightfall.

The sky was a thing of actual thickness, like a vast
layer of black cotton above her, stifling her. The wind
blew in pushing gusts. Suddenly, as though waiting for
this moment when she was halfway from the house, halfway to the tobacco shed, the rain pounced upon her, a
torrent. With it a twist of wind that whirled the little
plodding figure almost about-face, and jerked her thin
skirts above her head. Blinded, breathless, she threw up
her arms, her shawl was released, and away it whisked
across the wet black fields, swirling high in the air. The
witches had it, surely. She stood a moment, supplicat-
ingly, holding her arms up as though to clutch it out of

the air. Then the blackness closed in on her. She rushed forward toward the yellow light, her head down, her breath coming sobbingly. She was terrified, yet she was getting a delicious, a fearful excitement out of this. Anything was better than sitting alone in the empty haunted house. There, just ahead, waited Ondy, and warmth and shelter and friendly human contact. So she ran on, wet to the skin, shivering, a little hysterical, laughing, too. It was thus she burst in upon the Pole standing over the charcoal fire, the dull embers of which had died down almost to an ash. They cast a glow over his sun-browned face, his great throat rising out of the old brown jacket, work stained.

"Ondy! Ondy!"

He turned, his eyes dazzled by the fire into which he had been staring. The drenched little figure stumbled toward him, the water squashing in the muddy boots, her thin calico skirts clinging to her.

The very alarm in his face was comfort, was warmth. Her lips were drawn back from her teeth, what with breathlessness, terror, relief.

"Temmie!" He pointed in the direction of the house. "Is her? Miss Oakes?"

"No. No—she's all right. I was just—it was so lonesome in the house—I got scared—the wind blew so—everybody was asleep." Her teeth were chattering. Her bright soft hair was matted dark about her head.

He put his hand on her shaking shoulder, gently. Drew

her to the fire, fanned it a little with his hat. "Come by fire. You are wet like little fish in water. Come. Here. Ondy make you quick warm. Ondy fix fine. You see."

From a corner he fetched a piece of sacking and bade her sit on it by the fire. He drew off the sodden shoes and wiped them with another piece of sacking. There was a heap of dried cornstalks near by which was used to cover the stripped and bundled tobacco leaves so that they might not lose their moisture. He brought a handful of these to the dying fire and it flared into sudden flame. "Here, Temmie." He took off his coat and, kneeling, thrust her thin little arms into the great sleeves, warm from the heat of his body. She was lost in it. The sleeves came down over her hands, and he turned them back, deftly. He folded the garment about her. It wrapped her like a blanket. Its odor repelled and attracted her. It smelled of the tobacco Ondy smoked, of the pungent leaves in the shed, of the stable, of Ondy's body. It enfolded her like a warm human thing. "Oh, Ondy." She snuggled into it, safe. She smiled up at him, a bedraggled wisp, with her elfin face, her rain-soaked hair. Warmth. Safety. Someone to tend her—to tend her who was forever tending others.

He began to chafe her wet feet in their black cotton stockings. His face was very kind and earnest, his brow wrinkled. The fire was deliciously warm, the rain pelted the shed roof like bullets. His breath, as he bent over her, was sweet and warm like that of the cattle in the shed.

She said, "Oh, no, Ondy dear. I'm all right. I'll be dry in a minute." She leaned forward to touch his great warm hands with her cold little fingers. It was as though she had touched something from which the sparks flew. Hot prickling darts ran like pain through her body. Suddenly his hand that had been chafing her feet was gripping her shoulder, and it was not the same hand at all. It was a rough, compelling hand, insistent. It drew her to him. And Temmie's hand found itself creeping up to his breast, his shoulder, until it rested at the back of his powerful neck, and her palm could feel something pounding, pounding there at the side of that strong warm column of his throat. Warmth, glow, strength, protection— the acrid smell of the charcoal fire, the pungent prick of the dying tobacco leaves, the odor of the coat wrapped about her, her face crushed against him, the beat of his heart through the stuff of his shirt. Her hands on his throat, warm.

"Ondy," she heard herself whisper. She felt strangely faint, yet strong, too. Alive. "Ondy darling darling darling darling darling."

As he laid her gently on the pile of corn husks she saw the rows of tobacco leaves above her, a jungle of them.

X

FRIGHTENED—my foot!" Big Bella retorted, vigorously. "What's there to be frightened of? Ondy wants to marry you, and you him, don't you?"

"Oh, yes!"

"Well, then, what's there to grout about! Blowing hot and blowing cold, this week past. Person'd think Ondy'd sworn he wouldn't marry you, instead of anxious to."

Temmie, a wretched little heap of indecision, was huddled in one of the huge chairs in Big Bella's polychrome kitchen. "Aunt Jude," she now faltered, for the hundredth time, and shivered.

"Well, by the living jingo, Tamar Oakes, I thought you were a girl of more spirit. Aunt Jude, Aunt Jude—as if she could do anything, once you're married, tight and fast. Marry, I say, and tell her after. There's a time for being open and aboveboard, and a time for being mum and underhand."

"But she'll—she'll—what do you think she'll do?"

"Jude'll dance Beelzebub's own rigadoon, whether you tell her before or after. Might's well get it over with and have Ondy your lawful husband to stand back of you."

"Dr. Waite said no shock. He said another shock might kill her."

A tremendous sniff from Big Bella conveyed more effectively than words her acceptance of even this contingency. "No great shakes if it did," she muttered. "She'll probably send you packing, or threaten to, at first. And if she does scrouge you off the roost for a time, she'll soon wish you back. Ondy's known as steady and a clever farmer. He'll doubtless get a chance to work a farm on shares, even, which is what he's been aiming for this long time, as you well know. Besides, how can she make out without you and Ondy? That matter, you're both free to come here and live, and welcome. There's the tenant house, empty these years past. Ondy likely could fix it up, weather-tight and snug."

Temmie thought of the foxlike Mossop. "Oh, no, Cousin Bella. Thank you just the same."

Big Bella now made a great show of vexation. "Take your choice. Your aunt Jude was high and mighty and didn't marry—and she's come to a fine end. I married Mossop, a hired hand like Ondy. A pretty pass I've come to, as well. One way or t'other, life seems to bring you round to the same road in the end. There's as little to choose between us as two peas in a pod. Marry Ondy, and you'll likely have little enough of happiness. Don't marry him, and the same'll be true. Either way, you've a long road to hoe. Though I must say, Temmie, a man grown like Ondy Olszak, old enough to be your father,

[211]

or nearly, taking advantage of a child like yourself, all trembly and rathe——"

"He didn't take advantage, Cousin Bella. I've told you. I wanted him to. I wanted——" She spoke with a dignity that sat queerly enough upon the dejected little figure.

"Didn't know what you wanted any more than a babe in arms. Wanted somebody to cuddle and make a to-do over you, that's all. Well, now it's gone so far, get married is what I say, and tell Jude after. Tell her now and she'll be crowing like a cockerel. The neighbors will get wind of it—they always do—and first thing you know your wedding will be all over Oakesfield before it's happened, and they'll make a regular raree show of it."

It was amazing to behold Big Bella in this crisis, her own life a thing so ugly and deformed, now so full of wise saws for the living of other people's lives.

"I had to tell someone. I had to tell someone," Temmie had said, as she had entered Big Bella's kitchen that day, and had thrown herself, weeping, upon the vast bosom.

The past week had been a thing of terror for her. Jude's implacable eyes, as they fixed themselves upon Ondy's face, or hers, seemed to be boring into their brains. Temmie's heart was in her throat for fear that Ondy would blurt out their secret.

"You won't tell her, Ondy, please—please—not until I say so." At night, when Jude was asleep in the chill chamber upstairs, Temmie would argue with him in low, beseeching tones. "I do love you, Ondy. I will marry you. Only we've got to wait. Aunt Jude——"

"Aunt Jude, Aunt Jude," he repeated impatiently, much as Big Bella now did. "What I care for Aunt Jude! She is dead and breathes only. What for you let dead woman make unhappiness in our life, little Temmie? You think I am afraid for that woman! Me, Ondia Olszak!"

He took his relation to Tamar simply and as a matter of course. Sex, to the Pole, was nothing about which to make a great to-do. Its subtleties were not for him. His glance was warmly enveloping. His hand on her shoulder was the hand of the possessive male.

"Don't, Ondy! Don't!"

"Why don't, little Temmie?"

"She'll see. She'll know."

"What I care she sees! If you ain't marry with me pretty quick I tell her myself, by golly! Maybe to-night I tell her."

In desperation, then, she had made Big Bella her confidante. Big Bella had been intensely stimulated, flatteringly interested. Temmie's shy, halting recountal of the events of that stormy night had been interrupted from time to time by varying exclamations from Cousin Bella. "My, my! Do tell! . . . Sakes a'-mercy! . . . My poor ducky! . . . Gracious to goodness!"

At the end of the recital, Temmie's summing up. Ondy

says this, Ondy says that. "Ondy says we've got to be married. He wants Father Scully."

"That'll be nice," Big Bella agreed, placidly. "Nothing like a priest and a Catholic wedding to make you feel settled for life."

"But how can we? How can we get off without Aunt Jude knowing? Both of us at the same time. We can't."

Now even Big Bella's serenity began to crack under the strain. "Takes two to make a wedding—leastways, always has. Jude or no Jude, you and Ondy can't go off one to a time and get married to each other."

"Then I'll have to tell her first, that's all."

Mountainous in her great chair, Big Bella sat thinking, her fine gray eyes luminous, her pink cheeks like roses. Suddenly she slapped one enormous knee.

"I've got it! Saturday afternoon! That's the time. Here it is November, work's slack, tobacco's all stripped. I'll make out sick and send for you. She can't refuse, in human nature. 'Sides, she'll be et up with curiosity. Ondy, meanwhiles, has gone to Fenwick, we'll say, to dicker with the tobacco buyers. She can't forbid him going, a grown man. Ondy can meet you down the road a piece, with the team, and drive you to Fenwick. Father Scully'll be notified and waiting. His housekeeper will act witness. I'd go along, but climbing into the buggy's not for me, here of late, even if the springs could stand it, which they couldn't. Then back here you come, on the way home. I'll beat up a cake, proper as can be, for a little wedding feast. We'll have out the wild cherry wine, and drink the health of the bride and groom." Temmie's face was all aglow. "Then off you'll go to Oakes Farm, to tell her." Temmie's face fell. "Though," Big Bella finished, "I'd have my bridal night, such as it is, in peace, if I were in your place, and no harridan screeching the roof down to make me rue the day."

Temmie drew a long breath of relief. Her face that had been wan with anxiety and indecision now bloomed. "I'd like to get married in my best dress. How can I manage that? My best dress, at least. And, oh, Cousin Bella, up in the attic, in one of those chests, there's a wine-color silk, with pleatings, that Aunt Jude told me once, when I asked her, was the wedding dress of Charry Challons, her grandmother, that married Martin——"

"Should think you'd had enough of dressing up out of the attic chests to last you the rest of your life," Big Bella said, with a grimness unusual for her. Then, at sight of Temmie's suddenly stricken face, "There, there. But you've got to take your choice. Wine-color silk with pleatings and Jude Oakes thrown in, or married as you stand, in decent peace. I'd know which, fast enough, if 'twas me."

Thus Tamar Pring, known as Tamar Oakes, and Ondia Olszak, the Pole, were married by young Father Scully in the rectory of the Church of the Sacred Heart of Jesus, in Fenwick. When the time came it was Tamar who was calm and confident, and Ondy who, red and breathing fast, behaved at this, his second wedding, as if he were a bashful boy at a school exercise.

Strangely shy and silent now, this ill assorted pair, as they bumped their way over the rutted November roads toward Oakesfield. Her heart was heavy with apprehension. Once he laid a clumsy caressing hand on her knee.

"Don't." Then, with a little pang at the frown that wrinkled his usually placid brow, "I wish we hadn't said we'd stop at Cousin Bella's."

"We ain't got to."

"Oh, yes. I promised. She's baked a cake and everything."

When they entered the kitchen of Champion House it was all too plain that Big Bella already had generously sampled the cherry wine set out for the bridal feast. She sat in her great chair, quite incapable of rising, and waved a limp uncertain hand in the general direction of the table. "Health bri' an' groo'!" she called out in her high sweet voice. She had covered the stained yellow oilcloth of the kitchen table with a fine linen cloth, hand woven, aged, and priceless, and she had decked it with the remains of her creamy Royal Doulton plates on which were pictures of equipages of the eighteenth century—stagecoaches, barouches, postchaises—and figures in the costumes of the day. In the center of the table was the bridal cake, a depressing structure, sagging at one side and dented in the middle where it evidently had fallen in baking. Big Bella, a notoriously bad cook, had done her worst in honor of the bride and groom.

Worse still, Mossop was there, leering and sly and suggestive.

"Fill up your glass!" Big Bella essayed to rise, lurched like a ship at sea, sank back into her chair, smiling uncertainly. Temmie, in an agony of wretchedness, gulped down the heady cherry wine, finding it sweet. Almost immediately she felt more courageous about the waiting Judy.

Ondy tossed off his glass at a mouthful, smacked his lips, took another. Mossop's red-rimmed eyes followed his movements with malicious dislike. "Cut your cake, Temmie," he ordered, in his wheedling tone. "Cut the bride's cake, for luck." He tittered. His sharp gray beard waggled.

Dutifully Temmie plunged the knife through the soggy mass, sliced it, passed it, nibbled it, wishing herself home in the kitchen at Oakes Farm, Aunt Jude or no Aunt Jude.

Now Hen Mossop, emboldened by three drinks of the cherry wine, began to utter a stream of bridal obscenities, cackling. He slapped Ondy a resounding thwack, advanced on the bride, whether to pinch her cheek in his vise-like tweak or to kiss her, Temmie did not know. But suddenly she became the matron, Mrs. Ondia Olszak. She put down her plate, rose, came swiftly over to Ondy, eluding the pursuing Mossop. She took her husband's arm. She seemed to adjust her whole figure into new and dignified lines.

"Come, Ondy. We'll be going now." She walked over to the giantess, stooped, kissed her cheek. "Thank you, Cousin Bella dear, for all you've done." She went to the door, opened it. "Thank you, Mr. Mossop. Come, Ondy."

The Pole stared, blinked. Then he bowed a stiff little old-country bow to his hostess, to his host, and followed his young wife dutifully down the side path to the road.

The early November dusk had come on. The countryside, wrapped in its drab autumnal garments, lay awaiting its burial with the coming of winter. Soon, Temmie knew, the drifts would make the country roads impassable for days, and later, with the spring thaws, the sink holes of years' standing would be waiting to mire down the strongest team of horses. Ahead of her stretched the long Connecticut winter with this man beside her, her husband.

"Six o'clock, or nearly. She'll be wild. I hope Jot stayed with her, as he promised, till time to start the chores. Supper'll be late."

She glanced sidewise at him. The brow was knit.

"By golly, old woman begin yell I fix her. I get plenty job in Oakesfield."

"Ondy, darling, we won't tell her to-night. Not to-night."

"Sure thing I tell her to-night."

"No. Please. Listen. To-morrow. When it's morning. Not to-night, Ondy."

She lifted her face for his kiss. Already she had learned adult wiles. Mollified, he bent his head. She moved nearer, nestled close to him.

"What she is saying we come back like this together?"

"I'll tell her something. You met me on the road from town—or you stopped at Cousin Bella's, knowing I'd gone there. You just go to the barn and start milking. I'll manage, some way. Please, darling."

They entered the farmyard. She had climbed nimbly over the muddy wagon wheel and was opening the kitchen door before he could wind the reins over the whip.

She met the volley of interrogation calmly enough as she slipped into her work dress, and set about preparing the evening meal. Late? Yes. Cousin Bella? Better. Nothing the matter, really. Ondy? In the shed, milking. Supper? In a jiffy, Aunt Jude.

"Why don't you come wheel over here near the stove, Aunt Jude, and talk to me while I'm fixing supper?" She felt suddenly strong, confident, unafraid, as she moved from table to stove, from stove to cupboard, with plates, cups, cutlery. She looked with new eyes of pity on this withered and dying spinster. Poor Aunt Jude. Poor Aunt Jude. "Do you think we could kill a turkey for Thanksgiving, Aunt Jude? Well, I just thought it would be nice, just this once. . . . Did Jot remember to give you your medicine at four? . . . Mr. Mossop says tobacco will fetch a pretty good price, even if it is runty this year, because the drought's made it scarce as well, so that evens things up, doesn't it? Things always even up, don't they?" She wondered if she sounded foolish. She thought she did, rather. Maybe that cherry wine, all at a gulp. It seemed to her that the eyes of the woman in the wheel chair never left her face. Sardonic eyes, searching the girl's flushed face. The little golden flecks in Tamar's eyes seemed brilliant to incandescence to-night.

Supper was a grisly meal. Those searching eyes rested now on the Pole's smiling face. It seemed to Tamar that waves of electricity were dancing from Judy to Ondy, from Ondy to her. They rocked in them, these three. The whole kitchen, the house itself, seemed to undulate with them.

"My, it's hot in here!"

"Cold," said the thick tongue.

She cleared the table, washed the dishes, the eyes still on her.

"Come, Aunt Jude. It's bedtime."

"I'll thank you not to tell me when it's bedtime." Acid as ever.

"I can't help it, Aunt Jude. I'm tired."

At last the stubborn head lay on the pillow up in the chill room off the far end of the upper "saloon," where Jude Oakes had slept all her lifetime. Temmie was glad that this room was so remote from the great front chamber. She had plans of her own. The night light turned low, but not too low; the watch, the pills, the water, the cane, the tea.

Temmie returned to the kitchen to find Jot and Stas already off to bed, and her bridegroom yawning by the kitchen fire. He looked up sleepily as she came in, held his arms wide, she walked into them, lay on his knee.

"Listen, Ondy. We'll wait until she is sound asleep. This morning, early, while she was napping, I made up the bed in the big front chamber, and I've just slipped a hot bottle into it to take the chill off the sheets. We'll sleep there to-night."

"For why we sleep there?" he demanded, thinking of his own accustomed bed.

"Because, Ondy, I am a wedded Oakes now, and the wedded Oakes in this house always sleep in the big front chamber, where Captain Orrange Oakes and his wife, Judith, used to sleep when the house was first built, over two hundred years ago."

She thought, once or twice, during the night by the side of this strange man, in this great strange bed, that she heard queer scufflings and scratchings. Mice, probably, scampering in the old wainscotings or walls. Or ghosts of dead-and-gone Oakes. The man slept heavily, deeply. The girl lay, for the most part, wide eyed, staring into the darkness. But toward morning she must have slept soundly, for she awoke at dawn with a start, bewildered, unable to find herself. She sat up. Her eye fell on the portrait above the mantel, dimly seen in the Novem-

ber gloom. The portrait had been rehung in its place
after that night of the show in the tobacco shed. Tamar
Oakes, of the blue hooped petticoat, and the fan and the
rose, looked down with mocking eyes upon this other
Tamar in the bed. Temmie turned her eyes from the girl
in the picture to stare at the man on the pillow beside
her. He lay in deep sleep, one arm stretched possessively
toward her, his great chest rising and falling, his tumbled
hair giving him the look of a tousled schoolboy.

Well, thought Temmie, not without some grimness, I
am a wedded Oakes now, sure enough, and an amiable
consort. Here lie Ondia Olszak and Tamar, his amiable
consort. Tamar Olszak. Oh, my goodness. Rilly. Amaryllis Olszak. Orrange Olszak.

She slid out of bed in the freezing November morning, peered out of the window, which was tightly closed,
for Ondy had the proper peasant horror of the poisonous
night air. The valley below could just be faintly dis-
cerned in the dawn. She must rouse Ondy. They must be
downstairs before the woman in the chamber at the far
end of the hall should hear them. This was the day on
which she must be told. Tamar shivered in anticipation,
and at the bitter chill of the vast room. She put on her
garments, clammy to the touch, and thought, as she shivered, of the good fire she would soon have snapping in
the kitchen stove. Perhaps Jot was already astir and had
built it.

She tiptoed to the door, to see how the land lay, opened

it stealthily inch by inch, rather enjoying the dramatics of this early morning adventure. She peered down the hall, toward the great mahogany stairway, her goal.

A sprawled huddle on the floor halfway down the saloon. A grotesquely sprawled thing, its wide-open gray eyes staring with a terrible glare of suspicion and hate toward the door of the chamber which Temmie had just left. The gray hair was all wild about her shoulders, and one arm was outstretched along the worn carpet, so that a long bony forefinger pointed straight to where the dead eyes stared—pointed as though in dreadful accusation.

Temmie's voice, scream on scream, hurtling through the silent house, brought the Pole and the dwarf and the boy running to her.

XI

THOUGH the native New Englanders of the valley looked down their noses at the Polack farmers, and the Poles looked askance at their American-born neighbors, the two factions were united on one subject, at least. Those Olszaks up at Oakes Farm were a crazy lot; and that Temmie, she was the craziest of all. Mrs. Expect Greensmith, of up near Gallows Hill, could tell you a tale.

"I was around collecting for the minister and stopped by there last of all because it was on my way home, and anyhow I didn't know would I go at all or not, because of her being so odd, and all, and hasn't set foot inside the church for years, so a body is put to it to know whether she's Polack or American—and her an Oakes, too, and the family written up in the liberries, and got their land a grant from the Indians, hundreds of years ago. Though she does pay her church dues reg'lar, every quarter, prompt as can be, even though she doesn't attend. Well, it was later than I reckoned on, and when I got there they were eating supper, and where were they eating it but outside, mind you, in that old grape arbor that's fit to topple at a breath, side of the house. Like gypsies. It was that hot spell middle of May. Wait. That ain't all. There sat Temmie Oakes, big as life, in an old plum-color silk dress, like a valentine, with a tight basque and a bit of trimming around the neck and down the front, and a purple snood on her head and gold beads around her neck pieced together so the string showed. Don't tell me that isn't crazy. Dressing up in clothes out of the attic, like a child. It gave me a turn. I stood there, gawping, nervous as a bride, not knowing which way to look. They say she puts 'em on the girl, too—that Rozy they adopted off the Smentkowskis. Dresses her up, a figure of fun, out of the old chests."

Mrs. Expect Greensmith's hearer—it might be Miss Tryphene Foote, or Urania Dibble, or Mrs. Leere—always could cap this with a tale of her own.

"They're all odd—the Oakes lot. Look at Jude, died in a stroke when she found the girl was sleeping with the Polack, and in the front chamber, no less. And Big Bella roaring drunk up and down the road."

There never was lack of gossip about Oakes Farm. Sometimes they referred to its occupants as the Olszaks, sometimes as the Oakes. But it amounted to the same thing. The Olszaks were land poor, and no mistake. There they were trying to work that farm of nearly four hundred acres, most of it run to seed and wild as the day the Indians granted it, yet they wouldn't part with an acre—leastways, that Temmie wouldn't. Fought like a wildcat that time Olszak tried to sell Maks Kusak that sixty-acre piece side of the ridge, and wouldn't put her name to the paper, so the deal fell through, and they needed the ready cash, too.

Oakesfield raised its eyebrows over Temmie Oakes' first child, still-born, and before its time, a girl. Temmie had called it Amaryllis, after her ma, though it never drew breath, and for months she talked about it, Amaryllis this and Amaryllis that, as if it was alive. Give a body the creeps. Funny, they didn't have any of their own till years after that, when the boy Orrange was born. There was Ondy Olszak's boy, Stas, of course, and then they adopted that Rozia, over at the Smentkowskis, though goodness alone knows whose child she was, and a mystery if there ever was one; remember that woman died up there at Oakes Farm a few months after she came over from Poland, and no doctor till she was as good as dead. They adopted that girl, Rozia they call her, with legal papers and all, in the court at Stonefield, and she's Rozia Olszak now, and Temmie Oakes makes a to-do over her as if she was her own. Times I think she's none too bright herself, that Temmie. Near thirty and acting like a child.

They say . . . they say . . . they say . . .

They say that Jot Oakes, the dwarf, he went clean off his head—he was never right, anyway—after Jude Oakes died, and used to go looking for her through the house, all hours the day and night, and wouldn't eat.

He would forget she was buried in the Oakes lot in

the graveyard, and one winter day Temmie, to quiet him, took him and showed him where she was laid, with her name on the stone and all, amongst all the Oakes, and a sight of them there is, too, enough to fill a graveyard themselves. Well, she explained his sister Jude was there, sleeping, and he quietened down, but I always say you must keep a sharp eye on a dog that's bit you, and what does he do but run off that day of the blizzard, winter of '93, and they hunted high and low, never thinking of the graveyard, and there they found him, froze to death, on Jude Oakes' grave, though they do say midgets like Jot never live to be old, anyway. They buried him by her in the Oakes lot in a child's coffin, and his grave is tiny, like a child's, and gives you a start when you see it because the lettering on the stone says, "Jotham Oakes, aged forty-seven."

You can't tell me there isn't something funny about that Oakes place, what with this and that always happening, and kind of gives you the shivers when you go by, though I heard there was an architect up from New York saw the house and said it was the finest example of some kind of building or other in America, and wanted to buy that front door fanlight for a fancy price just as it was, like a piece of goods at the store, you might say, and at that Temmie Oakes put him out of the house as if he was a peddler, and threatened him with the dog if he as much as showed his face again.

You'd think she'd married the President of the United

States, instead of a good-for-nothing Polack who didn't even have the get-up to buy a piece of land for himself, till he married her and she fell heir to the farm, with Jude's death and then Jot's.

Thus the New England neighbors.

The Polish women, too, had their say.

"That Olszak, he caught for himself a fine one with that little skinny girl. He has a big farm, yes, with land enough, but he will end by the roadside. You will see. She uses the cream from their cows for ice cream and even for coffee. Pure cream, that brings in money. And they kill their chickens to eat themselves, and they eat eggs; she puts eggs in cake, and they have beef because she says pork is not good to eat every day. He caught himself a fine one, that Olszak. A Polish girl was not good enough. I could burst with laughing. Feliks Smentkowski writes his father and mother in Poland about Ondia, and they write Feliks should have Ondia's head examined. Why didn't he marry that Ewa Stefanska from Fenwick?"

And ten years went by. If you had asked Temmie about those ten years she would have said, "I've been happy. Happier than I've ever been before in my life." But she could not have told why; or if she could, her reasons would have sounded odd indeed, as a basis for happiness.

From the very first she had wanted to adopt the child

Rozia. Ondy had opposed this with all his Slavic stubbornness.

"That Rozia, she is *boginka's* child. She make black
luck in house. She is *topczyka,* that Rozia. Pfft!" He
spat, to express his repulsion.

Temmie had picked up a word or two of Polish; and
she accepted Ondy's strange Polish peasant beliefs as a
child accepts fairy tales. After Jude's death and Jot's,
Ondy had solemnly gone to the cattle shed, the barn, the
sties, the henhouse, and had ceremoniously informed
the cows, the horses, the pigs, the chickens, the geese, of
the passing of their old owner and the installation of the
new. If he failed to do this, he said, they would sicken
and die. After every happening, tragic or gay, at Oakes
Farm, Ondy wrote his people in Poland, and always the
letter had the same ceremonious beginning.

In the first words of my letter, beloved parents, I address you
with these words of God: "Praised be Jesus Christus," and I hope
that you will answer, "For centuries of centuries. Amen."

And now I inform you that I have married with the niece of
the woman who owned this farm and she is now dead and there
is only the brother, the one of which I wrote you, he who is a
dwarf and lacks the fifth stave. So soon I shall own this farm,
with my wife, it is as big as the whole commune of Dobrzykow.
Now beloved Father and beloved Mother, I kiss your hands and
legs. . . .

After their own child had been born dead Temmie's
thoughts turned again to Rozia. Then she learned that
Julka Smentkowski, the old girl, whom Feliks had mar-

ried for her dowry, and with little hope of children, was "expecting." The news traveled up and down the district like flame in the brush.

"Please, Ondy, please! Julka won't want Rozia now that she's going to have one of her own. She walks and talks, so cute. And if she lives here you'll save the board money you've been paying Julka to keep her."

Ondy saw the force of this argument. That little Temmie, they said in Oakesfield, could wind him around her finger, he was crazy about her and she about him, like a young couple courting, and it wasn't decent, hardly, they've been married now three years.

"And, Ondy," Temmie continued, "it can't be true, what you said about her bringing black luck, because, look, if she had been here in the house when Aunt Jude had her stroke, and when she died, and then Jot, and then Amaryllis, you'd have said it was her fault. But she wasn't even here. Maybe all those things happened because you wouldn't have her here. Doesn't it work that way, sometimes?"

So they adopted the girl, Rozia, legally. She was a handsome child, red-cheeked, black-haired, with strange, wild ways. Temmie used to dress her up, like a doll, in bits of faded finery from the attic, but the child resented this from the first, tearing at the bonnet strings, clawing the lace and passementerie, stamping her small feet and working herself up into a rage. Ondy regarded this with an amused and tolerant eye.

"Which is little girl, you or Rozia? I guess Rozia got more sense as her ma."

"Let's have a picnic, Rozia," Temmie would say, in the middle of winter. "Ondy's cutting wood down in the pine bottom. We'll surprise him."

She would hastily pack fresh-made doughnuts, and sandwiches of cold pork and store cheese, boil a pail of coffee, bundle Rozia on the home-made hand sled, and trudge off down the road toward the pine bottom, three miles away, leaving the work half done, the big house deserted. Breathless, her little face glowing pink in the frame of her woolly hood, Temmie would appear at noon in the hollow where Ondy was cutting pine wood. "Ondy, we're going to have a picnic." They would build a fire of fat pine chunks, and perched on a felled tree trunk they would drink the steaming coffee and eat the sandwiches and doughnuts, and ride home with Ondy and the team and the big bob-sled in the late afternoon.

Crazy as a loon, said the American housewives, peering out upon the passing sled from the shelter of their farmhouse curtains. That one, said the scandalized Polish farm women. Better Ondy had sent to Poland for a farm girl and paid her ship ticket and taken her as she walked, with no dowry, and debts, even.

No wonder that Oakes Farm did not thrive as did the smaller farms of the Poles thereabouts. Ondy worked fifteen, eighteen, twenty hours a day, in midsummer, and during the autumn stripping. Stas did the work of a man.

Rozia worked almost from the time she was able to walk.
Temmie worked terribly. It was incredible that that
slight childish body was capable of the tasks she accomplished. She actually did all the work of the great house,
cooked, washed, ironed, baked, churned. She sometimes
even worked in the tobacco, like the Polish women, topping in July, or nipping off the suckers in August. They
would all be there, in the hot midsummer sun, with the
rich green plants pushing out of the good red earth—
Ondy, the strong sinewy Pole, and Stas, sturdy and sullen, Rozia, the adopted one, Tamar, delicate, tiny, like a
sprite among earth creatures. Even Rozia's baby fingers
learned to pinch the suckers from the plant tips. They
worked rhythmically, silently. You could almost hear the
tobacco pushing up out of the earth. Now and then a saving breeze zinged like a zither through the hemlocks on
the ridge above them. The Still River sang and dimpled
in the valley, and the strong swift Housatonic rushed
valiantly to meet the sea.

Olszak's tobacco thrived as well as the rest, they were
content enough, but of spare money there was none. The
farm ate it up. Ondy was not spendthrift, but he was careless of money, like the other Polish men. He liked to
drink with the Poles, to buy a good horse, a good cow.
They were gayer, more light-hearted than the Polish
women, these men, and weaker. Like small boys, they
turned their money over to the women. Their greed was
not for money but for land. The women were formid-

able, domineering, and thrifty to the point of niggardli-
ness.

"Ma, let's have some money," the Pole would say,
when he went into town on Saturday. His Frania, or
Pecia, or Kazia would dole him out enough to meet his
needs, grudgingly.

These Poles lived on cabbage, potatoes, salt pork. As
they flocked in greater numbers to the valley the village
storekeepers were in despair. They raised their own pork,
their own cabbage, their own potatoes. Their money
went into the land, or back to Poland. They made their
own harsh wine, brewed their own beer; their cider, hard
as iron, came from their own juicy apples. Sometimes a
Pole dropped in at the village store to purchase, for a
few pennies, a little sack of cheap candies as a treat for
his brood of children. That was all.

But Temmie Oakes knew nothing of the ways of
thrift, as did these hard-headed Polish women. She set a
lavish table, and wasteful, compared with peasant stand-
ards. Chickens, eggs, cream; even meat from the store.
Ondy was good-natured, careless. Like his countrymen,
he begrudged the wage of hired help—or perhaps it was
that he could not bear to see his beloved land tended by
another. He was like a lover who is crazed at the thought
of alien hands on his mistress's flesh. His Polish neighbors were content with thirty acres, or sixty, under inten-
sive cultivation. At Oakes Farm, while the east hundred
was working, the west hundred lay barren, untended. The

old stone wall crumbled here while another section was being repaired there. The farm machinery was ancient, old-fashioned. The Polish farmer laboriously performed by hand the work that modern mechanism could have done in one tenth the time. Thus they had always worked in Poland. Long hours of labor meant nothing to them. They were serving the land.

"By golly, we sell sixty acre and got good money," Ondy sometimes said. "Here is too much damn land, this farm." Then, looking a little stricken and fearful, "Land is fine, big farm is good, but not too big, like here. Huh, Temmie? We sell east sixty and with money I buy you kerosene stove and new dress and all things for farm. Huh, Temmie?"

But Temmie, so slight, so timorous in other ways, was an iron woman in this. She set her face against it. "No. Oakes Farm is not too big. It used to be a thousand acres. It mustn't be cut up. It's to keep. For Orrange Oakes."

"Orrange? Who?" But he knew. He had heard the name many times. Sometimes—rarely—her stubbornness goaded him, usually so gentle, to an unwonted cruelty. He would look down at her, at her narrow childish flanks, the tiny waist, the flat, barren belly; his eyes rejected the strangely virginal figure. "You don't have no son. Never in your life. You ain't woman."

"I am! I will! I'll show you. You'll see. A son. Orrange Oakes, and his hair will be light brown, and his nose will be a little hooked, and he will be tall and strong——" She would stop, choking. The childlike face would crinkle into tears. He was ashamed, contrite. For a time he would drop his talk of selling the east sixty.

The birth of the boy, Orrange Olszak, was a dreadful, a grisly business. It was as though she had willed it against the forces of nature. It left her torn and old, with a pinched and haggard face set permanently on that elfin body. She could never have another child. That she actually had achieved this one was a miracle, like something out of the Old Testament.

So weak was she, so ravaged, for a year following her confinement, that Ondy was obliged to have a Swedish girl to help about the house.

Ondy was too much the Pole to show unwonted emotion at the birth of this, his son. But he was sufficiently jubilant to get drunk on hard cider. He stood at the side of the great oak bed in the front chamber and looked down at his wife's face, a wedge of gray-white framed by dank, stringy hair. He looked at the fragment of flesh that had but now been torn from her flesh. His brow wrinkled.

"By golly, he look like picture in hall is feller who is hang by Cromwell. Is I betcha feller in picture is his papa, not Ondy." He laughed at his own witticism.

Temmie's face was terribly serious. She could barely whisper, but what she had to say, she said. "Of course—he's an Oakes—Orrange—Oakes."

From the earliest days of the boy, Orrange Olszak,

two things were ground in upon his consciousness. The importance of tobacco was one; the importance of the Oakes family heritage was the other. Perhaps the first thing of which he was conscious was a little world of green rising above him—green that was worshiped and tended like a holy thing. Temmie would bring him out into the tobacco fields and plump him down there to dig and crawl in the warm earth. The first talk he heard was of these green things. For these green things meals were timed; one did not go to church because of these green things; if the green things were big enough and plentiful enough his mother could have a new dress, his father could buy a plow, there would be a new cow, Stas could go to the county fair at Stonefield. The green things were more important than any other object in the world.

"If the tobacco crop's good you can have it, Orrange. We'll see, when November comes."

The broad green leaves gave him shade as he crawled in the dirt. When he was able to stand, Ondy, laughing, guided his uncertain fingers to where the little sucker bloomed, waiting to be nipped off.

The stories his mother told him were the stories that she herself had heard in her childhood from the nostalgic memory of Amaryllis Oakes. The attic—the cellar—the great stones of the foundations—the carved cornice under the eaves—Black Esau—Tamar Oakes—old Chief Waramaug—Big Noel Champion—Captain Orrange Oakes——

"He's the one you're named after, Orrange—and he was named after the one in the picture—you know——"

And almost as soon as he could talk, his faltering tongue essayed the difficult, high-sounding words, long before his intelligence could grasp their meaning. "Turblan and visharytemermen came into clishun with cromwell beaded on tawr hill sixteen fify-seven."

"That's right, my darling!"

Big Bella, at his birth, had solemnly announced herself his godmother, self-elected, and had presented him with a pap bowl of solid silver, hand molded and exquisitely engraved with the name of Orrange Oakes. Originally, doubtless, the property of Oakes House, it had found its way, during the centuries, to Champion House attic, amid the welter of neglected treasure piled there in dusty corners.

Ondy, scowling, had surveyed this offering. "He is name Olszak, not Oakes."

"He's an Oakes from head to foot," Temmie had replied, happily, and not too tactfully.

When next she got out the pap cup to celebrate Orrange's first tooth she was horrified to see that Ondy had scratched out the name of Oakes and had etched beside it, with a nail or some other crude instrument, the name of Olszak in straggling, unformed letters.

From year to year—almost from day to day—the difference between the child Orrange Olszak on one side, and Stas and Rozia Olszak on the other, became more definitely marked. The small child's bone structure, temperament, tastes, reactions to given sensations, manner of growth, were all different from theirs. They two were Polish, through and through. Outwardly, in later years, they were to take on the aspect of Americans, but fundamentally they never changed.

It was curious, the thing that happened to the Polish children as they passed from babyhood into childhood, from childhood into adolescence. Temmie was at a loss to know how to cope with them. They were quite unlike the American-born child who develops, year by year, along certain plainly marked lines. No; Stas and Rozia, from being one kind of creature, suddenly changed into another. As a very small boy Stas had been busy, sullen, given to moods, dirt, and to frightening small girls. Then, suddenly, at twelve, he was sober, adult, secret. He worked on the old stone fences, he cut brush, topped and stripped tobacco—a man.

Rozia, in childhood, had been a pretty little thing, shy, wild, with deep-set soft eyes and a line from the cheek bone to the chin that was like the curve of a bird's wing. Then, suddenly, almost overnight, Temmie saw that she had taken on the look of the other Polish girls of the district. Their adult faces were hard, their cheek bones too high and broad, their eyes without depth, at once dull and cunning, like an animal's eyes. Little Rozia was now big Rozia, Polish, but still pretty enough, in a bold, colorful way. She was amazingly strong, her arms were long and the bones powerful, so that she could pitch hay like a man, lifting the laden fork and tossing it upward into the loft as though it were a blown feather.

At twelve Rozia had done a strange and terrible thing. From time to time Temmie had fashioned for the girl dresses and cloaks and petticoats contrived from the old silks and muslins and velvets and woolens packed away under the eaves of the attic. The chests and trunks were a treasure trove of finery. Much of this was too ancient, too time-worn, for use; some too precious; some too poor. But between the yellowed garments of a long gone day, and the shoddy stuff cast off by later Oakes, there were sturdy and fine materials waiting for Temmie's deft fingers and sly needle.

"I don't like it! I won't wear it! I hate it!" Rozia would yell, as these remade garments were thriftily being fitted to her figure. "They're old rags. They'll laugh at me."

Temmie, absent for a half day on some household business in Stonefield, returned to find her kitchen reeking with smoke and acrid with the smell of burning cloth. Over the kitchen stove, poker in hand, smoke-grimed, terrible, stood Rozia Olszak. About her, on the floor, lay odds and ends of garments—a silk bodice, a lace cap, one satin slipper, a bit of yellowed dimity. From the open top of the kitchen stove poured the thick yellow-green smoke of smoldering cloth. She had spent the afternoon burning, piece by piece, every scrap of treasured stuff on

which she could lay her sacrilegious hands. Everything—
anything—whether fit for the museum or for use as a
scrub rag, had been stuffed ruthlessly into the red maw of
the wood fire. Even the little rose chiné with the hooped
blue satin petticoat lived now only in Temmie's memory
and in the portrait of Tamar Oakes that hung on the
wall in the front chamber. It was ashes, with the rest.

"There!" Rozia had screamed. "I told you! You
wouldn't listen. Dirty old rags. Like a scarecrow."

She was glaring like a smoke-blackened imp from hell.
She was the Polish virago to the core. Temmie stood,
her arms bundle-laden, her pinched little face drained of
all color. She placed her bundles on the table, methodically, like a sleep walker, her eyes on Rozia. Then, suddenly, her legs refused to hold her. She sank into a chair
and buried her head in her folded arms on the kitchen
table and wept as she had not wept since the child,
Amaryllis, was held up before her, dead.

XII

OAKES FARM was a curious mixture, now, of Poland and New England.

Crudely bright Holy pictures hung on the discolored walls of the vast kitchen; and in the south sitting room, beside the delicate pastels of the old French prints, were the Virgin, the Christ Child, the Crucifixion, in glaring blues and orange and scarlet and yellow.

Temmie had learned to cook the Polish dishes that Ondy's palate craved—potato pancakes, prune soup, raisin bread, cabbage balls, sour milk cheese, duck soup. When Father Scully, of the church at Fenwick, made his annual rounds at Easter time to bless the Easter food, Tamar Oakes' table was ready and in proper order. There were special Easter dishes to be prepared, according to the Polish Old World custom, and she did them.

Father Scully always went from house to house throughout the parish at Easter time—a task that assumed colossal proportions as the Polish population grew. In the beginning the young priest had a smart little buggy and a fleet trim mare. In this vehicle he whirled from farmhouse to farmhouse about the countryside. Temmie looked forward to this visit. She liked the dramatic quality of it, as she loved all form and ceremony.

No Polish housewife could know the exact hour when Father Scully's brisk buggy would stop before her door, and the handsome young figure in its black robe stride into her kitchen. For a day and a night each Polish farmhouse was on the *qui vive*. The table must be spread with a clean white cloth—the best the household afforded. In the center, under an immaculate napkin, were salt, butter, bread. The actual Easter meal was uncooked at this early hour, but its main dish, ham or a leg of veal, was placed on the table, unroasted, awaiting the blessing. Usually a child, one of a numerous brood, was posted outside as lookout. Starting early, early Saturday morning, up the brisk little hills or down the valleys dashed the priestly visitor. He liked a good bit of horseflesh, did Father Scully, and his trim mare, with her dainty hoofs and quick slim legs and roguish eye, had more than a drop of blue blood in her.

"Ma! Ma, here he is!" the small Jan or Elzbietka would scream. Father Scully would descend, while an ecstatic farm child stood at his horse's head. His black skirts flying with the vigor of his movements, he would stride straight into the house to the table that had been prepared for him. The Polish housewife wore her freshest apron, bordered with old-country tatting or embroidery. Her hair was slicked back with a wet comb. Her high cheek bones shone with scrubbing and unwonted excitement.

"I greet you, Mrs. Lazowska"—in Polish. "Blessings

on this house." He stood before the clean white table. In Latin he uttered his Easter blessing on the food, on the house. His fee was tendered him, humbly. He accepted it, whatever its value. Sometimes, in the pinched household of a newcomer, or a farmer still in debt, it was a mere twenty-five-cent piece. In a richer household a dollar; sometimes more. From six in the morning until midnight he went his rounds. Perhaps a hurried word as he ' gathered up the reins. A shrewd man.

"This is a handsome house, Mrs. Olszak."

"Oh, isn't it, Father Scully!"

"How is it I never see you at Mass, Mrs. Olszak?"

"I—the house—the children—Ondy goes when he can —I belong to the——"

"I want to see you there, Mrs. Olszak." The keen eye rested on Orrange, peering from behind his mother's skirts. "The boy. You don't send the boy."

"Orrange," said Temmie, simply, "is an Oakes."

She never went to her own church, for that matter, with its Wren cupola and steeple, the jewel-like window, and the old high-backed pew wherein generations of Oakes had sat in chill worship. She had not the time. From week to week she saw almost no one outside her own household. The Polish women were ill at ease with her, clannish, suspicious. The sparse New England women eyed her with Brahmin disapproval from behind the stiff folds of their front-room curtains. That Oakes girl—the one that married the Polack A little scrawny, wrinkled woman, with the body of a very young girl. To see her, armed with broom and pail and rag, attacking that vast old house was to see a wren doing battle with a dinosaur.

Thicker and more thickly the Polish farmers spread over the valley of the Still River and the Housatonic, and the region bloomed like a garden. From time to time one of them cast a covetous eye on Ondy's broad acres, but Temmie fought them off like a fury. The valley prospered and throve as it had not since the splendid days of Captain Orrange Oakes and his slave-tended domain. Fields thick with tobacco, barns bursting with hay, silos oozing ensilage, cattle in the meadows; children and chickens and geese and dogs shouting, cackling, barking, squawking in the yard—that was a Polish farmhouse.

Cousins and cousins and cousins. Every Pole had a hundred cousins in Poland, and every cousin longed to come to America, and buy a farm, and be a rich American landowner. Even Maks Kusak, the little Polish tailor who had lived with his wife and his brood in one of the crowded downtown New York streets, now moved to Oakesfield. They took to farming as though the tailor's bench had never been. Only during each spring and autumn there were echoes of Maks Kusak's urban life. Then Mrs. Kusak, vast and wifely, aired her household goods on the clothes line, and there, in the breeze, with the workaday garments, you saw, in pompous minuet, a left-over Prince Albert coat, neat striped trousers, a black vest, black trousers too, advancing, retreating, in stately reminder of the days of Maks' more formal calling.

All seemed prosperous, serene. Yet underlying and permeating everything was a curiously sinister and hidden thing. There was about these alien people a strange opposition of moods. Now tender, merry; suddenly sullen, brutal. There were frequent family feuds; beatings, cries. Strange bruises appeared on a man's face or a woman's. Sometimes there was bloodshed. Fathers and growing sons quarreled, fought.

"That Stas," Ondy began to say, with increasing frequency. "I show him who is boss. I give him a licking, by golly, I betcha he ain't sit down so easy."

"Oh, Ondy, you're always quarreling—you and Stas. What's the matter?"

"He is big bum. All the time he is run, run, run to Fenwick, to Stonefield with that Savaty—that Jack Savaty—he got job in hat factory in Stonefield. Little Orrange, he work better in tobacco shed stripping as Stas. That big bum. Next time I lick him he can't walk, by damn!"

"But Stas is a big boy. He's a man, grown. You can't whip him any more."

"I lick the guts out him yet. You see." Ondy was not a brutal man. His was a kindly nature, and merry. Something was disturbing him deeply. Ondy's hair was grizzled now, his face a leathery brown, but his eyes were clear, steady. He was heavier, handsomer. In the district, and beyond in Fenwick, and even Stonefield, he was known as a reliable Polack, honest, fairly intelligent, but not shrewd like some of the others—like that Smentkowski, for example. He had a lot of land, that Olszak, but it didn't do him much good.

"Why don't you sell some of your land, Olszak, and get some ready cash?"

"Old woman she ain't like for sell." He looked a little sheepish. Sometimes he and Temmie would quarrel about this. Those were bitter times for her. The boy, Orrange, would take his mother's part against Ondy and Stas and Rozia, strangely united in this one thing. Ondy would raise a big brown hand to cuff him. Temmie would snatch the child away, a tigress.

"Don't you touch him, Ondy Olszak! Don't you dare touch him!"

"Ain't he my boy? Who you got him by, huh? Peddler, huh, like your ma?"

She and the boy faced him, hostile, quivering.

As Orrange grew from babyhood to childhood Temmie began to stir a little in her mind, to look about her, like something coming out of a long, long sleep. All her energies, stretching this way and that these last fifteen years, in her efforts to keep the house, the land, the family together, now seemed to relax, to sag, like a piece of worn elastic. One day had passed like another. Each morning the work loomed up like a mountain ahead of her. Each night saw it surmounted. During the infancy of the boy, Orrange, she slept three or four hours a night. It was ten or eleven before she could creep, numb with weariness, into the great oak bed. She was up at three or four. She took a fierce and childish pride in doing all the things that the Amazonian Polish farm wives did. She had been bitterly chagrined to find that she could not nurse the boy. The Polish women kept their children at the breast until they were three or four years old and running about in the yard. Theirs was the Old World belief that so long as they nursed the last child a new one would not be conceived; and they were weary of their seemingly endless child-bearing. A Polish farm child often was kept at the breast until it drew blood and pus for nourishment. Or you saw it nursing one moment and munching a hard candy the next.

Except for her size, and for the look in the gray innocent eyes, Temmie seemed no different from the Polish farm woman of the district. Nondescript calico, old boots, a shawl in winter, a sunbonnet in summer. Only on the rare occasions when she went into town did the little broken figure take on something of its old elegance. She would put on her plain black dress with the white collar; the black hat. And suddenly you saw that in this woman's body—in the articulation of the joints, in the bone structure, in the blood, in the carriage of the head or the set of the shoulders, in the look of freedom, perhaps, that shone in the clear gray eye—was breeding. No Polish peasant stock here.

XIII

SHE was seated flat on the ground, an old piece of sacking under her. It was November. Thanksgiving was ten days off. On her feet were old boots, on her head a battered felt hat of Ondy's, a piece of gunny-sacking covered the front of her dress. She had the neck of the huge white goose under her left arm. His yellow bill was open wide, her elbow imprisoned the bird's body while her left hand was on its throat, down which she was working corn methodically and patiently. The big white goose was being fattened for Thanksgiving, as Ondy had taught her to stuff it. The first hard frost had come. The tobacco was stripped and stored in the sheds. They would slaughter a pig next week, and salt it down for the winter.

Around the side path came two tobacco buyers from Hartford. Ondy was expecting them. He was awaiting them in the small shed. They glanced down at her as she sat there, her legs sticking straight out before her, her head bent over the bird. Her hands, blue with the cold, worked the corn down the bird's throat. The men nodded carelessly in her direction as she looked up. They did not touch their hat brims. They passed on.

"I thought Olszak married an Oakesfield woman—rich."

"Not if that's her. That's Polack."

She lifted her head slowly, stared after them. She released the great white goose with a push that sent him squawking. She stood up, cramped and stiff; brushed the corn from her lap. She was blushing like a girl. She went through the kitchen to the front hall, past the portrait of Sir Orrange Oakes, up the broad stairway to the cold front chamber.

She stood in front of the long gilt-framed mirror and looked at herself as one who has not seen herself in years. She looked at this woman in the long gilt-framed mirror.

She saw a withered woman with graying hair and a harsh skin and a small, almost childish body that seemed smaller still from the stoop that had come with standing slightly bent to ease the pain—the dull pain that had become part of her after the birth of the boy, Orrange. A shapeless woman in muddy boots, and a colorless dress, and a man's felt hat, battered, stained; hands rough, unlovely. How many years since that autumn day when Aunt Jude had flung open the door?

Who's this girl? I'm Temmie, Aunt Jude.

She turned her eyes from the drab figure in the long mirror. Almost as if against her will she forced herself to look up at that other Temmie mocking her from the wall. The portrait seemed to swim, then, in a mist.

"Forgive me," said Temmie.

Next morning—Sunday—she was up and about the kitchen even earlier than was her wont. She flew at her tasks like a fury. For Temmie and Rozia on Sunday as well as on weekdays there were the meals to be cooked, the beds to be made, the rooms to be tidied. The men of the household did no work in the fields on Sunday, but the live stock must be fed, and the poultry; wood must be carried in, fires started. The farm could never be left alone. If Ondy went to mass, Stas must stay at home.

The November day was lowering, the sky leaden, the air penetrating with the wet cold of impending snow. Orrange's best shoes, blacked and glittering, were warming behind the kitchen stove; his one decent suit, cut down from clothing outworn by Stas, was neatly folded over a chair. Breakfast smoking on the table, Temmie made her proclamation.

"We're going to church this morning—Orrange and I."

If she had announced herself as about to set out, with her small son, for China, she could not have met with greater astonishment or more varied objection.

"What for you want to go to church?"

"I got to stay here and do all the work! Dinner and everything, and dishes and beds! And Sunday!"

"I got to take buggy see feller in Milford."

"How about me getting off and going to church or something once in a dog's age, Sundays? The kid ain't doing nothing all week only sitting in school. Leave him do something Sundays."

"What is in church to-day you got to go all at once?"

"I'm going because I feel so inclined. Person'd think, to hear you carry on, that going to church Sunday was something of a crazy new idea, instead of the proper thing for decent folks to do."

"Next Sunday is just as good."

She set her chin. It was Olszak against Oakes. "I haven't put foot inside my own church, that my own forefathers built, not in years. I'm going, and nothing shall stop me. Orrange, too. He's fed the chickens and filled the wood box. I guess I can leave this farm, can't I, for two hours, without your acting as if I was doing a murder!"

Stas pushed his plate and cup away with a clatter. He got up, wiping his mouth on the back of his hand. A boy no longer, his face took on the look of a man in rebellion. Unrest was in the young Pole's moody face, and dissatisfaction, and hate.

"I'm good and sick of this goddam farm, myself, and don't you forget it, Sundays and weekdays and every other day. Good and goddam sick." He slouched across the room and out to the barnyard.

Ondy's fists on the oilcloth were clenched into hard brown hammers. He pushed back his chair and made as though to follow Stas. His eyes, usually a clear blue in his weather-beaten face, were dark now. A vein stood out on his forehead. "I make him sick, all right, that Stas, that *cham*."

"Now, Ondy, don't get all het up. . . . Rozia, stop clattering the dishes so. What's ailing you? I suppose you're sick of the farm, too, young lady. . . . He didn't mean anything, Ondy."

"Yes, I am, if you want to know," muttered Rozia, under her breath, as she carried a stack of dishes to the pan.

"Sick or well or dying, the lot of you, I'm going to church this morning, and so is Orrange."

"Don't want to go to church," Orrange announced, a last pleasing touch.

Now it was Temmie who pushed back her chair and rose, a figure of rebellion. "Well, you're going, young man. So march yourself into those clothes, and double-quick, too. All this slamming and mumbling and grouting because I said I'd a mind to go to church. High time I went somewhere. I may go every Sunday, if I feel so inclined. It may so be I'm sick of farming, too, along with the rest of you." She sounded astonishingly like Jude Oakes in that lady's more vital days. Indeed, words and tone were, unconsciously, patterned after the woman whose misdirected power had survived her death.

Once accomplished, it turned out to be a dreary and disappointing business, this churchgoing. As Temmie tied the mare to one of the old oak hitching posts outside the church she noticed how few and how decrepit were the vehicles similarly fastened; how shabby and neglected the paintless little church with its cupola and steeple, broken now, weather-worn, but bearing still the stamp of beauty given it by the master hand of its designer.

Church had already begun. Tamar took the boy's reluctant little fist in her grasp. Together they entered. Necks would crane, she knew. Eyes would slide round to her. As she opened the heavy oaken door it was as though the chill of the tomb rose to envelop her. The smell of an old church: damp, mold, dust, mice, incense, candle wax. At the doorway the old carpet was worn through to the boards, and a dreary tuft of whiskers sprang to catch the feet of the unwary. The pews were clammy to the touch. The pew cushions, once plump and well fed, were flat and meager as the pallets of the poor. Head up, Orrange at her elbow, Tamar Olszak marched down the center aisle in her shabby, outmoded black, straight to the Oakes pew, so long unoccupied: high backed, imposing, well forward, as befitted the pew of a first family. A little stir followed her, as when a breeze rustles through the boughs of dead trees on which a brittle leaf or two still clings.

Nine people only in the body of the church—six women and three men. Three specters in the massive hand-carved choir loft. A gray-haired, gray-faced, gray-surpliced man in the pulpit.

". . . meek . . . shall inherit the earth. . . ."

Fiddlesticks! thought Temmie. Orrange was wriggling and sniffling.

Sh!

"I'm cold."

Sh! She took his hand in hers. He wriggled his fingers free. He began a whispered count of something or other in a private game of his own; the panes in the altar window, probably—the jewel-like window of Captain Oakes' providing. One pane—blue it must have been, she thought, trying to recall the pattern—heavenly blue— had been broken and replaced with a piece of cheap milky white. It was like a patch of calico on brocade. Another tiny bit, broken, had never been replaced, and the November air slyly whistled through it. The draught must be directly on the rector's neck, she thought. Poor man.

". . . O God, the heathen are come into thine inheritance . . . we Thy people and sheep of Thy pasture will give Thee thanks forever . . . all generations . . ."

Sheep. Being a sheep does you no good, she thought. Slaughtered, in the end. Hope Ondy and Stas don't get to quarreling again and bickering. Rozia, likely as not, forgot to put the pork shoulder on at eleven, as I told her. Hope those pains won't be so bad this winter as last. He said operation. Newfangled notions. Old Dr. Waite never was one for operations; if he was still alive he wouldn't hear of it, and no more will I. Orrange has got to go to a school, not the country school, but a real school in Fenwick, and learn something. He's an Oakes.

The collection.

"Your dime, Orrange."

He fingered it, in an agony of relinquishment. Must he? A whole dime. Money was such a rare thing on the farm. He was saving—had been saving for months—to buy two pigeons that Jo Halicki had for sale.

"Can't I keep it?"

"No."

His lip came out in a pout of protest. Lingeringly he placed it in the basket so sparsely dotted with silver.

Two men of the meager congregation marched solemnly, stiffly to the altar with the poor offering. They deposited the baskets, stood, heads meekly bowed, awaiting the blessing. Tamar Oakes did not bow her head. Her eyes, fascinated, gazed on the figures of the two men. They were thin, scrawny, bloodless men, their shoulders sharply sloping, their legs spindling, their heads long and thin. She saw the backs of their necks rising from their ill fitting collars. Brown, stringy, sapless necks, the slack skin hung on sagging tendons. How feeble the pulse must be, there under the unvital skin.

". . . Bless this offering, O Lord, bless this congregation . . . let us come before His Presence with Thanksgiving and make a joyful noise unto Him with psalms."

They rose. They made a noise unto Him with psalms. It was not joyful.

The ghosts drifted up the aisle and out into the November noonday whose lemon-and-water sun was less chill than the indoor air of the church had been. They did not come forward to take her hand. Tamar Oakes who married the Polack.

"I hate church," Orrange announced, as they drove home.

"Orrange Oakes Olszak, don't you ever let me hear you say that again. Your ancestors built that church. It's beautiful. Captain Orrange Oakes himself, that you were named after, superintended its building."

"I bet he didn't like going to church, either."

"He liked everything that had to do with Oakesfield— the farm and the house and the trees and the hills."

"Oh, that's different. So do I."

"You ought to go to church every Sunday."

"Why?"

"Because it helps you to be good and to feel good."

"I don't feel good."

When she drove into the barnyard Ondy was nowhere about, nor Stas. She left the unhitching for Orrange, proud of his ability to accomplish it, and hurried to the house. The kitchen was empty. The fire was but a handful of dull embers in the kitchen stove. Of preparations for dinner there were none.

"Roze! Roze! Ondy! If this doesn't beat all! What in the world——"

A clatter of footsteps, the door flung open, Rozia, tear-streaked, wide eyed.

"Rozia Olszak, what's the meaning of this? Near one, no sign of dinner, the fire——"

"They had a fight. Terrible. Pa and Stas. He pret' near killed him."

"Who! Who killed who? Oh, God! Where——"

"In there. They fought in the barn."

White faced, shaking, she turned toward the door toward which Rozia was pointing. But as she stumbled toward it Ondy appeared in it. The sleeve of his coarse blue shirt was torn and hung in strips. His powerful right arm was bare. The accustomed brown of his face stood out now like a coating over white. Down one cheek there trickled a thin line of scarlet. He wiped it away with his big bandanna handkerchief, and another trickle came to take its place.

"Ondy! You're bleeding! Ondy!"

"Well, how was it by church? Good?"

"Roze, get the clean white rags in the cupboard there. Here. Sit here."

"What for I sit down! I ain't sit down. You better fix for that Stas some rags, by golly!"

"Ondy Olszak, tell me this minute if you've really hurt him. What did you fight about? Can't I leave this house once in ten years? Oh, my goodness!"

She was sponging his face with cold water. Rozia, meanwhile, enlightened her, eagerly. She seemed pleasurably excited.

"I was fixing dinner here and I heard them yelling and

cursing terrible and I run to the barn and there they were stomping and pounding and rassling on the floor and all over so I tried to get them apart and they wouldn't any more than if I was a fly, and Stas hit Pa and then they kind of rolled around and then Pa give Stas an awful crack you could hear it and down he went flat and just laid there like he was dead——"

At the look in Temmie's face—"He ain't dead," Ondy put in, rather sheepishly. "Old man show him who is boss. He is twenty year, me, I got more as fifty, I fight like son of gun, knock him down. Old man is hell of feller. I think now Stas he stay on farm, all right, and shut his mouth."

"But what for? What for? Why did you fight?"

"Oh, ain't he say he is sick of farm? He say farm is no damn good for him, he work by hat factory in Stonefield get maybe hunderd dollar week. I fix him."

Stas lay on the bed in his room, silent, sullen, bruised. Ondy's knockout blow proved, on inspection, to have been effective but harmless. "Fighting around," Temmie scolded, even while she applied healing applications, "like a lot of drunken——" She stopped, aghast. She had almost said like a lot of drunken Polacks.

Midday dinner was a late and melancholy meal, of which the vanquished Stas refused to partake. Gloom hung over the house throughout the day—endured, in fact, through the week.

"Oh, my goodness sakes alive!" Temmie exclaimed,

again and again. "You two sit there glaring at each other like a pair of fighting cocks."

"Who's glaring?" Stas growled. "You make me sick."

He went about his work sullenly, but what there was to do he did with his usual efficiency. There was the late autumn pig-killing, with all its attendant labors; there was wood to be cut in the pine bottom and hauled. The week was crowded with work. Each had had a share of hard labor—Ondy, Temmie, Stas, Rozia, Orrange. Saturday night found them weary, relaxed. The ominous cloud that had lain for a week over the household seemed, in a measure to have lifted.

"Is Men's Communion to-morrow," Ondy announced at supper Saturday night. "Communion breakfast, too. Father Scully he get after me I ain't come to Mass. I go to-morrow Communion and breakfast, is good time. Feller from Storrs Farm College make a speech to farmer about tobacco, by Communion breakfast."

"I'll go with you," Temmie announced, blithely.

"Communion breakfast ain't for women."

"I know. But the Guild ladies serve it, don't they? And even if I'm not a member, I can go and look on and see folks. I'm tuckered out with this week. Anyway, I'm going to go around more, from now on. Seems to me I've been like one dead, these ten years past."

Ondy appeared none too gracious, but she went, nevertheless, and even took Orrange with them. They crowded into the sagging old buggy. The Men's Communion was at half-past eight. Though they had risen early, they found themselves late arrivals. As they drew up before the Church of the Sacred Heart of Jesus, in Fenwick, they were hard put to it to find a post or tree to which they might tie the mare. It might have been more difficult still had there not been an astonishing number of squat, comfortable automobiles shining with paint and metal and glass under the wintry sun. The horse teams, Temmie saw with a shock, were actually in the minority.

"Why, look at all the automobiles! Who do they all belong to?" Oakes Farm was on a by-road, little traveled. The highroad lay a good mile beyond it. Few enough automobiles chose the rutted way past Olszak's.

"Is farmers like us," Ondy explained, and there was a new strange bitterness in the man's usually placid tone. "That Stas, he is all time say tobacco farmers got automobiles only us."

No Old World genius of a long-gone day had had a hand in the designing or building of the Church of the Sacred Heart of Jesus. A squat, substantial tan brick building, newly erected five years ago, set well back from the prim, comfortable New England street. A broad solid church front; broad solid cement steps; bright crude windows; a steeple with no nonsense about it, and an iron-throated bell.

The church was packed. It was not only that every pew was filled: men and women were standing at the back. The entry door was open, the entry was filled, there actually were people standing on the church steps.

Perhaps because she looked so slight, so frail, in the midst of all these broad-bosomed women and broad-shouldered men, Tamar was handed along, with Orrange in tow, until she stood in the front row of those in the rear of the church. Then a lad whom she recognized as one of the Kusak boys rose, awkwardly, and proffered her his seat in a pew at the back. She slipped into it, gratefully, though protesting a little. Orrange stood, with his father.

Smell of earth, of bodies at blood heat, of yellow soap and Sunday clothes.

Father Scully in the pulpit. A powerful red-cheeked man in his rich vestments, his black hair touched with gray, his voice harsh, compelling. Men and men and men, row upon row of them, close packed, shoulder to shoulder, down to the very altar rail. They sat quietly enough, yet it was as though their resilient muscles bounced back from the yellow pews. Their massive shoulders rose and fell with their full breathing. Men of fifty, grizzled, like Ondy; men of forty, thirty, twenty, boys of fifteen. Round headed, full blooded, their heads inclined slightly forward, like docile, listening animals. The backs of their necks were like the throats of bullocks, and weathered with little lines.

"I wish you fellows would give me a break," Father Scully was saying, surprisingly enough, in that authoritative voice. "I only got three hours' sleep last night.

And why? I was called to administer the last rites to Aleck Krupa and didn't get home till two in the morning and up at five to hear Confession. Now, why couldn't some of you fellows come to Confession Saturday night instead of standing on the street corner at Fenwick or Stonefield, and all crowding in on me this morning so that here I was hearing Confession till time for Men's Communion! Now then . . . after the services there will be a men's breakfast served in the Guild Hall by the ladies of the Guild for all who care to partake, followed by a talk by Professor Ben Nichols on tobacco raising in the Connecticut Valley—uh—'How Can The Leaf Be Improved.' "

From English he now dropped into the hard consonants of Polish, delivering the same chiding, making the same announcements.

The men began to be called up to take Communion. Pew by pew, on either side, they advanced as they were beckoned by the ushers—eight from this row, eight from that, down the aisle, four by four, their great brown hands meekly clasped in front of them, their steady eyes fixed on the altar. They were like splendid cattle. Men and men and men. The solid church floor creaked under their steady tread. Eight men, eight men, eight men, eight men. Back to their pews. Tamar began to feel a little giddy. Ondy advanced with his file, his Sunday coat stretched tight across his powerful shoulders. They ad vanced. The Poles advanced like a conquering army.

The Guild Hall, after the early Mass, was all house-wifely bustle and confusion. In the main room long tables on trestles were laid with plates, cups, saucers, hunks of bread, and bananas and oranges. In the little kitchen adjoining, the women were busy over boilers of coffee, great pans piled with fried sausage cakes, mounds of baked beans.

"Now then," shrilled the ladies of the Guild, their hats askew, as they heaped plates high, filled cups, whisked to and fro, all hospitable excitement. "Tell 'em set down anywhere and begin while it's hot." Plate after plate of steaming food, smoking hot coffee. Temmie, to her surprise, found herself pressed into service. She carried three plates of food at a time, replenished cups, passed the bread, skimming up the long hall, down again to the crowded little kitchen for a fresh supply. Ondy was seated between two other Polish farmers. They were reading a local Polish newspaper, and Ondy was pointing with one broad forefinger. Orrange was engaged inexpertly with a punching bag which was strapped to the wall in one corner of the hall, almost—but not quite—out of his reach.

The men continued to stream into the hall, they sat, they ate hugely. Father Scully appeared in the doorway. He put a hand on Orrange's shoulder. "What's your name, boy? Olszak? Oh, yes. Why aren't you eating?

[*263*]

Here! Give the lad something to eat. Sit you down, Olszak."

Father Scully was not sitting nor eating. He was up and down the hall, the skirts of his black cassock flying behind him as he strode. Another Mass to be said at ten. He smoked a cigarette to stifle the pangs of hunger which could not be satisfied until after the final Mass, long past noonday. Nothing in the Creed and nothing in the Bible about not smoking a cigarette.

Temmie gulped a cup of the hot coffee, standing. She listened to the college professor's talk on tobacco, thinking to keep Orrange in hand with her presence and a stern maternal eye, but the boy listened, interested. Tobacco. Here was something he knew from seedling to packing shed.

As they drove home at noonday Tamar felt warmed, stimulated. The warm feeling lasted through the wintry drive home.

Orrange unhitched the mare, led her into the barn. Together Tamar and Ondy entered the house, contentment upon them.

Rozia, red-cheeked and important, met them at the doorstep, for the second time the bearer of tidings, and relishing the rôle.

"He's gone."

"Who?" But they knew.

"He wouldn't stay. Nothing I could do, he wouldn't hear to me. The minute you had drove off. He was only waiting. Here." Full of importance, she held out a sheet of cheap blue-lined paper. "It's for Pa."

But Ondy Olszak only stood turning it helplessly over and over in his big brown hands, so Tamar took it from him. In her Sunday dress she stood at the kitchen table and read the note scrawled in Stas's unformed hand.

". . . stay on the goddam farm no longer . . . job in Stone-field . . . can't nobody make me stay . . . twenty-one and my own boss . . . the old man . . ."

The Pole, her husband, in his awkward Sunday blacks, stood with his head bowed, listening.

XIV

ORRANGE OLSZAK went to the public school in Fenwick. A simple enough proceeding, one would have thought. But its accomplishment had been marked with anger, tears, quarrels, recriminations.

"For why Orrange go to school in Fenwick?" Ondy demanded.

"Because he's got to have a decent education. I've made up my mind to that."

"Is school in Oakesfield."

"School! One room, with a lot of snuffling brats of all ages, all mumbling together just anyhow. It's worse than a Chinese school. Second reader talking its lesson out loud while fifth reader's studying its arithmetic. Five years old and fifteen years old, all in a heap together. He's going to a real school and learn something."

"Oakesfield school was school you learn in, and Stas learn, and Rozia. Is good enough for them, by golly, is good enough for Orrange."

"He's different. He's going to school in Fenwick. Matter of that, he may go to college, as well."

"You are crazy like old Judy Oakes she was crazy."

"That's as may be, and I thank you. But crazy or not, my boy's to have a proper education, and not brought up just anyhow, like a clod."

"He don't go with my money."

"Then with mine."

"You ain't got money."

"Then I'll get it. I'll sell the thirty, down by the Ridge, that that Teofil Wolski's been after, for pasture land."

He had the stubbornness of a bull, but she had the tenacity of a flea. It was strange that with the passing of the years the difference between them had become more and more strongly marked. Tamar was increasingly the New Englander; Ondy more markedly the Pole. In their youth propinquity and passion had brought them together. There remained an accustomed fondness, and even a measure of tenderness. She was used to him. He was used to her. Their marriage had been as thoughtless and inevitable as that of any two young animals thrown together. Passively they accepted the years that followed. Temmie rarely opposed her husband in his personal conduct or in his conduct of the farm. But on two subjects she was adamant: Oakes Farm was a sacred thing and must be kept an entity; Orrange Olszak, their son, was somehow pure Oakes—a reincarnation of that Captain Orrange Oakes whose history had so stirred her in her childhood. As Orrange grew from childhood into boyhood there seemed to be some excuse for this hallucination. The boy, Orrange, had the dolicocephalus English head, the piercing blue-gray eyes, the easy grace, the imperious manner of that Orrange Oakes of centuries ago. Her determination to see him properly educated met with as much derision and opposition as had the announcement of old Judith Oakes, wife of Captain Orrange, when she was for sending her granddaughters to the Moravian boarding school conducted by the Countess Benigna Zinzendorf. And Tamar overcame that opposition as triumphantly. She sold thirty acres to Teofil Wolski, and it was like cutting off a finger of her right hand. She hoarded pennies, dimes, and quarters from the sale of hens she had bought and eggs they had laid. She had made up her mind that she would, if necessary, sell this piece of rare mahogany or cherry wood, that bit of precious old china or glass, to one of the ghouls who were increasingly prowling the neighborhood farm attics, seeking such treasures as they could lay hands upon for city selling.

For three winters—from the time he was fourteen until he was seventeen—Orrange Olszak actually went to school in Fenwick, leaving the farmhouse when the morning was still gray, returning at night just in time to do his share of the arduous chores in barn and shed and sty.

"Listen. If we had a Ford I could get there and back in a tenth the time."

"You want Ford go earn money and buy him," Ondy said.

"I will. You wait. Wait till I get this farm going right."

"Yeh, you smart feller all right, sit in school all day like baby boy."

The Olszaks were land poor, all right. The neighbors agreed about that. That crazy Temmie Oakes, hanging onto the land, and all the time it was eating them out of house and home, with taxes and repairs and all. Certainly the other farms for miles all about were prospering. But they were farms of thirty, fifty, sixty acres at the most. Oakes Farm, with its hundreds of untilled acres— that was different. And the Olszak farmhouse, with the gay, improvident, childlike little Tamar to run it, was different, too.

Truth was that Ondy, though willing to dispose of a slice of land here, a slice there, was vain of being known as proprietor of the largest single farm in the whole district.

The Smentkowskis were prospering. Julka's daughter, Helena, was going to Stonefield to learn to be a nurse at the hospital there. Julka was very grand about it. Helena Smentkowski was strong as a horse, an indefatigable worker, doubtless would make a rough, capable, tireless nurse. On her rare visits home to the farm she had great stories to tell. Her hearty hospital jokes were, queerly enough, almost never on the subject of sex. Sex jokes did not amuse the Poles. They looked on the processes of sex in the stolid Polish peasant way, a humorless and commonplace proceeding. But jokes about the digestive tract were considered gorgeously funny. When Helena described certain intimate hospital equipment, and explained the use of a bedpan, farmhouse after farmhouse throughout the Polish district rocked with mirth. On Sunday morning, after church, Helena's mother, Julka Smentkowski, gathered a group of Polish farm women about her, a fascinated knot, heads close together, while Feliks was the center of a group of men. Loud guffaws, then. They wiped their eyes and stamped their feet with laughter.

Fundamentally they had changed little, these peasant Poles. But with prosperity they had taken on certain outer manifestations of success. Kusak's farm bloomed, and Wolski's, and the Markiewiczs', and the Halickis', and the Boreks'.

Every day Temmie saw Mrs. Wolski driving home the cows, pastured in the thirty she had sold them. The Wolskis owned a touring car that was painted a deep rich blue, a mud-spattered vehicle, but sound enough. Every

evening Mrs. Wolski drove past Oakes Farm in her touring car. In the back seat squirmed four Wolskis whose
ages ranged from three to eight. In the curve of Mrs.
Wolski's arm, as she sat at the wheel, was the latest Wolski infant. The Wolskis had fourteen cows and were
planning a more ambitious herd. The meadow reached,
the small Wolskis in the back seat spilled out pell-mell.
Their combined efforts opened the pasture gate. Through
this, as they stood aside, Mrs. Teofil Wolski jockeyed
expertly. Driving round and round the pasture she neatly
encircled the cows with the touring car, until, herded together, they headed toward the open gate, the automobile nipping at their leisurely rumps. Through the gate,
into the road. Again the combined Wolskis tugged at the
heavy gate, closed it, scrambled into the back seat. Down
the road to the Wolski farm ambled the herd, and just
behind them was Mrs. Wolski at the wheel, the sleeping
infant cradled in the curve of her bountiful bosom.
Temmie in the farmyard, perhaps, taking in the wash,
old boots on her feet, a shawl pinned over her head.

"How-do, Mrs. Wolski."

"How you do." A gracious nod from Mrs. Wolski,
driving grandly by.

In the midst of this pastoral peace along came the
war, and tossed five decades over its Gargantuan shoulder. Orrange was too young to take active part in it, too
nearly a man not to feel the shock of its impact. He and
Ondy and Temmie worked the farm like slaves, like ma-

chines. The young men came back from France, they looked about them, they looked at the farms with lackluster eyes. Let's go somewheres. Let's drive over to Hartford, let's drive over to New Haven, let's drive over to Waterbury, let's drive over to Bridgeport, let's drive over to Springfield. Let's go somewheres. What the hell!

Then Rozia Olszak, grown more and more restless, left Oakes Farm as defiantly, as abruptly as her half-brother Stas. She, too, wanted to go somewhere. She longed for the city, and she fled to it, a red-cheeked, bold, handsome girl. It was not sudden revolt. Her rebellion had smoldered for years. A trifling quarrel was enough to set it flaming.

"Oh, Rozia, you were such a sweet baby," Temmie said, helpless before the girl's hard peasant stubbornness.

"Yeh, baby! Sweet baby is all right, but it don't get you nowheres on this farm."

It was easy enough to get a job as servant girl in Stonefield. A year of that. A job at the Five-and-Ten and a room with two other Polish girls. Stockings rolled, hair bobbed, orange rouge overlaying the farm-girl coloring. Fresh-looking in spite of it, big-boned, strong and tireless as a man, and as well able to look out for herself. Ambitious, too, and hard-headed. A job behind the busy soda fountain and lunch counter at Linnick's Drug Store on the busiest corner in Stonefield. Cooking, it seemed, was essential to a drug-store job.

"Can you cook good?"

"Sure I can cook."

She loved it. The boys from the hat factories came in, perched on stools at the counter, consumed incredible messes called chicken à la king, tuna fish salad, Lover's Delight.

"Hot bacon and egg on toasted rye with piccalilli and a chocolate sundae plenty of pecan nuts hot chocolate sauce and whipped cream. Howsa girl?"

"Fine and dandy. How's yourself?"

"Finernat."

"What'll it be?"

"Whattya got?"

"Say, got! Can't you read?"

"Ham and cheese on white butter both sides cup of coffee. Howsa girl?"

"Fine and dandy. How's yourself?"

"Fine."

But she had her eye out for marriage and did not make herself too cheap, conducted herself with a kind of dignity—or perhaps it was just the way she carried herself, what with shoulders broad and straight from pitching hay, and head high, mark inherited from generations of peasant women ancestors who had carried heavy loads atop steady heads set on strong columnar throats.

She bore Temmie and Ondy no ill will. She was, after all, no part of either of them. Sometimes—rarely—she came back to the farm on Sundays in her city finery.

Good-naturedly enough she helped with the dinner, and even commanded the little shriveled woman to take her ease while she prepared the food and served it.

"Go on sit down rest yourself. I'll dish up. Why'n't you and Pa sell this place and go live in town where you see something? Orrange, too. Always reading a book."

"Read one yourself some time, Roze. You can't tell. You might like it."

"Yeh, I'd look good reading a book after I been working all day. I got plenty time to read books when I'm an old woman like Ma. Not when I can go to the movies and go driving I don't read books, believe you me."

The Oakesfield boys of Orrange's age met in the Grange Hall. They talked. They had a room fitted up as a gymnasium. They had begun to look about them, speculatively.

"I want to go to Storrs a winter or two," Orrange announced, one October night, at supper. "I'd like to start next month, when the tobacco's all stripped." Storrs was the State Agricultural College.

"You crazy," Ondy said.

"We're not getting anywhere with this farm. It's just where it was fifty years ago, only more worn out. Old-fashioned methods you used in Poland. Another ten or fifteen years and it'll be finished."

Temmie clasped and unclasped her hands, a nervous trick she had acquired of late years. The gray eyes went anxiously from the boy's thoughtful face to the old man's stubborn one. Ondy had risen, had clumped across the kitchen, cigar in mouth. Removing the stove lid he spat into the fire. The contempt of the seasoned farmer for smart young kids.

"Yeh, finish. Like hell is finish. Fine farm like here! Is best farm in whole county, by golly. Is finish when world is finish. All other farms in county is finish too, huh?"

"Pretty soon. Not as soon as this, though. They've all got big families, lots of kids, and they all work, and their farms are a tenth the size of this. The boys won't stick for long. The girls won't, either. Look at Stas and Roze."

"You ain't got money for college."

"I wrote them about that. They say I can work my way through, doing odd jobs. Other fellows do it. They help you out, if they know you mean it." He looked straight at his father. "I can try it for one winter, anyway, from November to April. And I'll expect you to pay me the wages of a hired hand through the summer from now on."

"You crazy son of gun, you!"

"Now, Ondy. Don't start quarreling with Orrange. Orrange!"

"We're not quarreling, Ma. It's all right. Pa doesn't understand."

"Yeh, you understand, you smart feller. You think I am crazy pay my own kid wages!"

"No. And I'm not crazy, either. I could hire out to any farmer around here for sixty dollars a month, if they're short of hands, and they are, in the busy time. But I don't want to hire out. I want Oakes Farm to be the finest farm in Connecticut, and it could be, too, if you'd listen. Not in five years, but maybe in ten or fifteen. Here on this land, with two rivers draining it. Old Orrange Oakes knew what he was doing. I know just the way he felt about it."

"Oh, Orrange!" Temmie's voice was young again, like a girl's. "Oh, Orrange!"

"Look. You can't go on sticking things into the ground and hoping they'll come up all right. Farming is going to be as technical as manufacturing. It was all right, twenty-five years ago—what you did with this land. But not now. When you came to this farm it was all broad leaf. There wasn't any shade-grown. But even that's no good, now, because cigar smokers have got it into their heads that a light-colored cigar isn't as strong as a dark one. It isn't true, but you can't make them believe it isn't. Our leaf's dark. All through the Valley, it's dark leaf. We've got to learn to raise light broad leaf. Cuban is light, and they're buying Cuban. We've been getting seed from Cuba. We ought to raise our own. Ten years from now, if we don't do something, our tobacco will be used for nothing but fillers and binders, and all the wrappers will come from Cuba. We need horses and automobiles and plows and tools and new lathes and wagons and curing sheds. I am going to get them, but first I'll have to learn to grow tobacco and run this farm technically."

"Ondy, he's right. I know he's right. Listen to him."

Ondy threw himself into a posture of elegance. He mimicked Orrange's voice and tone. " 'We need automobile, we need horse, we need plow, we need shed.' By damn, I guess you better work for Henry Ford, he fix you plenty automobile."

"I'm telling you. You go on running the place like this and we'll lose it. We'll lose it, I tell you."

Ondy leaned forward, very earnest, his blue eyes dark, his seamed face serious. "I come this country, I get eleven dollar a month job. Plenty pork. I get so much salt pork I am sick of it so I don't want never eat salt pork. Then I get eighteen dollar month. Pretty soon I get dollar and quarter a day. I think I am rich like hell. Now I am boss biggest farm in Oakesfield and in whole state Connecticut, I betcha. You are crazy feller."

"Oh, God, it's no use!" groaned Orrange Oakes. He stood up, his face drawn. "Look here. If I lose Oakes Farm, and this house, because of you!"

"Oh, no!" Temmie's voice was almost a scream. She looked about her, as though alien hands were already laid upon the old mansion; as though the old bricks were already tumbling about her ears.

When Orrange Olszak returned from his second winter at Storrs he was taller than his father, and as broad shouldered, but he did not look it, lacking the older man's solid bulk and thick waist. Beside the two men Temmie was like a child. She was years younger than Ondy, but she looked older than he. He seemed almost as strong and lusty as when he had come to Oakes Farm, so many years ago. He could do a day's work with the boys of twenty, and beat them at it. He drank his home-made beer and hard, rough six-weeks' wine, and his applejack, he ate well, he worked his fields all the day.

"By golly, is good tobacco crop get good price I buy you gasoline stove sure thing this year," he promised Temmie. But it was Orrange who bought it. It was Orrange, too, who arranged that Temmie no longer churn by hand, as she had done, laboriously, for so many years. Many of the neighboring farms had electric appliances now. The Wolskis' dairy was the talk of the district. It was so elaborately equipped that at first sight the uninitiated might be hard pressed to know whether this was a cow barn or a factory. Milking was no longer done by hand, but by machine. The Wolskis' cows were Holsteins, yielding bulk rather than richness of cream, to be sent to the city daily. Overhead and all about was the intricacy of pipes, hose, nozzles, metal caps, tubes. Hum. Whir. Buzz. In their stalls, row on row, stood the gentle ruminant creatures, symbol of all that is pastoral, now helpless in the grip of the machine age.

Sometimes Orrange talked of an artesian well and their own water.

Oakes Farm. Oakes Farm. All his life he had had it ground into his consciousness. Nothing came before Oakes Farm. No matter what happens, Oakes Farm must never be sold. Promise me you'll never sell an acre of it. You'll never cut it up and sell it. The great farm, acre upon acre, soared up toward Pequot Ridge and over it, leaped Gallows Hill, ran toward Fenwick, embraced hills, rivers, woods. For over two centuries it had dominated a family, wrung from them oblation. Now it held the last of them clasped to its withered bosom. The old Pole, the sick and ageing woman, had nothing more to give it. It turned to the boy who was now a man. Love me, it said. I am still beautiful. I am still fertile. Love me, and I will reward you.

Sometimes Orrange said strange things, bewildering to Temmie. She would sit in the kitchen doorway, the boy would squat on his haunches at the old stone doorstep. She talked of Big Bella one evening, sadly. Big Bella moved with great difficulty now. When she walked at all it was with the aid of a great stave, like a man. Her feet were terribly calloused and her ankles swollen, from bearing her enormous weight. She drank, now, anything she could get her hands on, and you sometimes saw her being very sick indeed over a roadside fence. She still managed to go, somehow, to the woods once or twice a year for her herbs. Ponderous, wheezing, she plunged among the tender green of the early spring leafage and the bridal white of dogwood like some vast mythological monster. Yet one part of the befuddled mind remained clear. She still gave the farmers' wives physic for themselves and their children. They gave her, in return, their hard cider and their blackberry and cherry wine. Sometimes she fell into a drunken stupor as she sat there. Usually there was no chair big enough to contain her enormous bulk, so she sat on the state sofa that every Polish best room boasted, and there, often, the beautiful gray innocent eyes would become misted, would close, she would topple asleep, and there they would allow her to stay, all day or all night. It was impossible to move her. They would cover her over with a coarse gray blanket. Sometimes, when Temmie came to see her, she became confused. She called her Rilly.

"It's terrible, the way Cousin Bella is. The way she drinks. The Polish boys hoot at her when she walks in the road. She oughtn't to be allowed to go around alone. They'll find her in the ditch one day, dead, or bogged down in the woods somewhere. And the way that little Mossop looks at her. It makes my flesh creep. He'd be glad of it, I've no doubt."

"It's all right, Mother. It doesn't matter now. It's finished."

"What's finished?"

He did not reply at once. He looked up across the farm land, toward the Ridge, painted against the sunset. "Captain Orrange and his wife Judith, and Big Bella and Aunt Jude and all those. It's like the begats in the Bible. It ran so thin after two hundred years that there wasn't any blood left. A good job, your marrying Pa."

"I've never regretted it," Temmie said, not knowing in the least what he meant.

"You and Ondy begot me, see?"

She looked at him, worshipingly, but she mocked him for his own good, with something of her old gay spirit.

"Oh, I suppose you're something rare."

"Well, I'm pretty good. Not as good as old Captain Orrange, and the bird with the satin coat and the ringlets, there in the hall. No, sir! Giants in those days. But I'm pretty good, with Ondy's blood in me, and yours."

"I've often thought, Orrange. You don't go with the girls enough. Not that I want—I don't know—I suppose you'll get married. But you're not the same. I mean, who can you——"

"I don't know, either," said Orrange, simply. "But when I do I'll have kids that'll know where they're heading in. This business that old Orrange started, it's finished, I mean, as far as we go. End of the line, like a street car. The Polacks, too, like Pa. Their kids don't want the farms, most of them. They want to go to Stonefield, and around, like Stas, and work in the factories and get into politics, and run things. They'll have a Polack mayor in Stonefield one of these days. You'll see."

But she was not interested in this. "To-morrow I am going to see Cousin Bella. She's got to be looked after. That Hen Mossop! I'm worried about her more than ordinary."

So that the very next day, when one of the Halickis stopped by in the car to say that Hen Mossop had sent for her, for Big Bella was taken bad, she was spared the shock of surprise.

"I had a presentiment," she said, as she hurried, just as she was, in her calico work dress, to the dying woman.

Big Bella's kitchen, always a welter of disorder, was now a nightmare. It was as though a maniac had wreaked his insanity upon it. Unwashed dishes lay piled all about, chairs were overturned, crockery, smashed, lay on the floor. In the midst of this sat little Hen Mossop, like an evil gnome, neck stretched forward, tense, his scraggy pointed beard sticking straight out like a weapon.

"How is she? I had a presentiment." She made straight for the bedroom off the kitchen.

"Don't you go in there!" squeaked Hen Mossop.

"What's to prevent me, I'd like to know?"

"She's gone."

"Gone!"

"Dead." Then, quickly, "She wouldn't hear to having a doctor. Always cooking messes of those yarbs of hers. I fixed it for her, her medicine, best I knew how."

She looked at him. She turned her honest gray eyes on him. Hen Mossop's hot, mean little eyes dropped before the sudden awful conviction he saw in her gaze.

As she turned the handle of the door and entered the unaired room where the dead woman had lain for two days, the stench was like a physical blow.

They buried her in the Champion plot, a curiously long grave, and wide. They had to have a special casket made for her. The old Oakesfield burying ground was a dreary, neglected wasteland. Its crazy tombstones leaned this

way and that, or, tottering, had fallen completely and
lay disintegrating with the clay whose memory they were
meant to preserve. The grass was coarse and high and
weed choked. Cows grazed through the broken fences.
The old carving was almost obliterated except where a
slab, harder than the rest, had resisted time and weather,
or where a protecting tree had borne the brunt of the
fury of the elements. You could barely decipher a name.
Clarifa, with the old s. Zeruah, wife of Darius. A bare
half-mile down the road toward Fenwick the Polish
cemetery was spruce and almost gay. It was like a pleasure park in bad taste. Pequot Ridge looked down upon it,
frowning. There were fine granite stones, solid and rich,
embellished with carving, crosses, angels, doves, wings.
The well kept graves bloomed with floral pieces of wire
and colored glass, glittering in the sunlight. The graveled
paths were neat, the grass smooth and trim and green.
Wladyslaw Kustosz. Zygmont Wolinski. Zofia Skrzypek.
Stefan Gorski. Jozia Terlacki.

The news went round that Hen Mossop had sold
Champion House. It was to be moved four miles Fenwick way and used as a dance hall and roadhouse. The
old site of the house was to be a filling station, and the
farmland was to be cut up into small parcels. Word came
that they were moving Champion House. The moving
crew was there; they had got the rollers under the huge
structure.

"Take me there," said Temmie. Orrange drove her

over, and Ondy dropped his work to go, too, for he wanted a glimpse of the spectacle.

Hen Mossop had ordered them to chop down the two gigantic elms that had stood for centuries before the old house. Except the oak trees that stood in front of Oakes House, there were no trees like them for miles around. Each branch was in itself as large as a tree. Chained like heroic vanquished captives they had been hauled down the road by four-horse teams. The great stumps remained, bleeding.

As the Olszaks came up they saw that quite a sizable crowd, for a farm district, had gathered to watch the house-moving. The magnificent old structure, on rollers, trundling down the highway, was like a duchess on skates. They had got it out of the yard, across the ditch, and had set its startled staring face toward the foot of Gallows Hill, where a spy had been hanged during the Revolution. Temmie descended from the Olszak buggy. She stood by the roadside looking up at the old house in its shame. Just so had she looked when she heard that dirty little boys had hooted at Big Bella lurching by. She covered her face with her two hands.

Then, as though this were a signal, the old house suddenly ran amok. With a lunge and a shiver it tore away from confining ropes and pulleys and rollers, crashed down the gully, uprooted small trees, telephone poles, and overhead wires, and came crazily to rest as though for a breathing space in which to survey the ruin it had wrought. The front porch was ripped off, one of the grand old chimneys had toppled, broken windows stared like sightless eye sockets.

Orrange put an arm around the bent, thin little shoulders. She was weeping. Ondy laughed aloud, like a delighted boy.

"What for you cry, Temmie?" said Ondy. "Is only old house." He was enjoying the spectacle immensely.

Orrange and Temmie looked at him with hostile eyes as one regards an alien.

Temmie turned to Orrange, looked up at him. "Promise me," she said, as though continuing a conversation well understood between them.

"Not as long as I can prevent it," Orrange said.

For a month the old house refused to budge, though they brought all manner of modern appliance to bear on it. The main road was blocked. Annoyance and expense began to make the movers wish they had never begun the project. No sooner would they manage to extricate the great house from its self-chosen resting place and hoist it again on rollers headed toward its destination than it would again go crashing into fences and trees, coming to a halt in a spot so fiendishly selected that to move it again was almost impossible. The purchasers of the house talked of abandoning it. They said it was bewitched. Months went by. It lay, tipsily, in a ditch by the side of a field.

Hen Mossop had sold the household goods, and the

old pieces were put up at auction in Fenwick. The voice of the auctioneer was heard by Polish housewives with a thrifty eye for bargains, by interior decorators from the city, by passing tourists. Much of the fine old furniture originally belonging to Champion House had long ago vanished, but there still remained enough to make a goodly showing. Much of it had been piled away and forgotten in barns, sheds, or attic. There were old wooden mortars for grinding grain by hand; there was the great gong that had summoned the slaves and field hands in the days of Noel Champion. The kitchenware came into its day of splendor—ruddy copper basins that had been used in buttery and pantry now were keenly inspected by ladies with a business eye. "Daffodils or zinnias," they chirped, "are so sweet arranged in copper. Or wax fruit. Such a lovely note of color."

"Now, ladies *and* gents, here's a nice little lot. You don't see them things often now'days. Real genuine antiques, they are. They're what you call star candlesticks. You can't knock 'em over. See!"

To prove which, he gave one of the pair of star candlesticks a smart push with his hand, and sure enough, it suffered the indignity, maintained its balance, head up, like a lady who has been jostled by a street-corner loafer.

XV

STAS OLSZAK'S pay check at the end of each week represented a sum that would have made Ondy's eyes, when he was Stas's age, pop with unbelief. Stas was tireless and ambitious and reasonably intelligent. It hadn't taken him long. He had not been three years at the Ludlowe Hat Factory before he was working in the coning room, the best-paid department of the great rambling structure whose acids and offal had for years polluted the river. The little dimpling stream, that had so long smelled of the woods and the flowers and the clean earth and the rocks, was black there, and bitter. The Ludlowe Hat Factory prided itself on the quality of its hats. The least you could pay for a Ludlowe Hat was ten dollars. In Captain Orrange Oakes' day Jabez Ludlowe had made caps of fustian for the laborers. Each proud pasteboard box now containing a Ludlowe hat bore on its front a crest which was a pleasing and impartial mixture of the armorial bearings of the various royal houses of Europe, in which lions rampant clawed plumes supported by bars sinister on field of blue dotted with fleurs-de-lis.

The floor of the room in which the coners worked ran wet, day and night. You were paid by piece work. Stas's clear peasant coloring was tinged with greenish yellow now, and his eyes had a curious lack-luster glaze. But he was a fine workman. He and the other coners scarcely stopped for a bite of noonday lunch during the rush season. They wolfed a sandwich and drank milk out of pint bottles—good rich milk which the doctor had prescribed —but their skin remained that odd pasty clay color. There was, to working as a coner, one slight drawback which balanced the advantage of its high pay. The fine Ludlowe felt hats were made of rabbit fur. In this seemingly downy hair of the animal is a tiny spiral which is oily fiber and which, if not broken down and destroyed by some artificial means, would have made the Ludlowe hat stiff and hard as ordinary felt hats, instead of as soft and pliable as velvet. Long ago it had been discovered that a combination of nitric acid and quicksilver performed this splendid service for Ludlowe hats. Unfortunately, the workers in the coning room inhaled this into their lungs, absorbed it through the skin. They developed a disease known as the shakes. The hand shook, the head shook as with palsy, the skin became yellow. Stonefield came to recognize a hat-factory worker laid off with the shakes. He stopped work for a time, took prescribed treatments, and returned to the nitric acid and quicksilver.

So, very soon after coming to Stonefield, Stas could have been seen standing, with a group of fellow hat-factory workers, on the busy corner in front of Linnick's

Drug Store on a Saturday night, smoking a cigarette and watching the girls go by on the sidewalk and the automobiles go by in the street. Stonefield was choked with automobiles. You could scarcely cross the street on foot. They drove round and round and round. Stas soon had one of his own, and a bright blue suit, and tan shoes, and a good Ludlowe hat. These hat-factory workers were mostly Poles. They became strangely unvoluble, for Poles. They seemed not to have much energy, outside the shop. Their speech was blurred, like their eyes. In their mouths, on the street corner, "all right" became "aw—I—" or nearly that. Stas married a Polish town girl who had worked in the packing room of the factory. Three children—a boy and two girls—a radio, an automobile, a house of their own; on monthly payments, all. Evenings and Sundays they went driving in the automobile. They were pretty good at engines, not like their Polish fathers on the farms outside Stonefield. The old Polish farmers never quite got the hang of the wheel's manipulation or the feel of the engine. Their great slow hands, thick-fingered, were accustomed to the manual processes of planting, sowing, reaping. They were familiar with the smooth palm-filling feel of the scythe, the sickle, the hand plow. They were likely, these old fellows, when they drove, to meet with accidents and land in the ditch, especially if they had been drinking their own home-made wine and beer.

Ondy was forever essaying to drive Orrange's old

second-hand Ford, making off with it like a mischievous boy and leaving it stalled somewhere on the road.

"Listen here, Pa, take the horse. You'll get there sooner. Last Sunday you gummed her up so I couldn't get her straightened out for a week."

"Aw, what's matter with you! That old Ford is no good, is like plow. Next year I betcha I buy me fine automobile like Wolski. Ma and me we go ride every day. Huh, Temmie!"

"You make me nervous, Ondy, driving. Clawing around there in the brakes, or whatever they are, so uncertain. Not like Orrange. He hardly moves his hand. Rozia says it's dangerous, the way you drive."

Certainly Rozia was in a position to know. Rozia drove a glittering sedan with her monogram on the door. In it she arrived grandly at the Stonefield cash-and-carry market, mornings, stowing her bundles away in its capacious tonneau, where the baby's ingeniously contrived cradle swung suspended in midair. Rozia had caught for herself a widower, Jake Gosciak, forty, with three children, an automobile, a seven-room bungalow in Stonefield, and a fertile piece of farm land out Oakesfield way. He was a boss hat-factory worker and a friend of Stas. She had done well for herself, had Rozia. Everyone said that Jake had made a bad bargain, marrying a girl who stood and joked with the men all day behind the drugstore counter. But, as it turned out, they were wrong.

Rozia had planned the wedding. She had thriftily saved

some money, and the infatuated Jake generously contributed what was needed. This was no small matter, for her ideas, gleaned from the movies and the Sunday rotogravures, were magnificent indeed. Not in vain had Rozia studied Laura Lovely in *Make Me a Bride*.

Ondy, Temmie, and Orrange were graciously invited, though they were to take no part in the wedding ceremony. It was to be a church wedding, followed by a breakfast at Kosciusko Hall.

The wedding was at nine on a cold drizzling November morning. "I'll drive you in," Orrange said.

"Drive us in! You're going, aren't you?"

He shook his head. "You and Pa go. That's enough out of one family."

He sensed the vulgarity of the wedding; shrank from witnessing its display. Between Orrange Olszak, working the old farm in Oakesfield, and Stas and Rozia, deep in their urban pursuits in Stonefield, the gap had so widened with the years that it was now no longer to be bridged. There was no feeling of ill-will. Rozia was eight or nine years older than Orrange; Stas fifteen years his senior. There was no point of contact, except the dim and forgotten past.

Outside the church of St. Stanislaw, as Orrange drove up in his rattletrap Ford, there were a score of plump motor cars; and clustered about the steps in the cold rain a little crowd of rag-tag and bob-tail—children, bedraggled neighborhood housewives—scenting excitement, curious for a glimpse of the bride.

Orrange turned and drove off as Ondy and Temmie, two uncertain and somewhat awkward figures, ascended the steps. Inside, the church was chill and damp. The wedding guests only half filled it. The two old people took seats in the rear. The guests were bundled in their stout coats. The tapers, in their ruby glass holders, made a false glow of warmth. The eyes of the congregation rested gratefully on that red glow.

"There is no one I know," Temmie whispered, and shivered a little.

Ondy looked about him furtively. His black felt hat was clutched tight in his two hands. Strange, among strangers, at Rozia Olszak's wedding. "There is Stas and Josie." His son and his son's wife entered. Josie Olszak, a great strapping woman, larger now with the child she was soon to bring forth, wore a light beige coat with a good fur collar. She held the garment wrapped modishly about her. The two nodded to acquaintances here and there.

A thin cheering outside in the drizzle, followed by sibilant whispers from the rear of the church, shuffling feet, half-subdued hysterical gigglings. The organist, taken unawares, scurried into the wedding march, then struck the proper pace. The Reverend Bronsilaw Vladek appeared from the vestry; took his place at the altar. Down the aisle came Rozia Olszak's wedding party, planned by her to the last detail. Rozia Olszak, determined to be as American as any of them.

First came Adam Gosciak, the ring bearer, seven. He had on a new suit of black, with white cotton stockings and square-toed shiny black shoes. He walked cautiously, heel and toe, as though balancing an overfull glass of water, for in his two hands he held a small white pillow on which the wedding ring slid precariously. As he walked he twisted his bullet head and slid his pale eyes this side and that to satisfy himself of his proper meed of admiration. Occasionally he even managed to twist his head all the way round to the rear, to see if they were behind him, like a game of follow-the-leader. At his heels came the small Misses Gosciak, flower girls in white, with their hair newly trimmed and the backs of their necks well shaved. They carried little baskets of rather brown-looking rose petals which they strewed spasmodically and untidily in the path of the bride. The maid of honor then, Helena Smentkowski, in rose-color satin, very mod-ish, cut very low, front and back, and sleeveless, her dark arms and breast contrasting sharply with the bright stuff of the gown. Long white kid gloves came to her elbows. On her head was a tiara of diamantes. In her arm a bou-quet of roses that matched her gown. Her other arm rested in that of Frank Rzepkowski, son of the August who owned the old Baldwin farm out Oakesfield way. A bridesmaid in blue satin, a bridesmaid in green satin, a bridesmaid in yellow, all with slippers to match, and bouquets, and long white kid gloves and tiaras of diamantes on their brows, each on the sturdy arm of a groomsman. Now Rozia herself, on the arm of her bridegroom. Rozia Olszak, the bride, was giving herself away. No old people fumbling at the altar. Her white satin gown might have been something of an anticlimax, after the blaze of color that had preceded it, had it not been for the long voluminous folds of her white tulle veil training behind her, and for the steady look of triumph and determination on her strong dark face. White gloves, tiara, satin slippers, bouquet of white roses.

Rozia Olszak and the other four women of the party were incredibly composed. The men, in their best blacks, were stiff, self-conscious, wretched. They wore generous boutonnières. Their great hands, gloveless, were clenched tight. Their eyes, glassy, unseeing, were fixed straight ahead in a catalepsy of embarrassment.

The fat middle-aged Polish women, and the plump young Polish matrons with parcels of children awaiting them at home, leaned forward in their pews to gape at this glittering display. In their eyes envy, pity, and mockery mingled. You wait. You'll see. Satin and white gloves and bouquets and diamond crowns. You'll come to be like us, to-morrow.

It was a long mass. Father Vladek's exhortation to the breakfastless party seemed endless, in the dim chill of the church. The Communion, then. At last, the peal of the organ.

As they turned and marched up the aisle Rozia's eyes were cold and steady. She walked with her head well up. Easy to see who was to be boss in that household. Temmie, looking at the woman's face, saw no resemblance to that Rozia who had come so tragically into the world in the back bedroom of Oakes Farm more than a score of years ago.

Long streamers, tin cans, old shoes, and other bits of barbarity were tied to the tail of the bridal automobile. Bride and bridesmaids, in their satin finery, coatless in the sharp November morning air, scrambled into the waiting automobiles, were off in a bedlam of screams, shouting, rice, laughter. The bare arms, the bare bosoms, the white kid gloves, the huge wilted bouquets, the cheap glass tiaras, the tulle, were off to Kosciusko Hall. The new Poles.

The crowd began to disperse, briskly. The show was over. Temmie and Ondy stood on the pavement before the church, gazing after the bridal party. Ondy, a square, solid peasant figure, a little round-shouldered now, but powerful still. He had forgotten to put on his hat. The fine cold mist fell on his grizzled head.

"Put on your hat," said Temmie. A little old lady in shabby black. "Come."

"There is time," Ondy reminded her. "They go first to take photo, all of them, before dinner. Up in hall is band playing, and lots of good things for eat and drink."

"Come," said Temmie again. "It's raining harder. We'd better start walking."

Round the corner came the rattletrap Ford. Orrange caught them up, grinning. "Kept on raining, so I did my errands in town and thought I'd come back for you. Thought maybe Roze might—but I didn't know. Anyway——"

Gratefully they crept into the back seat of the crazy Ford.

"Where to?" called Orrange.

"Kosciusko Hall," shouted Ondy, as though in defiance.

When they reached the hall the Polish band was blaring. The sound came down the narrow wooden stairway to the street. Ondy stepped out, heavily. But Temmie stayed as she was. The little heart-shaped face under the outmoded black hat was pinched and gray. "You go, Ondy. I don't feel—it was so cold in the church. I'll just go on home with Orrange. They'll never know. You go."

XVI

THE Polish girls of fourteen, fifteen, sixteen, and their strapping mothers still worked in the tobacco during July and August, topping. But they worked grudgingly. About them was a new elegance. The granddaughters of women who, in Poland, had been hitched to the plow, side by side with the ox, the whip applied to one as to the other, now worked daintily in the Connecticut tobacco fields. They wore broad-brimmed black hats to shield them from the sun. Over their muscular bare arms they pulled the legs of discarded black cotton stockings.

All his life Orrange Olszak had seen women working like men. He never remembered a time when his mother was not working. In his boyhood he had taken this for granted. But of late years he had remonstrated.

"Don't lift that. . . . Look here, Ma, get in out of the sun. . . . Don't cook a lot of hot stuff. Let 'em eat cold. . . . Listen, you've got to have a woman in to help. Get that Swede woman—Gussie—the one you had last year, haying time."

"Next year," she said. "Next year, when times are better."

It was Orrange, not Ondy, who had got her the gaso-line stove so that the big kitchen, during July and August, should not be like a blast furnace with the heat of the range. He had got her some proper cooking utensils, too, from Stonefield, but often as not she neglected these for the heavy old copper pots and iron skillets. He was handy with tools and a born mechanic. He pored over books and catalogues showing patent devices, electrical fixtures. He showed her the picture of a little electrical plant which could be set up in a shed, and that would pump water, light the house, churn the butter.

"It's wonderful," he said. "Like an electric servant. I'm going to buy you one, some day, you'll see. Then all you'll have to do is to sit in a chair and press a button."

She looked up at him in her wren-like way. She was so small, so small. It was absurd that this little creature, with her delicate bones, her thin fine skin with the little freckles dotting the nose, her little wrinkled hands and tiny feet, should be a farm drudge. There were odd brown splotches on the skin of her temples now, and on the backs of the gnarled hands.

"That'll be fine," she said. "That'll be grand. And if I don't have it your wife will."

"Who's she?" demanded Orrange.

"Oh, she's somebody wonderful. Between the two of you you'll make Oakes Farm as fine as it was in the old days, long ago, when Captain Orrange and Judith——"

"—amiable consort," he put in, laughing.

"—amiable consort, had it, a kind of American court."

It was incredible, the tenacity with which she had clung to the farmland. Many of the older Polish farmers were selling, now, to city people. The Pole moved to the city, and the city people moved to the country. It was like a game. Some of these city people, Temmie learned, were descendants of old New England families—even old Connecticut, a few of them—whose forebears had scattered to the Mid-West, to the Far West, and who now were trekking back to find refuge in the very land which, hundreds of years ago, had served as refuge to their ancestors. They fell upon the sticks of old furniture, the crumbling old houses, with glad cries. It was rumored that they paid absurd prices for the farms.

Orrange's plan for the growing of the light broad leaf had not turned out so well. "But it hasn't had time," he argued, desperately. "I didn't say you could do it in two years or three. Five, maybe, but you've got to stick together."

The trouble was that the Polish farmers could not be made to stick together. They would gather at the Grange Hall and fix upon a price for the year's crop. So much a pound. Sixteen hundred pounds to the acre—then thirty cents a pound. That's fair enough. They all agreed to that. They would stand by it. Then, after the November rains, the buyers would come round to the tobacco sheds while the leaves hung limp on the laths, or, perhaps, while they were being tight-packed into bundles. From farm shed to farm shed, offering a price. No, the tobacco farmer would say. No.

Then one farmer, weaker than the rest, or more driven by need for money, would break. Then they must all go down together, or hold the entire year's crop in the sheds throughout the coming winter and the next summer, to be sold for a still greater loss in the end.

"But if we've got the best light broad leaf in the world," Orrange argued, "they'll have to pay our price. And we can have, if only——"

" 'If only,' " growled Ondy. "If only we got million dollar for tools and sheds and machinery, huh!"

It had not been a good year. A hailstorm in the early spring, a hot dry summer. Temmie had been in the stripping shed with Ondy and Orrange. It was Indian summer. The first frosts had come, but not the bitter frosts of November. She plodded heavily across the field to the house. Supper time, or nearly. The day was almost as hot as a midsummer day. A haze hung over the hills, the woods, the meadows. She looked out over the meadow to Pequot Ridge and Wepawaug, their slopes ablaze with the last wild flames of the Connecticut autumn. It was the time of year she loved best. Yet she dreaded it, too, for just at its heels came winter, black and bitter. The old house loomed up ahead of her. It was part of the natural landscape now. Its faded brick, the magnificent old oaks standing before it, the chimneys, the roof, all blended into the background. Oakes House seemed as immova·

ble, as much a part of the soil, as much a piece of Connecticut, as Pequot Ridge itself.

Temmie had helped with the topping this summer, in the August heat, though Orrange had made a great fuss. All over the valley the women had worked, pinching off the little flower that would retard the leafy growth. All the young girls had helped, and the women, and the old women. The countryside had been a carpet of deep rich green. The sun had beat down, fiercely, on Grandma Wolski, and the youngest walking Wolski, and on the whole family of Maks Kusak, the erstwhile tailor.

And now the tobacco crop was in. Well, it was in. Not a very good crop. Next year, though, it would be better. Next year, Orrange had said, the light leaf would be broader and stronger, like the old dark leaf. Or the year after, anyway.

November. How many years since the child, Tamar Pring, had come to Oakes Farm with the little tin trunk, and the ridiculous Indian dress saved from Pring's Indian Miracle Medicine Show. Winter was here again. They were so long, so cold, these New England winters. The old house had no proper heat. All those fireplaces that had to be stuffed with wood, and yet you froze. Maybe if she had a long sable cloak, such as Judith Oakes had had, years and years ago.

She came into the kitchen and sat down to rest a minute in one of the old ladder-back kitchen chairs. She had heard they were paying crazy amounts of money for chairs just like these in the city. Not her chairs. Not ever. Well, supper to get. She might fix something extra for Orrange. He often liked a Polish dish. He was enough of a Pole for that. It was cooler now. Maybe cool enough for those potato pancakes he liked, crisp and brown. In a minute she would get up from her chair and get the potatoes out of the bin and wash them, and peel them and grate them and fry them in real butter. Not fat. Real butter, for Orrange . . . Oakes . . . Ol . . .

When Orrange and Ondy came in she still sat there, leaning over one side a little against the delicate hand-wrought arm of the chair, so very tiny that she looked like a child that had fallen asleep in the dusk.

When Orrange saw the lettering on the stone it was with a shock of surprise.

TAMAR OAKES OLSZAK
Aged 52 yrs.

He had always thought of her as a **very old woman.**

XVII
1930

WHAT I can't understand," said old True Baldwin, in his best business manner, "if it's such a hell of a good farm, why're you so anxious to sell it? And if you're so stuck on farming I should think you'd have pride in it enough to keep it. Even if your name is—uh —mean to say, it's been in the family years, on your mother's side, anyway."

"Father!"

"Now, now, Candy. This is business. The price you name, young man, is ridiculous—nothing but wornout land and this old house."

"Father!"

"Well, yes, it's a grand old house. I don't deny it. And Candy—my daughter, here—is stuck on it. But just the same. Why, there isn't a foot of plumbing in the whole place, nor a line of heating pipe. Cost, lowest, a hundred thousand to make the old shack livable."

"More than that, I should think," said Orrange Olszak, politely. "And then," he turned his cool gray Oakes gaze on Candace Baldwin, pink and chic and urban, "you'd want a swimming pool, a tennis court, and

[*303*]

your own private golf links. You could use the east sixty
for golf links."

"He's kidding you, Dad," said Candace.

"No, I'm not, Miss Baldwin. I have no sense of
humor."

She returned his cool gaze with her own. "You admit
it!"

"Yes. An inheritance from my father, the Polack."

"That's marvelous. Simply marvelous. Nobody's ever
admitted it before. You ought to be stuffed and sent to
the Smithsonian."

"Look here, stop your wise-cracking, Candy." He
turned to Orrange. "She's a smart aleck."

"But a heart of gold," said Candy.

Orrange Olszak said nothing. In his shirt and trousers and his old field boots he sat there, unsmiling; and
something about his quiet dignity made them feel a little
foolish and even cheap. Candace covered this with flip-
pancy, old True with brusqueness. Stripped to the waist,
glistening with sweat, he had stood on the running board
of Candy's smart car as they drove back across the fields
to the house. The cool quiet of the vast old kitchen had
received them. He had sluiced himself with cold water,
rubbed himself briskly with a towel hung outside the
kitchen door, and had disappeared for a moment into a
room off the kitchen. When he reappeared he had pulled
a clean blue shirt over his bare body, and wore trousers
with a belt.

"What price you asking for this farm?" True Baldwin had demanded, bluntly.

Orrange Olszak told him.

"Whew! Gold mine on it?"

"No. In it."

They had talked, then, of crops, of acreage, of the soil, of the tobacco market.

"Of course you'll want to go over the house. I'll be glad to show it to you. It doesn't look very—I live here alone, and I just use these two rooms, really, and the room we call the south sitting room. Once a week a Swede woman comes in and cleans up and bakes. So it doesn't look very—but if you'd like to go over it now?"

"What I'd like," said Candace Baldwin, "more than anything in the world this minute, is food. If you could give us a little lunch—just anything. I'm dying. Dad hasn't been so well. We've driven since eight."

He grinned. He jumped up. "I'm hungry myself. There isn't much. Eggs, and some lettuce from the garden, and cheese and milk and honey."

"Why, it's Biblical, that's what. I'll help. I'm not a very good cook."

"That's all right. If you'll wash the lettuce I'll beat up the eggs. Oil up there on the shelf, for dressing. I usually eat lettuce just plain, like a rabbit. But that's good oil. The real stuff. Italian stores in Stonefield. You can get all kinds of swell stuff, imported, if you've got the price. I haven't, but the fellows that work in the hat factories live high."

Candy opened the cupboard door. She took down three plates. "Good God!" she exclaimed, piously. She was looking at the plates.

"Yes," Orrange said. "There aren't many left, though."

Old True wandered about the kitchen, squinting at the old gin closets, peering into the vast cavern of the unused fireplace, running a hand over the ancient wood. He came to the outer door. He looked up at it. He placed his hand on it, passed his hand over its breadth. "Why, say, Mr.—uh—why, say, Olszak, this door is one solid piece of old oak. One solid piece."

"All the doors in this house are."

They ate at the kitchen table. "The dining room hasn't been used in years. Big enough for a Peace Conference. I'll show you, after lunch."

And after lunch he had shown them. The hearthstone in the dining room. Tamar Oakes—1693–1708. The great stones in the cellar foundations. The attic, like a ballroom, oak raftered. The saloon. The glass house, broken and littered with débris, where Judith Oakes once used to sit, writing verse and reading Italian and French. The big front chamber, overlooking the valley and the river and the ridge, with its vast oaken bed, its posts mortised into the floor.

"You say you're an architect? This house was built

after the old scribe method, which you probably know about. Every stud was marked or scribed for the particular place it was to occupy. I studied about it in the library at Stonefield. Then there are some old plans I found, and prints. I'll let you see them if you're interested. The oak posts of the house are nine by nine inches at the bottom and ten by fifteen at the top, mortised about halfway up for the cross beams of white oak, eight by twelve. Those beams are thirty feet long, and they carry the weight of this second floor without any studding to support them. The king rafters are five by six, white oak, and twenty-two feet long." He looked a little apologetic, for she was so silent. "I just thought you might be interested, being an architect."

"Interested!" she said, in a small voice. "Would you, as a farmer, be interested if somebody showed you the Garden of Eden?"

"Well, I thought you'd be. You see, it isn't just a house. It's a—maybe it's just the way I feel about it—I—uh— they've papered over this room, time and again, but the original paper is still under the layers—the paper that old Captain Orrange Oakes imported from England over two hundred years ago, heavy and rich. It's under there, all right. Some day I'm going to peel the top layers off——"

He stopped then, abruptly, and flushed a painful red.

She sensed now, surely, that agony was mingled with pride as he showed them his house; that tragedy lay in his parting with it. She sought to divert him. "This bed would about fit you, Father. You're always complaining they're not big enough." She put a hand on one of the great polished oak posts.

"Oh, no!" said Orrange Olszak, quickly. "Oh, no!" Then he again flushed more painfully than before.

"I see," she said, quietly. "There is some family custom about it. Is that it?"

"Well, yes. You see, it's the main bedroom. It's for the married couple at the head of the house. No one but a wedded Oakes, they say, has ever slept in it. My mother slept in it." He pointed to the portrait of Tamar Oakes —the Van Oogstraat portrait over the fireplace.

"Your mother! That!"

He looked a little sheepish. "Not really. But she looked just like that when she was a girl. They say she was so much like that it might have been a portrait of her. They say once she put on the dress—— But you wouldn't be interested. Excuse me."

"Will you tell me, some day?"

"Yes."

They descended to the saddle room, off the wide main hall. The hall was so dim that he went on ahead down the great mahogany stairway to fling open a shutter, so that they might have light. Sir Orrange Oakes looked down upon them from the wall.

Old True Baldwin's keen eyes narrowed. He turned from the portrait to the young man in the blue shirt.

"When it comes to likenesses," he said, "that might be a picture of you, almost, in fancy dress. Eh, Candy?"

"Don't, Dad," she whispered. Then, as Orrange went ahead to open the door of the saddle room: "He feels terrible. Can't you see?"

"This used to be the saddle room," Orrange called to them, "if you'll just come this way. Careful. Two steps down. It's always cool in this room, some way. My great-aunt Judith Oakes used it as an office. There are papers here, and plans you'd probably want to see."

But True Baldwin could stand it no longer. "Look here, young man. You seem to be quite a feller. And the way you talk about this place. I'm no fool. How does it come you're so anxious to sell?"

Candace Baldwin saw a sharp white ridge spring out then, like a scar, along his jawbone. Orrange Olszak had set his teeth, as if in sudden pain. "Sit down, won't you? Here, let me wipe this off, Miss Baldwin. Everything's pretty dusty." He himself sat at the old desk, with its papers in order now, neatly pigeonholed in sheaves. The saddle room was cool and quiet. The scented midsummer smells came in on a little breeze wafted down from the cool shadowed places on Pequot Ridge. He looked down a moment at his two brown hands; looked up into True Baldwin's face.

"I'm not anxious to sell. I've got to. I'd give twenty years of my life to keep this place and run it the way I want to. I'll tell you. It's this way: This place has been

in the family ever since—well, you know. You lived
around here years ago, you say. My mother felt the way
I do about it. She was an Oakes, through and through.
After she died my father and I ran the place, but he had
one idea about it, and I had another. He was a good
farmer but he was all for using old-fashioned methods,
like the ones he had always used in Poland. But I showed
him that in ten years at the most, with any break at all,
we could have the place on a paying basis—not only that,
but one of the finest farms in the state. Farming. That's
all I know. Well, they brought him home dead one day
about a year ago. He ran the car—my Ford—into a
truck. It was night, and he was—there'd been a Polish
celebration, and he'd had a glass or two of applejack. He
didn't drink. Just a glass or two. But he always was a
bad driver. No driving sense. No feel of the wheel. Some
people are like that—old people, especially. I've got a
half-brother and half-sister in Stonefield. They're older
than I am, a good deal. They've always been after us to
sell the farm. But my father and I stuck. When he died
they went after me. I tried to show them that if they'd
only let me—but they wanted the cash. They're ambitious. My half-sister Rozia wants to send her boy to prep
school and to Yale; and my brother—well, anyway, they
got pretty upset about it, and finally they got a lawyer
to prove I was withholding money that rightfully belonged to them, because I wouldn't sell. He was a smart
Polish fellow, a big political boy there in Stonefield, and

he fixed it for them. The court ruled that I had to sell the farm if they wanted it sold, two against one. I tried —I——" He stopped. He cleared his throat. He stood up and reached in a high cupboard of the fine old desk for some papers under lock and key. Hs spread the papers on the desk. Candace and her father leaned forward so that the three sat close.

Candace Baldwin looked down at his hand spread out on the maps and plans. It was a brown strong hand, work-calloused, but not clumsy. Curiously, the fingers tapered almost delicately. The hairs on his wrist were a golden brown, like the hair of his head. She stared at this, fascinated. The hand was lifted to shut the cupboard door —a puff of wind—the papers blew—the hand flung out impulsively to rescue the papers; it struck her breast a light blow.

"Oh," she cried, as though in pain.

He was all contrition. "Oh, Miss Baldwin! I'm so sorry. I didn't go to hit you. The wind—did I hurt——"

"You didn't hurt me. I was just startled."

But she had felt the most frightful, the most delicious pain, like a sudden stabbing knife through her bowels.

They pored over the papers. Orrange talked, briefly. He answered True Baldwin's questions. True Baldwin knew how to ask a question.

"Look here. I like this place. I don't say I'll buy it, just off-hand, like that. But I like it. They can all have their Long Island estates and their make-believe farms.

Shucks! My folks were farmers here, and I was a farm
boy. Yes sirree! And now I'm coming back to the farm
again. It's the—uh—the complete circle. I want to run
this place as a farm, by God, and make it pay. No gentleman farming, with the upkeep eating the profits, but a
real farm. Look at George Washington. He rode around
his farm every day, overseeing everything. I've pitched
hay and slung swill to the hogs in my time with the best
of 'em. Now, what I want to know is this, Olszak: If I
decide, after going into it from every angle, that I want
to buy—and I don't say I'll plank down your price, exactly—but, anyway, if I decide to buy, do you think you
can run this place, and make it pay, and manage it, as
superintendent, kind of?"

"Manage it?"—dully.

"I want to buy another hundred acres or so, one side
or another, and make it an even five hundred. By God,
we can make it the finest farm in America. Let 'em have
their cities. Not for me. Eh, Candy? You can move your
business to New York, if you've got to be an architect.
But, say, this house would be a job for you, what?" He
turned again to Orrange. "You don't have to give me an
answer now. Of course, nothing's decided. But the way
you feel about this place and all. We'd fix up the loom
house you showed us, or the tenant house for you to live
in—Candy'd make it a swell place for you—and you
could boss the whole works———"

Suddenly Orrange Olszak's head came down on his

folded arms across the desk. True Baldwin stared. Candy put out a hand, as though to touch his shoulder, but the man's head came up quickly, he rose, his eyes averted. He looked like an embarrassed schoolboy. "Excuse me—I——"

"Say, I hope I haven't hurt your feelings. I guess the way you feel about this place——"

"I—no, you haven't—it's just that I thought I'd have to leave Oakes Farm, and then, when you said that maybe—— Excuse me." He left the room, abruptly.

"Kind of emotional, isn't he, that young man, for a Polack?"

"He'll be all right in a minute," as though she had known him for a long time. "He's upset. He'll be back. It's relief from the strain. He'll be all right."

"Well, what do you think? Seems to be a likely young fella. What do you think?"

"Oh, very likely," agreed Candace Baldwin, her eyes on the door through which he had vanished. She heard his footsteps, returning. "Ve-ry likely indeed, Mr. B."